Mialkovsky casuall_____s
still-restabilizing rif_____'s
head. *Possibly a great deal of money; but who would have
the nerve to issue the contract? They'd have to know that
the other CSIs would never stop looking for the killer . . .
or the people who set it into motion.*

The idea of being known among his peers as the
only assassin ballsy enough to take the internationally infamous Gil Grissom out with a single shot and
then successfully evade the subsequent all-points
search by vengeful legions of detectives, CSIs, and
forensic scientists appealed to Mialkovsky in an
oddly twisted Special Ops sort of way.

But he wasn't about to give in to the macho impulses that had once fueled his most outrageously
risky and successful missions. He'd long since outgrown those youthful flashes of insanity. Or, at
least, he assumed he had.

The truth was, Viktor really didn't know; and he
only vaguely cared.

But of one thing he was certain: playing the odds
with a clever and resourceful crime scene investigator like Gil Grissom was a Las Vegas long shot, indeed. Something he'd sworn not to do, but then
accepted the Clark County contract anyway because
the money had been too good to resist. . . .

Original novels in the CSI series:

CSI: Crime Scene Investigation
Double Dealer
Sin City
Cold Burn
Body of Evidence
Grave Matters
Binding Ties
Killing Game
Snake Eyes
In Extremis
Serial (graphic novel)

CSI: Miami
Florida Getaway
Heat Wave
Cult Following
Riptide
Harm for the Holidays: Misgivings
Harm for the Holidays: Heart Attack

CSI: NY
Dead of Winter
Blood on the Sun
Deluge

CSI:

CRIME SCENE INVESTIGATION™

IN EXTREMIS

a novel

Ken Goddard

Based on the hit CBS series "CSI: Crime Scene Investigation" produced by CBS PRODUCTIONS, a business unit of CBS Broadcasting Inc., and ALLIANCE ATLANTIS PRODUCTIONS, INC.

in association with Jerry Bruckheimer Television.

Executive Producers: Jerry Bruckheimer, Carol Mendelsohn, Anthony E. Zuiker, Ann Donahue, Naren Shankar, Cynthia Chvatal, William Petersen, Jonathan Littman

Series created by: Anthony E. Zuiker

POCKET **STAR** BOOKS
New York   London   Toronto   Sydney

Pocket Star Books
A Division of Simon & Schuster, Inc.
1230 Avenue of the Americas
New York, NY 10020

First Pocket Star Books paperback edition November 2007

POCKET STAR BOOKS and colophon are registered trademarks of Simon & Schuster, Inc.

For information about special discounts for bulk purchases, please contact Simon & Schuster Special Sales at 1-800-456-6798 or business@simonandschuster.com.

Manufactured in the United States of America

10   9   8   7   6   5   4   3   2   1

ISBN-13: 978-1-4165-7476-7
ISBN-10:   1-4165-7476-X

In memory of San Bernardino Sheriff's criminalist John Davidson, an amazing fellow who taught me long ago to reconstruct shooting scenes with a slide rule and a set of trig tables . . . and of Whittier (CA) PD Sergeant Tom Lamping, a recently lost buddy who faced life and adversity with the heart of a devoted husband, loving father, skilled craftsman, and tough cop.

Acknowledgments

My sincere thanks to my editor, Ed Schlesinger, who has a very keen sense of suspense and mystery, not to mention a questionably evil gift for keeping readers guessing; and to my literary agent, Eleanor Wood, who has remained amazingly supportive and encouraging all these years.

And a special thanks to my longtime criminalist buddy, Luke Haag, who brought the entire science of shooting scene reconstruction forward in his wonderful—and aptly named—new reference book that, in my certainly biased view, ought to be required reading for all CSIs—trainees, practitioners, and dinosaurs alike.

Luke, like many other "old-timers" in the field (myself included), is an advocate of the idea that while performing their work in a carefully methodical, analytical, and ethical manner, forensic scientists should never forget that their proper role in the lab or at a crime scene is to *think* about the significance of the evidence that lies before their eyes. The following comment regarding the accreditation-driven trend of crime labs in the U.S. (and throughout the world) to establish rigorous protocols for each and every examination their scientists perform; thus—intentionally or otherwise—establishing "menus" of tests for the investigators to select from when they submit their evidence is apt and timely:

> "In this strictly reactive role the forensic scientist is no longer functioning as a scientist at all. Rather he or she has been reduced to the role of a technician. . . .
>
> He or she may be doing the requested tests correctly and in accordance with some approved, standardized, certified, or accredited methodology but they are not fulfilling the true role of a forensic scientist."

—Lucien C. Haag, 2006,
SHOOTING INCIDENT RECONSTRUCTION

1

LIKE THE YOUNG MULE DEER in his rifle scope, Viktor Mialkovsky was a patient creature who preferred to spend a great deal of time monitoring his surroundings before making a decisive move.

But unlike that timid mammal—who now sat trembling in fear approximately two hundred yards from his high-point position overlooking the rocky clearing below—Mialkovsky was the furthest thing imaginable from harmless.

Thanks to a considerable amount of progressively intense training and experience, all paid for by the United States government, Viktor Mialkovsky was perfectly capable of killing human and wildlife alike with a wide range of lethal weapons that specifically included his bare hands. As a result of that same training and experience, he was also considered an expert hunter, tracker, and survivalist by the small number of peers and supervisors who were personally aware of his skills. On the summary sheet in his personnel jacket, the words "mission-oriented" and "emotionally detached" had been highlighted and underlined for emphasis.

Had Mialkovsky possessed a similar degree of camaraderie, and respect for teamwork and authority, he would have been the ideal government hunter-killer: an infinitely adaptable human weapon to be judiciously applied to the most difficult tactical problems. That was certainly the plan, as far as the succession of people responsible for his training and duty assignments had been concerned.

But it hadn't taken each of these veteran supervisors long to conclude that their supposedly ideal hunter-killer was indifferent to authority and regulations in general, to the rules of engagement in particular, and to the other men and women attached to his missions without exception. Most of them were convinced that Mialkovsky's heralded "emotional detachment" had far less to do with his ability to control his emotions than with a general lack thereof.

These were serious flaws that should have terminated Viktor Mialkovsky's government career long before his skill set became unmanageable; and certainly would have, had he not also possessed from early childhood an almost feral ability to conceal himself—both his mind and his body—within the organizational structure of his environment.

No aptitude or personality test ever confirmed the suspicions of his supervisors, none of his questionable actions had ever been documented, and no eyewitnesses had ever stepped forward to report what they had heard or seen.

In effect, to his supervisors and to his external world at large, Mialkovsky remained irrefutably who and what he chose to be at any particular moment.

And that, in addition to his formidable skill set, made him extremely dangerous to anyone or anything that happened to cross his path.

Thus the fact that Mialkovsky and the young mule deer had chosen to conceal themselves on adjacent sets of narrow rocky mesas overlooking this particular high-mountain clearing on this particular night certainly bode nothing good for the animal. But the presence of the terrified deer seemed only to amuse the supposedly emotionless hunter-killer, who had briefly held the deer's head in his crosshairs before methodically shifting his view to the next sector.

It was a casual decision that would have undoubtedly intrigued the legion of government psychiatrists who had diligently probed Viktor Mialkovsky's psyche over the years with their batteries of standardized but ultimately unrevealing tests.

This particular decision by Mialkovsky *was* revealing, because it would have taken the hunter-killer only a fraction of a second to send one of his modified 7.62x51 NATO hollow-pointed bullets through the deer's exposed head. In doing so, he would have confirmed the functionality of his primary weapon, acquired some extra meat for his freezer, and reduced the number of unpredictable factors at the scene by one; all positive results achieved at minimal risk to his intended task.

Very "mission-oriented," indeed.

And, in fact, during that brief and thoughtful moment, he had considered squeezing the trigger of his silenced bolt-action rifle, for the simple purpose of double-checking the accuracy of the 80mm-wide-aperture ATN 4-12X80 day-night telescopic sight . . . and to make the next few hours a bit more interesting.

But, ultimately, he chose not to do so, for five very specific reasons.

First of all, he'd come here to hunt a different species.

And he'd already sighted in the scope after he'd parked and concealed the dune buggy back down the trail.

And he really didn't need another deer for his freezer, because he didn't have a freezer; at least not in this state.

And he didn't consider the animal a significant issue in terms of the overall scene.

But more to the point, Viktor Mialkovsky really wasn't interested in the concept of mercy killing, one way or the other. He viewed that as a job for the other predators in the area—the cougars and coyotes—who would eventually hone in on the deer.

No need to upset Mother Nature's balance. At least not any more than was absolutely necessary for his purposes here tonight.

So he remained in his high-lookout position here in Nevada's Desert National Wildlife Range, methodically searching the sectors of his three-hundred-and-sixty-degree perimeter for any sign of the individuals who could easily show up on a random basis, but who more likely were not going to be out patrolling a remote and desolate stretch of high desert on a Friday evening when they could be enjoying dinner with friends or family.

The weatherman had been predicting a big storm coming in from the north, so who in their right minds would be out hunting on a night like this?

Only the truly dedicated hunters, Mialkovsky thought, smiling to himself.

As the sun began to settle in the western sky, he observed what appeared to be a group of outlaw bikers—eight grubby-looking figures, barely discernible in the scope, six on motorcycles and two others in a battered and dirty jeep—come about halfway up the dirt road, turn off on a small side road, and proceed to set up a crude off-road campsite. He monitored their activities with the rifle scope for a half hour or so; but they were a considerable distance from his position, and seemed intent on fiddling with their motorcycles, lounge chairs, cigars, and whatever was in the big ice chest, so he canceled them out of his calculations.

When the sun finally set down over the high ridge of the Sheep Range, he removed the daytime eyepiece from the rear of the telescopic sight that cost five times as much as the rifle it was mounted on, and replaced it with the larger night-vision eyepiece that provided a clear and sharp field-of-view in shades of bright green. Then he went back to the routine and boring but absolutely critical task of monitoring his surroundings.

If the dedicated federal wildlife refuge officers, or their plainclothed special agent counterparts, who worked this area were going to conduct a surprise patrol in their ongoing effort to keep poachers from killing the prized Desert Bighorns that thrived on the high ridges of the Sheep Range, Mialkovsky figured this was when they'd probably show up. So he continued to maintain his sector searches as the slivered moon arced high overhead and grew brighter.

But there was no sign of activity from the U.S. Fish & Wildlife's Corn Creek Field Station—the official entrance to the range some six miles to the west of his location—or from the intersecting dirt and gravel roads that wound their way south to that ultimate bright-light emitter: Las Vegas. And the biker group camped out on the distant side road had built themselves a small rock-ringed fire, and—apart from a couple of apparent motorcycle joyrides in the nearby sand-filled gullies—showed no signs of going anywhere.

Maybe we'll have a peaceful night up here, all to ourselves, Mialkovsky thought, an idea that was unlikely at best. In his experience, things never worked out as planned. There was always a need to adapt to the some unexpected event, and that was perfectly fine as far as he was concerned.

In truth, he enjoyed the adapting part far more than the hunt . . . or even the kill.

The scopes and sensors he had brought with him on this particular night were state-of-the-art, so it was especially ironic that Mialkovsky was first alerted to the approaching SUV when the mule deer's ears suddenly cupped and swung around to focus on the distant new sound.

Six minutes later, Mialkovsky's far-less-sensitive ears finally detected the noise of the Escalade's muscular engine. But he'd had the bouncing and swerving off-road vehicle in his night-vision-enhanced telescopic sights for five of those minutes, and was now chuckling to himself as he watched the driver hit the ruts and bumps that would have been a lot easier to see—and avoid—with the head-lights on.

"Back off it, you idiot," Mialkovsky muttered irri-tably. The last thing he needed on this particular evening was an unplanned accident with unpre-dictable consequences.

But the heavyset driver of the Escalade showed no indication of halting his aggressive, high-speed ascent of the narrow dirt road, in spite of the fact that he was completely dependent on his front-seat passenger—a broad-shouldered man who ap-peared to be using a pair of night-vision-equipped binoculars—to guide them along the otherwise pitch-black roadway. On three separate occasions, the wildly driven four-wheel-drive vehicle missed careening off the road and tumbling down the mountain by mere inches.

Mialkovsky shook his head in amazement.

Some people just can't help doing things the hard way; it's their nature, he reminded himself as he watched the dark-painted Escalade finally come to a sand-and-dirt-and-gravel-spewing stop behind a mass of boulders down near the base of the trail.

Moments later, in a chorus of slamming doors, clanks, curses, and general stumbling, intermixed with audible hissings to "be quiet," the two men began working their way up the narrow winding trail.

From his high-top position overlooking the clearing and the trail, Mialkovsky was able to follow their movements in the glowing green view field of his night-vision scope with a minimal amount of moving. Not that he was overly concerned that the two men would actually spot him. Between the desert-camouflage Ghillie suit that blurred his features into an indistinct mass and the desert-camouflage cloth interwoven with branches of the local flora that accomplished the same thing for his extended rifle and other pieces of equipment, the two visibly overweight and poorly conditioned men would have had to trip over him to see him, even with their modern night-vision gear.

And to do that, they would have to do a hell of a lot more climbing up some extremely difficult terrain.

Given their antics so far, not to mention the possibility that the strained heart of the larger of the two men—who appeared to be carrying at least three hundred and fifty pounds on his short, squat frame—might give out at any moment, Mialkovsky didn't think that was very likely.

Predictably, when the two men finally made it up to the clearing, they chose the easier route up to the surrounding rocky ledges—the one to their right—instead of the far more difficult route to the left that Mialkovsky had taken.

In doing so, they never saw the old and wary Desert Bighorn ram quietly move away from them with practiced ease, instinctively keeping large boulders between it and these intruders who had disturbed his normally quiet evening. Instead, they began to work their way along the narrow rocky mesa on the far side of the clearing with a sense of purpose, the heavier man—the Escalade driver—in the lead, slowly searching the surrounding crags and boulders with his nightscope-equipped rifle while the second broad-shouldered man made a wider search of the area with his night-vision binoculars.

So, are you really worth all of that effort, old fellow? Mialkovsky wondered as he briefly set the crosshairs of his scope on the steadily retreating ram, the distinctive scar from a ricocheting bullet clearly visible on the animal's cracked left horn, before returning his attention to the two men across the clearing.

It would have been an easy two-hundred-and-twenty-yard shot, but Mialkovsky wasn't ready to start shooting just yet. In a situation like this, positioning was everything, and patience the key.

So he continued to methodically shift the scope's aim-point, monitoring the position of all of the possible targets around the clearing, until the mule deer's ears suddenly cupped and swiveled back toward the road once again.

This time he heard the vehicle moments after he had it in the view field of his telescopic sight: an old nondescript pickup truck with a poorly tuned engine, cautiously working its way up the dirt road with all lights off except for a pair of dim running lights mounted under the front bumper, and seemingly following the tracks that Mialkovsky had made with his dune buggy.

You've been here before too, haven't you, pal?

The thought came to Mialkovsky unbidden—his subconscious already working on the angles—as he focused his nightscope on the creeping truck. The only occupant appeared to be the driver, who was wearing some kind of helmet on his head; and he could see what appeared to be a bolt-action rifle cradled in a rack mounted behind the driver's head.

High above in the rocks, the veteran hunter-killer smiled as he made a quick sweep with his rifle scope to see how the other occupants of this high mountain habitat were reacting to the new visitor.

As he'd expected, the two men across the clearing had dropped to their knees behind some small boulders, exposed from the waist up, and were staring back in the direction of the trail with their modern night-vision devices. The old ram was standing still, watching and listening from his far-better-concealed position. And the young mule deer seemed to have turned into stone.

Another quick check of the distant biker group suggested that the figures sitting around the small fire—Mialkovsky could see only six, but there was intermittent movement on the opposite side of the jeep where the motorcycles were parked—had no interest in old trucks wandering around in the dark, or were completely oblivious to the situation. More likely the latter, he figured.

Moments later, the pickup came to a halt about fifty yards down the dirt road from the start of the narrow trail leading up to the clearing.

The sound of a rusty door slowly creaking open echoed across the cold mountain air, causing the two men across the clearing to crouch a little deeper behind their quasiprotective boulders.

Then silence . . . broken only by the intermittent sounds of a single set of footsteps carefully working their way up the narrow trail, moving like a man in good condition who had made the climb many times before.

In the brief moments that he was visible between blocking boulders and trees, Mialkovsky was able to identify the newcomer as a Hispanic-looking male wearing dark ski clothes and what now looked like a Vietnam War–era helmet strapped to his head. There was a small tube duct-taped to the helmet—so that it hung in front of the man's right eye—that looked like one of the obsolete first-generation nightscopes frequently sold at military surplus stores, and some kind of long object in his right hand that was mostly hidden by his body.

Across the clearing, it now appeared as if the two crouching men with the modern night-vision gear were arguing quietly with each other, clearly agitated by the unexpected appearance of this newcomer.

Mialkovsky smiled in pleasant satisfaction.

In all of the years that he'd been forced to adapt his tactical plans at the last minute, he couldn't remember a single time when the random movement of individuals had worked to his advantage. But tonight, the happenstances were lining up in his favor as if they'd been choreographed by fate itself.

As the Hispanic man neared the crest of the trail where it opened out into the clearing, he suddenly moved off the trail to his right and began to climb through the rocks, heading in the general direction of the small and narrow mesa where the young mule deer was hiding.

Humming silently to himself, Mialkovsky reached out and made a final check of the flash repressor he'd mounted a few inches in front of his silencer with a duct-taped wire frame, making sure it was aligned properly.

Wouldn't it be interesting if— the hunter-killer had started to muse before he blinked in surprise as the mule deer—startled by the now-rapid approach of the Hispanic man—lunged out of the darkness into the clearing . . . stumbled on its rear leg . . . and then came to an indecisive stop between Mialkovsky and his target.

Stunned by the incredible appearance of the one piece of evidence that he had wanted from the very early stages of his planning—but whose chances of happening with any degree of predictability were nil, he'd figured—Mialkovsky had barely a second to make his decision.

He made it as he always did: based on instinct and a constantly updated awareness of his environment.

In a series of reflexive motions, Mialkovsky reached forward, bent the flash repressor rig aside, and sent a 150-grain hollow-pointed 7.62x51 NATO round ripping through the fragile neck of the young deer.

Feeling the comfortable sense of calm that he always felt when the action started, Mialkovsky smoothly fed a second round into the rifle's chamber, reached forward to bend the flash repressor back into position, aimed and triggered a second hollow-pointed bullet into the lower neck of his intended target, jacked a third round into the rifle chamber, and then paused to watch the succession of events that would follow.

The Hispanic newcomer and the broad-shouldered man saw each other at the precise moment the obese man with the silenced hunting rifle crumpled to the ground.

Seemingly puzzled by the sudden collapse of his companion, the broad-shouldered man allowed the neck-strapped binoculars to drop against his chest as he knelt down, pulled off his right glove, quickly put his bare hand against the prone man's neck, and then seemed to recoil in horror.

Three seconds later, the broad-shouldered man lunged to his feet and began running back down the narrow ledge pathway, pulling his glove back on and fumbling for something inside his jacket.

Moments later, the still night air erupted in a jackhammer burst of 9mm rounds as the charging broad-shouldered man fired an Uzi submachine gun in the general direction of the already frantically retreating Hispanic.

As Mialkovsky watched from his across-the-clearing position, the broad-shouldered man came to a halt beside a large boulder, triggered a second blindly aimed burst from the Uzi that audibly emptied the magazine, tossed the spent magazine aside, pulled another one out of his jacket, rapidly reloaded and charged the weapon, made a quick sweep of the area with the night-vision binoculars still strapped around his neck, and then began to quickly work his way back down to the spot where the Hispanic man had suddenly disappeared along the trail.

Surprised, seriously confused, and pissed. Mialkovsky checked the details off reflexively in his mind as he continued to watch the drama he'd instigated with his second bullet unfold.

The 9mm bullets were still ricocheting off rocks and boulders high over his head when the desperately fleeing man lost his footing on the narrow trail and tumbled out of control for at least twenty feet, striking his helmeted head against a large boulder that halted his fall but appeared to leave him dazed and even more frightened.

When his Uzi-armed pursuer started screaming and cursing high above him at the upper end of the trail, he fell a second time, slamming his right forearm and then his helmeted head again into another boulder. The dual impacts sent the Hispanic man tumbling down the trail again, where he finally came to a halt in a sprawled and seemingly unconscious pile.

Mialkovsky had already started to incorporate this unexpected fatality into his calculations when, to his amazement, the man managed to regain his senses, staggered to his feet, and continued stumbling down the trail . . . undoubtedly propelled by the crashing, cursing, and gasping sounds his pursuer was making as he tried to descend the trail with the Uzi in one hand and the binoculars loosely held in the other.

By the time the injured newcomer reached the bottom of the trail, the broad-shouldered man was halfway down and closing the distance rapidly when his right boot appeared to slip on a rock. The sounds of violent cursing, shattering glass, and clattering metal told Mialkovsky that any advantage the outraged pursuer might have had in terms of night vision and firepower had just been negated.

And, in fact, by the time the broad-shouldered man finally reached the bottom of the trail, empty-handed and visibly shaking with rage and exhaustion, the fleeing Hispanic man had managed to reach his truck, wrench the driver's-side door open, pull himself inside the cab, turn the engine on, and send the ancient pickup roaring down the dirt road, headlights off and dirt and sand flying in all directions.

Enthralled by the comedic drama playing itself out in the view field of his nightscope, Mialkovsky watched the furious broad-shouldered man stagger around in the darkness for almost a minute before he finally found the dark-painted Escalade.

Moments later, the Escalade's engine roared and its headlights came on as the infuriated driver sent the heavy vehicle into a sliding and spinning turn, and then accelerated in the direction of the dirt road.

Anticipating the blinding and scope-sensor-damaging headlights, Mialkovsky had already shifted the aim of his scope back on the fleeing pickup truck that was now halfway down the winding dirt road. He was just in time to see the pickup suddenly swerve toward a large boulder on the left side of the dirt road.

A second before impact, the pickup's headlights

snapped on, and the truck made a sharp dirt-and-sand-spewing left turn . . . missing the boulder as it continued forward for about fifty feet on the side road . . . and then suddenly accelerating straight at the bikers' makeshift campsite, where the six figures were out of their chairs and milling around, probably alerted by the echoing sounds of the Uzi gunfire and the revving truck engines.

At that moment, as Mialkovsky blinked in surprise, the distant campsite erupted in a blaze of gunfire, billowing flashes streaking from the hands of all six figures in the direction of the accelerating pickup.

A professional part of Mialkovsky's mind reflexively started counting the individual shots, one sounding louder than the others; but he gave up when the number reached twelve and the echoing concussions began to merge into one loud roar. As he watched, the pickup truck, still visibly the focal point of the streaking fireballs, slowly ground to a halt, its headlights blown out and engine stilled.

"You . . . assholes," Mialkovsky whispered, incredulous that his carefully thought out and nicely adapted plan had suddenly come apart, thanks to a handful of dirtbag bikers who had taken offense to a stray pickup truck suddenly driving into their campsite.

But even as the words escaped his lips, the hunter-killer's mind was rapidly sorting through his options.

The notion of said dirtbag biker faces appearing, one after the other, in the crosshairs of his night-scope appealed to Mialkovsky's inherent belief in violent and immediate retribution. But he also knew the complications would be significant, and the logistics both involved and time-consuming, none of which he could afford right now. He sensed that time had suddenly become a critical aspect of his calculations.

The sudden roar of the rapidly receding Escalade told the hunter-killer that the broad-shouldered man had also seen the gunfire directed at the fleeing truck. Apparently no longer interested in revenge, he accelerated the powerful off-road vehicle past the large boulder at the side road turnoff in a billowing cloud of dirt and sand that would have undoubtedly blinded any pursuit, had there been any.

But as far as Mialkovsky could tell, none of the distant figures had any apparent interest in going after the escaping Escalade.

Instead, as the hunter-killer watched in sudden realization, two of them pulled portable radios out of their jackets as the other four approached the truck in a manner that suggested a great deal more training and experience in small arms tactics than one would expect from the average dirtbag biker.

"Oh shit," Mialkovsky muttered to himself as he reached into his jacket pocket, pulled out a small cell phone identified by a small strip of masking tape as #1, and punched in a number.

"About time you called. How did it go?" the gruff voice on the other end of the line demanded.

"The primary event occurred as planned," Mialkovsky replied calmly, "but there's been an unexpected complication."

"What kind of complication?"

As Mialkovsky stared out across the dark land-scape, the first set of flashing reds-and-blues suddenly appeared at the edge of the Las Vegas lights . . . and then a second . . . and a third . . . all heading north in the general direction of the Desert National Wildlife Range.

Mialkovsky nodded thoughtfully, thinking the situation might not be quite as bad at it had first appeared—depending, of course, on who was re-sponding to the scene and what they'd find, the em-phasis definitely resting on the "who" and the "what."

It had suddenly occurred to Mialkovsky that the one thing he'd been determined to avoid when he grudgingly agreed to do this job might actually hap-pen now, because nothing was currently making any sense.

Random movements by random people will screw up a good plan every time, the hunter-killer reminded him-self, echoing the long-memorized words of a name-less drill sergeant, as he began to seriously reconsider his options in light of this new possibility.

"I said what kind of complication," the voice on the other end demanded.

A lightning bolt suddenly flashed in the distance, followed—eight seconds later—by rumbling thun-der, an act of nature that caused Mialkovsky to pause and then smile briefly.

"Hopefully a minor one," he replied calmly even as his mind churned. "This is just an advisory call. The basic story should hold together just fine. But you should be prepared for a police contact some time this evening."

"The *police*? Here, tonight?" The person on the other end of the connection sounded shocked, as if the possibility had never been considered.

You really are incredibly dumb, Mialkovsky thought as he watched one of the four distant figures cautiously pull open the truck's driver-side door.

It always amazed him that outwardly successfully men who routinely used violence as a primary tool could be so stupid when it came to forward thinking. *But,* he reminded himself, *that's why they pay people like me to handle the complicated work.*

"It's highly unlikely that they'll discover the body on their own, and make the connection; but you need to be prepared, just in case."

"But I thought you said—?"

"Shit happens. You're paying me to deal with it," Mialkovsky snapped, a dangerous edge to his voice. "I'm going to stay out here for a while to monitor the situation. After I hang up, you destroy phone number one. Use a hammer on the chip, and then run it through the garbage disposal in the manner we discussed. If you need to contact me in the next twelve hours, use phone number two. Don't forget, you only have four secure phones for this project, so don't waste them."

"But—"

"I'll contact you again if and when I learn something useful. Right now, I've got things to do," Mialkovsky said flatly, and then disconnected the call.

Working quickly now, the hunter-killer disassembled the cell phone, removed and wadded up the strip of masking tape, smashed the chip and the phone parts with a handy rock, removed the flash suppressor system from the end of his silencer and buried it—along with the pieces of the crushed phone—under a large rock about ten feet away from his lookout point, located the two expended casings and placed them in one of his jacket pockets, put on and activated a set of night-vision goggles, and then began working his way across the narrow mesa to a scene that would have to be carefully re-arranged in a very few minutes.

The storm developing in the northern mountains could be useful, if it continued to come this way; but that was another random event that would simply have to play itself out.

There was only one thing Viktor Mialkovsky was absolutely certain of now: time was no longer on his side.

2

GIL GRISSOM AND CATHERINE WILLOWS had driven the entire twenty-three miles from the crime lab to the State Highway 95 turnoff leading to the Desert National Wildlife Range in comfortable silence, much like a long-married couple. Grissom was lost in thought about the recent article in *Science* about domestid beetles that he really disagreed with, but wasn't quite sure if he wanted to—

"I was supposed to have the night off, you know," Catherine said, interrupting her supervisor's train of thought as she pulled the black GMC Denali up to a stop at the Corn Creek Field Station entrance.

"What?" Grissom blinked and then looked over at her quizzically.

"You haven't heard a word I've said, have you," the slender, strawberry blond CSI said as she lowered her side window and waited for the uniformed U.S. Fish & Wildlife Refuge officer waiting at the entrance to approach their vehicle.

Grissom looked thoughtful for a moment.

"Well . . . oh, I'm sorry. Once this is all over . . ."

"Yeah, yeah, I know. Another comp day I can add to the pile."

There was an argumentative edge to her voice, but Grissom ignored it, smiling as he considered the visual imagery.

"This time, I promise you. Once this situation is resolved, take a few days. Seriously," he said, his eyes twinkling with amusement. "And besides, Brass was pretty insistent."

"That's what concerns me, more than anything," Catherine admitted. "You know how he operates. He never tries to tell us how to do our job. So why—?"

"Good evening, ma'am, are you the folks from the Las Vegas Police Department Crime Lab I'm supposed to meet here?" the uniformed refuge officer asked, gesturing with her head back at the two other almost identical black GMC Denalis that had pulled in behind Grissom and Willows. The woman's long blond hair, very youthful features, and deep southern accent seeming jarringly incongruous with the holstered pistol on her hip, the glistening badge on her new down uniform jacket, the four-cell flashlight in her gloved hand, and the surrounding Nevada desert.

"That's right," Catherine said, nodding and holding out her credentials—and then shielding her eyes irritatedly in an effort to maintain her night vision—as the young refuge officer focused the glaring beam of her flashlight on her ID case and then Grissom's. "I'm Senior Investigator Catherine

Willows and this is Supervising Investigator Gil Grissom. The CSIs in the other two vehicles are Warrick Brown, Nick Stokes, Sara Sidle, and Greg Sanders."

"Shanna Lakewell, and I'll take your word for the other investigators' ID's," the youthful officer responded as she removed her glove and extended her right hand in a quick handshake. "Connor asked me to wait here and lead you up to the scene," she added as she put the glove back on and shut off her flashlight. "He's definitely going to be happy to see you folks up there tonight."

"Oh, why's that?" Grissom asked, his curiosity piqued by the sudden edge in the young officer's voice.

"Things were really pretty tense when I left the scene a few minutes ago," Lakewell said uneasily, "and I really doubt they've improved a whole lot since."

"You mean things were tense among the investigating officers at the scene?" Grissom pressed.

"Well, I guess I'm not really sure what you mean by 'investigating officers,' " Lakewell responded hesitantly. "The officers involved in the shooting are pretty upset; but that's because they want to go looking for some drugs they think a big shot dealer dumped out of his truck somewhere on the range, and your Captain Brass won't let them leave the scene."

Grissom's thoughts flashed back to his phone conversation with Brass; Grissom had already explained to Catherine and the other members of the graveyard team as they were loading up their crime scene gear into the Denalis that Brass had been extremely brief in his description of the scene:

"A buy-bust investigation has gone bad at the Desert National Wildlife Range, and I need the entire graveyard team to respond to the location ASAP with all of your shooting scene reconstruction equipment. Yes, that's what I said, Gil, the entire team . . . as soon as you can get here."

And that was all he'd said to Grissom before hanging up. Everything else Lakewell was now revealing was new information to the two senior CSIs.

"Some of our Metro officers got involved in a shooting on a federal refuge, and Captain Brass won't let them leave?" Grissom continued to press Lakewell from the front passenger seat, determined to find out as much of what she knew as possible. He was getting an uneasy feeling that reliable info might be difficult to obtain once up on the mountain.

"Well, no sir, not exactly," Lakewell said, chewing her lip nervously. "In fact, I don't think that any Metro police officers were involved at all; just Connor—the supervising refuge officer out here—a couple of state narcotics officers, and two DEA special agents."

"DEA agents?" Catherine turned to stare at Grissom. "Brass is holding federal and state agents on a federal facility, and not letting them leave?"

"All of them, and their snitch, too; she was definitely involved in the whole mess," Lakewell added.

"You're saying an informant was involved in this shooting?" Grissom interjected calmly. "Presumably meaning an informant was allowed to be at a federal-state buy-bust scene *armed*?"

"I think that's what happened, but my information is all secondhand . . . from Connor." Lakewell nodded her head nervously.

"Connor is your supervisor?"

"Yes, that's right."

"And he was also involved in the shooting?"

"That's correct." The young refuge officer nodded again. "Listen, this is probably none of my business, and I'm brand-new to the job so I may be way off base; but if it was up to me, I wouldn't have let that woman have a sharp pencil in her possession during an arrest situation, much less a Glock . . . and at least one other pistol that I couldn't ID. But I really don't think that's the major issue up there. In fact, I think the entire situation is a whole lot more complicated than that."

"I'm sure you're right," Grissom said. "And roughly, how far are we from this complicated situation right now?"

"It's about ten miles up the Pine Nut Road, which is mostly dirt and a pretty tough climb during the day, and a whole lot more interesting in the dark. Plus, we've probably got a serious storm coming in anytime now," Lakewell added, glancing up at the sky, "so you'll want to be in four-wheel drive and right on my rear the whole way."

As Officer Lakewell walked back to her official green-and-white-painted truck that was parked a few yards away, Grissom pulled a cell phone out of his vest pocket and thumbed in a multi-dial code.

"Nick, Sara, I'd strongly suggest you switch over to four-wheel drive, have everyone double-check their safety belts and weapons, and then follow us up the road, staying tight on our"—Grissom glanced over at Catherine, who had her eyebrows raised in an 'I dare you' look of anticipation—"bumper." As Catherine rolled her eyes skyward, he added: "I have a feeling things are about to get interesting."

When the four-vehicle caravan arrived at the turnout point a few minutes later, the scene looked like something out of an early Quentin Tarantino movie.

The shot-up truck—mired in the sand with four deflated tires and illuminated by two sets of LVPD patrol car headlights—was the visual centerpiece, and impossible to miss or ignore. The driver's side portion of the windshield had been shredded. Some cracked, starred, pulverized, and bloodied sections of the laminated glass—held together by the partially ripped and stretched pieces of the internal plastic layer—dangled loose from the windshield frame, while other like sections lay scattered across the truck's hood. The headlights, both side windows, and the driver's side portion of the rear cab window had been struck by dozens of projectiles. The sun-faded and rusted front and side panels that might have been painted red twenty years ago were pocked with dozens of apparent bullet and pellet holes. Cubic chunks of tempered glass and irregular-edged paint chips littered the ground.

All said, the ancient vehicle looked like it had been the objective of a head-on assault by a very determined military fire team.

Between the truck and the campsite, and well back from the temporary perimeter line of yellow scene tape that had been set around the truck, two LVPD patrol cars had been carefully placed so that their headlights lit up each side of the truck at forty-five-degree angles to the center line.

The campsite, about forty feet from the front of the truck, was illuminated by four hanging propane lanterns, revealing six seated figures—all wearing greasy jeans and an assortment of dirty and torn winter jackets—who looked a great deal like disgruntled outlaw bikers. A uniformed LVPD patrol officer stood next to the rock-ringed fire with his gloved hands resting lightly on his heavy belt buckle; a virtually identical officer was standing at the opposite end of the campsite; a third patrol unit with two additional uniforms standing watch outside was parked a little way up the road; and an LVPD patrol sergeant had placed himself in a center position between the two illuminating patrol units and the scene tape where he could keep a casual eye on everyone in general . . . and, seemingly, the one slouched female figure in particular.

The overall impression was that of a giant three-dimensional puzzle that desperately needed the attention of a patient and inquisitive mind.

Or, better yet, six patient and inquisitive minds, Grissom thought, an anticipatory smile crossing his face as his slowly sweeping eyes began to absorb relevant details.

One thing he noticed immediately was the fact that none of the six seated figures looked especially pleased by the arrival of the CSIs.

Behind the campsite, some fifty yards away, a pair of helicopters—one dark, military-looking, and marked only with an aircraft number, and the other clearly identifiable as an LVPD Search and Rescue airship—sat facing each other with drooping rotor blades, looking like a pair of glaring fighting cocks conserving their energy for the next round. The two overall-uniformed flight crews were standing next to the LVPD chopper, appearing to be sharing coffee and engaging in amiable conversation.

But the focus of Grissom's and Catherine's attention, as the six CSIs emerged from their vehicles wearing matching thick black nylon jackets over their vests, was Homicide Captain Jim Brass—a physically and bureaucratically tough police commander who the night-shift CSIs trusted to keep them out of trouble whenever possible.

Brass was dressed in his standard winter field garb—polished boots, pressed jeans, and a warm down coat—and standing next to a pair of fiftyish-looking men, both of whom were dressed in expensive suits, ties, and overcoats that really didn't match their more rugged-looking desert boots. And the conversation the three of them were having appeared anything but amiable.

As Grissom and Catherine approached Brass and the two visibly angry men, Warrick Brown and Nick Stokes stood side by side, arms folded across their chests as they slowly took in the entire scene, while Sara Sidle and Greg Sanders began the less-confrontational task of unloading the crime scene vans.

"This is Gil Grissom and Catherine Willows, the night-shift CSI supervisor and deputy supervisor I told you about," Brass said to the two overcoats.

"The other four CSIs over by the vehicles are Brown, Stokes, Sidle, and Sanders. Gil, Catherine"—Brass gestured with his head at his apparent adversaries—"this is Assistant Special Agent in Charge William Fairfax, from the DEA's Los Angeles Division Office, and Lieutenant John Holland from the Nevada Department of Public Safety."

The two commanders nodded at Grissom and Willows, but neither man made any effort to extend a welcoming hand.

"What we have here," Brass went on in a deliberately controlled voice, "is a questionable-shooting scene that I need you and your team to reconstruct."

Both Fairfax and Holland started to interrupt, but the DEA ASAC—a formidable-looking man with a carefully trimmed gray-flecked beard—was a half-second quicker off the mark.

"I want to go on record as adamantly objecting to the word 'questionable,'" Fairfax said flatly, his dark eyes filled with rage. "Three federal and two state officers engaged in a shoot-out with a major drug dealer known to be armed with automatic weapons, and with a long history of violence against law enforcement officers and resisting arrest. He aggressively drove into their campsite, instead of waiting for them to meet him at the road intersection, as planned, and immediately commenced firing on their position. Our team responded in a manner that was both proper and effective. There is no way this shooting scene meets the 'questionable' standards defined in the Tri-Lateral Agreement."

"And I agree with that assessment," Holland added emphatically. "This is not a questionable shooting, and your officers do not patrol federal refuges. Therefore, as far as I'm concerned, you have no jurisdiction over our officers."

"Would you like to talk with your captain again?" Brass inquired, holding up his cell phone. "Or your SAC?" he added, turning back to the DEA supervisor.

Both men briefly glanced at each other, but neither responded.

"According to the rules of the Tri-Lateral Mutual Assistance Agreement," Brass explained to Grissom and Catherine, "the questioned-shooting standard is met when one or more primary elements of the underlying investigation are not present at the scene. The undercover investigators here got into a shooting situation, and properly called for Metro backup. When our responding patrol officers arrived, the UCs stated they were here to make a purchase of ten kilos of high-grade cocaine from a known-to-be-armed-and-violent drug dealer named Ricardo Paz Lamos. As far as I'm aware, no one has positively identified the body in that truck as Ricardo Paz Lamos, and no one has pointed out so much as a single kilo of anything at this scene."

"How are we supposed to positively identify the bastard when his face is no longer recognizable, and his prints aren't on file?" Holland protested. "Hell, the guy's been an unknown for five years—no address on record, and apparently he never goes out anywhere in public. We're lucky to have this one vehicle stop photo." He held up a crumpled and grainy black-and-white photo in his gloved hand.

"And it's standard procedure for dealers making a big sale to conceal their main load some distance away from the buy site until they've verified the money and the right players are on site," Fairfax said heatedly. "You know how it works, Brass. You haven't been out of the field that long."

"You guys don't have to tell me how a buy-bust operation is supposed to go down," the LVPD captain shot back. "But, the presence of illicit drugs is a required element of the deal, no?"

"You bet. And that's precisely why our investigators need to be out there, looking for those keys"— Fairfax gestured with one gloved hand at the surrounding expanse of darkness—"instead of sitting here on their collective asses having every move they make second-guessed by you and your CSI team."

"What I also understand," Brass went on firmly, "is that we have a dead man in a truck who may or may not be your drug dealer, and who may or may not have done anything to justify a sixty-some-round barrage of what may or may not have been 'return fire.' "

Fairfax started to say something, but Brass held up a silencing hand.

"I count three missing primary elements in your underlying investigation, Agent Fairfax. And under the agreement that our sheriff and your agency directors have all signed and established as standard operating procedure for officer-involved shootings in Clark County," Brass stated pointedly, "the senior officer at the scene with the least number of subordinate officers involved in the shooting is to take control of the scene until a supervising officer with no involved subordinate officers can respond and assume command. At that point, the scene commander immediately conducts a shooting reconstruction to verify the facts of the incident. I'm not wrong about all this, am I?"

Fairfax looked like he was about to interject something, but remained silent.

"Since I am aware of no Metro officers involved in this officer-involved shooting, that makes me the scene commander here until relieved by higher authority; which, presumably, would be my boss, because both of your supervisors specifically placed your men under my command approximately, oh"—Brass glanced down at his watch—"fifteen minutes ago."

"He didn't place me under your command," Fairfax responded bitterly.

"No, he didn't," Brass agreed, "and neither did your captain," Brass said to Holland. "Which means you're both welcome to leave this scene at any time; or you're welcome to stay, so as long as you don't screw around with my investigation."

"I'm staying," Fairfax remarked.

"Me too," Holland added.

"Fine, just stay out of our way. I think you have enough problems as it is."

"I'm glad you're on our side," Catherine murmured to Brass, giving him a wry smile.

"You should see me *without* the coffee," Brass replied as he turned to Grissom. "Are you ready?"

"You bet," Grissom said as he and Catherine walked over to the six dirty and disheveled figures still sitting around the remains of the campfire, followed by the other four CSIs, Brass, Fairfax, and Holland.

"Okay," Grissom began as he stared down at the visibly disgruntled figures, "we'll begin with introductions. I'm Gil Grissom, from the crime lab. This is my deputy supervisor, Catherine Willows; and this is Warrick Brown, Nick Stokes, Sara Sidle, and Greg Sanders. They're all going to be assisting me in this shooting scene reconstruction. And your names are, and who you work for, starting with you?" He nodded at the relatively clean-cut figure at the far left end of the circle of chairs as Sara Sidle began to take notes.

"Connor Grayson. I'm the supervising refuge officer here at the Desert National Range. You'll have my complete cooperation in this matter."

"Thanks, Connor," Grissom commented, motioning with his head at the next figure.

"Jeremy Mace, detective, Narcotics Unit, Nevada Department of Public Safety. I disagree with the need and specifically the timing of this investigation, but I'll cooperate."

"John Boyington, detective, Nevada DPS. I'm Jeremy's partner, and I agree with everything he just said."

"Russell Jackson, special agent, DEA. Far as I'm concerned, this whole deal is pure bullshit. I'll leave it at that."

"Chris Tallfeather, special agent, DEA, ditto."

Grissom turned to face the last figure, a sallow-cheeked woman who could have been in her early twenties or thirties, with acne-scarred features, bleached-blond hair tied back in a loose ponytail, and a pair of large bloodstained bandages on the right side of her face, covering her cheek and ear, and who had remained slouched down in the camping chair, staring down at the ground, the entire time. "And you are?" he inquired.

"Jane." She directed the comment to the expanse of sand between her boots.

"Do you have a last name, Jane?"

"Smith."

Grissom cocked his head curiously, started to say something, and then shrugged.

"What happened to your face, Jane?"

"I got shot," the young woman muttered.

"You were wounded here, at this location, this evening?"

"Yes."

"Who shot at you?"

"He did." She gestured with her head in the direction of the illuminated truck.

"You're saying the deceased individual in that truck, presumably a man named Ricardo Paz Lamos, shot at you?"

"Yeah, sure," the woman mumbled, her head turned away from the CSI.

Grissom turned to face the men.

"Did any of you specifically see this incident?"

The five seated men all looked at each other and then shrugged and shook their heads.

"*Nobody* saw her get shot?" Grissom asked in a voice tinged with incredulity.

"I heard her yell 'Oh shit, he's here!' right when the truck arrived on the scene," Grayson finally said, "and then I heard her scream like she was in pain right after I started shooting at the tires. Or, at least, it sounded like Jane screaming; but I can't say for sure because I was behind that big rock over there, taking a leak." He pointed to a large irregular boulder that was about five feet high and ten feet long. "Now that I think about it, I never actually saw her during the shooting . . . not until we all came out of our barricade positions and approached the truck."

"And no one else heard or saw Jane at the time she was shot?" Grissom continued to press.

"I definitely heard her yell that Paz Lamos was coming, and then heard her scream, right after the shooting started; and I think I might have seen her fall backwards out of the corner of my eye—just the top of her head, and only for a split second," Detective Boyington spoke up. "She'd gone behind that big rock over there, to take a leak too, right after Connor headed over to the guy's side." He pointed to a larger boulder off to his left, in front of the right-truck-side-illuminating patrol car, that was approximately five to seven feet tall and at least fifteen feet long.

"Is that correct, Jane? You were over by that rock when the shooting started?" Grissom asked.

"Yeah, that's right." She nodded sullenly, her eyes still focused on the ground.

"She was pretty much obscured by the boulder," Boyington went on, "which was the whole idea of picking a big one, I guess. That's all I can testify to, as far as her shooting or being shot at. I'd already fired two rounds at the truck headlights—and maybe at least one at the carburetor by then—trying to stop the damned thing from running us over."

"So you're not sure about the timing of your shots, before or after you heard Jane scream?"

Boyington thought for a moment.

"No," he finally said, shaking his head, "I'm really not sure about the sequence. The headlights were directly in my eyes, so I know I fired at them first. Right after that, things got pretty hairy."

"I'm sure they did," Grissom said, nodding. "Did anybody else see Jane fall backwards?" He looked around at the rest of the seated group.

Mace, Jackson, and Tallfeather all shook their heads.

"Okay, now that we've more or less resolved that," Grissom said, turning his attention back to the snitch, "who do you work for, Jane?"

"I'm freelance; I don't work for anybody. These guys twisted me so I'd help them nail Ricardo." She was still staring at the ground, but she gestured with her head at the two DEA agents and possibly the two state narcs; Grissom really couldn't tell.

"So you'd define yourself as an independent party, not affiliated with any law enforcement agency?"

"That's right." Smith's head snapped up, her eyes widening in defiance. "I'm not a government employee and I really don't want to be here. So what happens if I refuse to cooperate?"

Grissom glanced over at Jim Brass, who shrugged, and then went on matter-of-factly: "We would take you into custody as either a material witness to a shooting, or as a suspect in that shooting."

"So I can't leave whenever I want?"

"No, you can't leave until we release you," Grissom affirmed.

Jane Smith emitted a long, exasperated sigh and went back to staring at whatever interested her on the ground.

"Okay," Grissom said, "now that we've got that out of the way, the next thing we need to do is collect your gloves, swab your hands for gunshot residues, collect all of your weapons, and then take elimination sets of your fingerprints. We'll collect your boots and clothing back at the station."

"You're going to disarm these men, here, in the field?" Fairfax interjected from the far side of the campsite, sounding incredulous.

"That's right," Grissom said, turning to face the DEA commander. "Standard procedure is to collect all firearms that may have been involved in the questioned shooting at the *onset* of the investigation. That means all firearms in their possession, including any and all backup weapons. You understand why, I assume?"

"I understand the reasoning; but why here, and why now?" Fairfax demanded. "You know drug dealers don't operate alone, especially out here in the middle of nowhere. For all we know, Ricardo could have a half dozen of his people out there watching us right now."

"Even if Lamos's men are still out there, which I seriously doubt," Brass snapped, "and they see us collecting your agents' weapons, they will also observe that this scene is protected by an additional twelve armed law enforcement officers—which doesn't include the armed helicopter crews, and the fact that both you and Holland are carrying. I make that out to be two-to-one odds in our favor at the very start, not counting our advantage of night-vision-equipped air cover, and, of course, all the backup we'd ever need from Metro and local military . . . if it came to that."

Fairfax looked like he was about to say something, but then thought better of it.

"That ought to be more than enough firepower to deal with a handful of Ricardo's men, in the unlikely event they really are out there, and really are stupid enough to approach this campsite. But I can't think of a single logical reason why they would, because their drugs don't seem to be here, and no one's going to pay them to retrieve the dead body of their boss under fire," Brass added.

"Yeah, but don't forget, half of our armed twelve are CSI," Holland protested.

Grissom's team stole glances at one another with knowing grins. They all qualified more or less regularly with their weapons, and were accustomed to the dismissive "science geek" comments they occasionally ran into with some of the more badge-heavy cops. It had long since become the equivalent of splattered water across a duck's back.

"If things get out of control, we'll try not to hurt anyone." Grissom smiled pleasantly as Brass motioned for Fairfax and Holland to back away from the area. "So, here's how we're going to work it. One at a time, each of you is going to go over to CSIs Sidle and Sanders, who will take your gloves and then swab both of your hands for gunshot residues. Then—"

"What's the point of that? We've all admitted to firing our weapons," Detective Jeremy Mace said.

"Reconstruction of a shooting scene requires a great deal of basic information that has to be collected as close to the actual time of the shooting as possible," Grissom explained. "Since we don't know what will later turn out to be meaningful, we routinely collect a great deal of evidence, much of which is never used."

"Okay, fine." Mace nodded, making a dismissive gesture with his hand. "I said I'd cooperate."

"So then," Grissom acknowledged, "you'll continue over to CSIs Brown and Stokes, who will collect your weapons and ammunition, provide you with an evidence receipt for your records, and take your elimination prints." Grissom looked down at the still-slouching Jane Smith, and smiled patiently. "Starting with you, miss."

Smith reluctantly rose to her feet.

"Now please walk over and give them your gloves, and then hold out your hands."

The young woman shuffled over to Sara and Greg, who were waiting with plastic-gloved hands, a pair of manila envelopes, and a gunshot-residue collection kit. Jane held out her hands and glared at Sara as the alert and wary CSI carefully removed her insulated gloves and placed them into the individually marked manila envelopes, and then continued to watch sullenly as the two CSIs gently tapped sticky-taped discs against the dirty palms and the backs of her hands, while Catherine methodically photographed the process.

"See, nothing to it," Greg said, offering up one of

his patented charm-enriched smiles, but getting only a brief, dismissive snort in return.

"I'm willing to go along with this part," Jane Smith whispered with a dangerous edge to her voice, "but I'm not giving up my guns as long as Ricardo's still out there."

"What did you say?" Catherine asked.

"I said I'm not going to give up my guns, because Ricardo could still be out there," Jane snarled, glaring her adrenaline-widened eyes at the CSI.

"No, you said 'is' out there, not 'could be,'" Catherine corrected. "That implies you don't think the dead man in that truck is Ricardo Paz Lamos. Right?"

"I . . . I do think that's Ricardo in the truck, or at least I hope it is. But I'm not giving up my guns until I know for sure, so *you* can just forget—"

Jane Smith made the mistake of jabbing her bare finger into the center of Catherine's chest.

Grissom saw Catherine look down at the finger pressed deep into her Kevlar-filled vest in disbelief, and then back up at the wide-eyed snitch. In a single smooth motion, she grabbed Smith's offending wrist with her right hand, twisted it around, and then wrist-locked the stunned young woman to her knees.

"You don't get to do that," Catherine said emphatically.

Jane Smith erupted. She first tried to fight her way out of the wristlock. And when that didn't work, she furiously slashed her booted foot at Catherine's leg.

An instant later, Smith found herself being

slammed face-and-solar-plexus-forward against the left front panel of the nearby LVPD patrol vehicle by Warrick and Nick. Before the stunned snitch could recover her breath, Warrick had her hands handcuffed behind her back while Nick and Catherine quickly and methodically searched her for weapons.

"Don't push your luck," Nick advised her calmly as the enraged informant started to bring her foot back up again . . . and then hesitated when the smiling CSI reached over and took a controlling grip on the center handcuff links as Warrick stepped back out of the way.

"Hey, what do you think you're doing?!" a voice in the background protested.

"Two pistols—a hip-holstered 9mm Glock, and a hammerless snub-nosed .38 Smith & Wesson from her right jacket pocket—two extra magazines for the Glock, and a pair of speed-loaders for the Smith, left and right jacket pockets. Nice," Warrick reported, ignoring the voice as Catherine and Nick first handed him the discovered armaments, then pulled the door of the patrol car open and strapped the still-cursing Jane Smith into the rear seat.

"I said, what do you think you're doing?" Fairfax repeated, starting toward the three CSIs and then hesitating when Jim Brass stepped in his way.

"They're arresting her, for assault on a law enforcement officer; *that's* what they're doing."

"But she's—"

"Ms. Smith is a material witness in a questioned shooting, and also under arrest. And if anyone else would like to interfere in this investigation and join her in custody, this would be an excellent time to speak up." Brass looked around at the other seated officers, but received only wicked glares from the four federal and state narcs. Connor Grayson, the supervising Fish & Wildlife Refuge officer, looked stunned.

"And speaking of interfering," Brass went on, turning his attention to Fairfax and Holland, "you were concerned about the possibility of Ricardo Paz Lamos's men being in the area, and making a timely search for the missing drugs. This might be a good time for the two of you to make a general search of the area with your helicopter; and I'm guessing our Search and Rescue team would be more than happy to help."

Fairfax and Holland looked at each other, and then at their seated investigators.

"I'm sure your men have a far better understanding of their rights, and the general shooting reconstruction process, than Miss Smith," Brass added. "I don't expect any further difficulties. But, if something should come up"—he held up his cell phone again—"I'll give you a call, and you can be back here in a few minutes."

"Come on, let's go," Holland said after a moment, grabbing Fairfax's arm and pulling the still-reluctant ASAC toward the makeshift landing zone.

Grissom waited until the agitated commanders were climbing into the dark-painted helicopter, and the blades of both airships were starting to rev up, before turning his attention back to the five seated law enforcement officers.

"Now then," the CSI supervisor went on as if nothing especially interesting had happened yet, which was pretty much the way he saw it, "while the rest of you continue to cooperate, Catherine and I need to examine the vehicle that appears to be the center of so much attention around here."

3

THE INITIAL ARRIVAL OF THE MILITARY assault helicopter had caught Viktor Mialkovsky out in the open, working on his scene, and the familiar rumbling of the Black Hawk's heavy rotor blades echoing off the canyon walls had sent him scrambling for cover.

By the time he'd gotten back into position with his night-vision scope, the armored airship had landed on the far side of the distant campsite, amid the flashing lights of the responding LVPD patrol vehicles and their Search and Rescue helicopter that had touched down in the same general area some fifteen minutes earlier.

With all of that ambient light, it had been easy for Mialkovsky to visually confirm the large bright LVPD logo on the elongated-egg-shaped Hughes helicopter, and the complete lack of any visible markings on the dark-painted Black Hawk.

The earlier arrival of the Metro officers and their helicopter hadn't concerned him much at all. These officers were trained and equipped to deal with drunks, dopers, thieves, and other relatively unprofessional idiots, and thus tended to act in a highly predictable "police" manner. But the possibility that an Army Special Forces team from the adjacent Nellis Test and Training Range had also been dispatched to the scene, for whatever reason, had been an immediate concern. Mialkovsky knew from hard-earned experience that the military Special Ops teams were superbly equipped and trained to deal with individual snipers dug into rocky hillsides. If such a group had responded, he could easily find himself surrounded by radio-coordinated pairs of night-vision-equipped spotters and shooters whose skills paralleled his own.

If that happened, Mialkovsky knew, his mission would be irretrievably compromised in the best of circumstances, and his hard-earned reputation for reliability severely damaged.

All things considered, he'd be lucky to escape with his life.

Accordingly, he'd spent the next hour carefully relocating his primary surveillance site to a reasonable-compromise site that included a pair of juniper trees for additional overhead cover, a reasonable line of sight on both scenes, and at least three escape routes he might be able to withdraw through if and when that tactic became necessary.

Focused on his work, Mialkovsky had ignored the animated interactions of the growing number of figures—uniformed and otherwise—at the distant campsite below. It was only the arrival of the three nearly identical GMC Denalis following behind the brightly marked Fish & Wildlife Refuge truck that caused him to pause in his careful preparations.

The campsite had been too far away for Mialkovsky to discern any markings on the Denalis, much less identify any of the individuals who emerged from the dark SUVs, but he had little doubt as to who they were, or why they were arriving at this particular shooting scene.

Vegas's legendary CSI team, called in to make a reconstruction, he had nodded to himself knowingly, his mind churning relentlessly as he watched the six identically uniformed green-toned figures exit their vehicles and begin to engage with the other figures at the scene. *Is that you down there, Grissom?* Mialkovsky had wondered, observing the lead figure directing the other five members of the responding team for a few moments before going back to work. *Wouldn't that be ironic—our paths intersecting once again?*

As he'd continued to move quietly and carefully among the rocks, making minor adjustments, Viktor Mialkovsky had felt his mind and body responding to the enhanced sense of danger in a manner that was almost feral.

Finally satisfied with the distribution and arrangement of his equipment, Mialkovsky had been working his way back to his scene, determined to make a final double check of all of the critical elements, when he heard the echoing rumble of the distant Black Hawk's rotors revving up again.

Cursing to himself, he barely managed to scramble back to his relocated position and pull himself under the thin desert-patterned canopy—a thermal blanket specifically designed to conceal the heat of his body from high- and low-altitude IR-equipped night-vision systems—when the Black Hawk came roaring overhead in a wide loop across the eastern face of the Sheep Range.

As Mialkovsky watched with the lens of his night-vision spotting scope, sticking out from under the canopy, the two helicopters made a series of carefully choreographed sweeps around the campsite, the LVPD chopper working outward in a north-westerly direction toward the Sheep Range at an increasingly higher altitude, while the Black Hawk extended its loops in a south-easterly direction toward Las Vegas.

Every now and then, the Black Hawk appeared to hover just above ground level or to actually land—Mialkovsky couldn't tell which—for a few moments and then take off again in its determined quest.

Mialkovsky had no idea what the Black Hawk was looking for, or doing; but its initial rapid pass across the lower face of the Sheep Range, and the slow and methodical movements of the Search and Rescue helicopter as it neared the mountains, made it easy for him to spot the night-vision camera system, illuminating infrared search beam, and thermal imaging system mounted on the undersides of both airships.

He immediately recognized both sets of night-search gear as being enhanced—but far less armored—versions of the equipment normally mounted on military helicopters.

This new insight caused Mialkovsky to pause for

a moment and reflect on his situation with a sense of both relief and concern.

The quality of the night-vision and thermal imaging search systems mounted on the Black Hawk—high-resolution equipment routinely used by federal law enforcement agencies to track criminal suspects—strongly suggested that he didn't have to worry about a visit by an Army Special Ops team.

That was a good thing.

But the presence of a federal law enforcement helicopter at this particular scene, arriving shortly after the violent shooting of the frantically fleeing Hispanic man, was a strong indication of a federal drug deal gone bad.

That was not a good thing.

The drug agents would undoubtedly be searching the general area for other suspects, thereby severely limiting his tactical options.

And the arrival of six CSIs on the scene, rather than the normal two or three, suggested the shooting situation was complicated, and that they would probably be working all night to reconstruct the events, trying to resolve whatever developments had brought the larger-than-normal team there in the first place.

That could turn out to be a *very* bad thing indeed.

4

GRISSOM AND CATHERINE CAUTIOUSLY approached the hastily rigged perimeter line with big bundles of bright, wire-mounted evidence locator flags tucked into their vests and high-intensity flashlights and strobe-mounted digital cameras in their gloved hands. As they moved forward, they continuously swept the beams of their flashlights across the ground in front of their feet, a routine double check to make certain the initially responding officers had set the perimeter far enough out to contain all of the relevant evidence.

They were stopped at the perimeter edge, examining the multitude of boot prints, churned sand, and expended casings on the ground between the truck and the bright yellow tape, when Jim Brass came up beside them.

"How's it going?" he asked.

"Bad time to be doing this," Grissom commented as he paused to take a broader look at the scene.

"We don't have enough lights to illuminate the entire scene properly, so we're going to have to work it in sections."

"Do you want to wait until daylight?" Brass inquired uneasily.

Somewhere in the dark sky that was rapidly becoming overcast and clouded, the threatening ripple of a distant lightning bolt offered a whimsical answer.

"I'd love to," Grissom said, gesturing up at the sky with his head, "but I don't think we'd have much of a scene left by morning. If you want us to reconstruct the shooting sequence with any degree of accuracy, we'd better get at it right now."

"I need this scene worked as quickly and as thoroughly as humanly possible," Brass replied.

"Getting pressure from the boss?" Catherine queried.

"The sheriff called in to let me know that he's definitely expecting 'quick and thorough' on this one," Brass responded, "but he's not the problem."

Grissom raised his right eyebrow quizzically.

"Mostly because he's out of town and won't be back until tomorrow afternoon," Brass explained, a pained expression crossing his face. "Mace, Boyington, and Tallfeather are the problems. Mace is the son of a Nevada state senator, Boyington's parents are wealthy and tightly connected to the governor's campaign staff, and Tallfeather is the youngest son of the chief of a Paiute Indian tribe living on the Moapa River Indian reservation."

"Oh," Grissom finally said. His interest in local politics was infamously and invariably limited to the degree that such nonsense might impact his crime scene investigations. "Well, it looks like you hit the trifecta then."

Brass gave a tight-lipped grin before responding.

"It would be nice if the body in that truck belongs to a drug smuggler named Ricardo Paz Lamos, we find ten kilos of coke, and the shooting turns out to be clean; but—"

"You don't think so," Grissom suggested.

"No, I think there's something wrong with their story—possibly several things. I just don't know what."

"I'm surprised Jackson's not one of the problems," Catherine commented. "He was pretty aggressive during the initial questioning. I got the impression he might have something to hide."

"Jackson *is* his own problem," Brass said. "According to Fairfax, he's been involved in three previously questioned shootings, and is technically still on probation, whatever that means."

"Probably means he shouldn't have been out here involved in a shooting tonight, which presumably makes that *Fairfax's* problem," Catherine said with a knowing grimace, nodding her head in understanding.

"Jackson was the assigned team leader on this deal, but I gather he was supposed to have run the operation from their field command center," Brass said. "That being the case, it would be nice, for Fairfax and the DEA's sake, if Jackson was the last one to fire his weapon, and only fired to stop the truck; but that doesn't seem to fit his M.O."

"So what do we think we know?" Grissom asked.

Brass pulled out his field notebook. "We think we know that Ricardo Paz Lamos called Jackson twice on his cell phone to explain he was running late, which was why the buy-bust team was relaxed and not set up for his arrival. Everyone agrees they heard occasional engine sounds coming from the base of the Sheep Range, roughly west to northwest of this site, but it was hard to tell directions because of all the echoing effects. No one saw any head-lights, but Grayson said that wasn't unusual because poachers frequent the area, trying to shoot one of the last Desert Bighorns on the planet. So no one got real concerned about the engine-noise situation except for Grayson, who wanted to go check the area, but got talked out of it by Jackson and Mace."

"They probably didn't want to blow their big drug bust over a couple of endangered sheep," Grissom said disapprovingly.

"Exactly," Brass said with a nod. "So everyone's sitting around talking, and the informant—our dear Jane Smith—is acting increasingly paranoid about something, when all of a sudden, maybe fifteen minutes before the truck arrives here, they hear what sounds like automatic gunfire coming from somewhere in the general direction of the Sheep Range, again roughly west to northwest of here."

"Automatic gunfire? That doesn't sound like poachers," said Catherine. "I'd think they'd want to be a little more subtle than that, especially with wildlife refuge officers like Grayson on the lookout. Maybe Ricardo Paz Lamos was taking care of some side business before he made his deal with Jackson and his team."

"Possibly, but don't forget, the Army does test and train on the west side of the Sheep Range," Grissom pointed out. "I would imagine they have a considerable number of very loud automatic weapons that need to be test-fired on a fairly regular basis. Maybe the sound carried?"

"But why would they test-fire them in the middle of the night?" Catherine asked.

Grissom shrugged—he didn't have the slightest idea of what the Army might or might not do, much less why.

"Grayson said night firing does occur at the test and training range on occasion, but the sound rarely carries this far," Brass said. "Anyway, after the shooting stops, they hear a car engine revving up in the same general location, the noise gets louder—like a vehicle was coming down the dirt road from the base of the mountains—and then, all of a sudden, this red truck appears, turns on its headlights at the road intersection, makes a sharp left, heading straight toward this campsite, and then accelerates right at the UCs."

"And that was when all the shooting started?" Grissom asked.

"Apparently," Brass acknowledged. "And there was a second vehicle that made a mad dash down the same road a few seconds after the shooting started, with its lights on; but that one didn't make the turn toward the campsite. It just kept on barreling down the road toward Las Vegas."

"Trying to escape a barrage of automatic gunfire?" Grissom asked.

"Very possible," Brass agreed. "Everyone at the

campsite saw the second vehicle drive by; but the only one who got a good look at it was Boyington, and that was for a split second. He thinks it was a dark-painted SUV, possibly an Escalade, definitely a late model, and big; but he admits that's mostly a guess because dust was flying everywhere and they were all still concentrating on the truck. We put in a call to the local hospitals, just in case."

"Could have been Ricardo Paz Lamos, making his getaway with the coke?" Catherine suggested.

"Another reasonable possibility, I suppose," Brass said, "except it's hard to believe that he'd make a run like that—especially with his headlights on— right past the road intersection where the deal was supposed to take place. Grayson said there are several dirt roads leading out of the refuge that he could have easily taken without being observed. And Jackson and Smith both describe Ricardo as the kind who isn't the least bit reluctant to get into gunfights with Mexican or American cops. With a rep like that, I'd have expected him to at least fire off a few rounds during the drive-by, for self-respect if nothing else."

"Speaking of shooting, has anyone claimed they actually saw the suspect in the truck firing a weapon?" Catherine asked.

"Smith, Tallfeather, Jackson, and Grayson are all insisting that they saw gunfire coming from the cab of the truck before they returned fire at the suspect," Brass replied after consulting his notebook. "And both Smith and Mace are certain that they were shot at—Smith because of her head wound, and Mace because he heard at least one bullet whizzing close by his head. All six UCs admit to firing their weapons at either the truck tires or the engine compartment, trying to stop it. But the five who say they shot at the cab—that would be Smith, Tallfeather, Jackson, Boyington, and Mace—all insist they only did so when they started getting shot at by someone in the truck."

"Did anybody open one of the truck doors or get inside the cab after the shooting?" Grissom asked.

"Jackson ordered Tallfeather to call for backup while he, Mace, Boyington, and Smith approached the truck," Brass said. "They all looked into the cab through the shattered windows, but, supposedly, no one actually touched the doors or got into the cab."

"Jackson let Jane Smith approach the truck with a loaded weapon?" Catherine said, her eyebrows furrowing in concern. "Isn't that a little unusual?"

"Jackson said she's the only one of the group who's actually met Ricardo Paz Lamos face-to-face," Brass explained. "That's why they had her at the scene in the first place. She's terrified of the guy; claims he put a price on her head—which is why Jackson let her stay armed on site. They wanted her to make a positive ID of the body in the truck, but she couldn't because the guy's face was blown apart."

"What about Grayson?" Catherine asked, looking up from her notes.

"He's pretty sure he was the first one to fire at the tires of the truck, trying to stop it when it first arrived on site," Brass said. "He also says he didn't fire at the cab because he didn't have a clear view of the suspect; and after the truck headlights were blown out, he couldn't tell where the other UCs and Smith were positioned. Immediately after the shooting stopped, he got on his radio and called Metro for backup."

"I thought you said Tallfeather called for backup," said Grissom.

"That's what Jackson said, but I confirmed that with the dispatcher that it was definitely Officer Grayson who made the call."

"So who do you think Tallfeather was calling? Fairfax?" asked Catherine.

"Probably," Brass said. "It would explain why he and Holland got here so fast. But if I wanted immediate backup on a buy-bust shooting in the middle of the night, I don't think calling my boss would be my first choice—even if he was riding around nearby in a Black Hawk."

"So, basically, you'd like some answers to all of these questions before the sheriff stands you up in front of the proud parents to hand out commendations for a job well done?" Grissom said with a smile.

"Be tough to put out a recall on the plaques if the D.A. starts handing out indictments," Brass agreed. "So what can I do to help?"

Grissom gestured with his gloved hand in the direction of the parked CSI vehicles. "In the back of Warrick's vehicle, you're going to find two stacks of weighted traffic cones—an 'A' stack and a 'B' stack—with large black-and-white alpha-numeric identifiers and circular photo-alignment markers on the outside surfaces."

"Okay, so?"

"Once we're finished swabbing and collecting firearms, we're going to want to place paired sets of those cones—'A-one,' 'A-two,' 'B-one,' 'B-two,' and so on—in the precise locations where the shooters were standing or sitting or squatting when the truck arrived on scene . . . and where they ended up at the actual time of the shooting. 'A' cone set for Shooter Number One, 'B' cones for Shooter Number Two, etc; the 'dash-one' cones for the truck-arrival locations, and 'dash-two' cones for the shooting locations."

"And I assume you'd like those locations based on an individual interrogation of each shooter—one that takes place out of hearing range of all of the others—and includes their general sense of where all the other shooters were located?"

"That would be ideal," Grissom replied. "And while you're asking questions, we're going to need to know how tall each of these shooters are, and if they were standing, kneeling, or prone when they fired their weapons."

"And if they shot right- or left-handed," Catherine added.

Brass made the appropriate entries in his field notebook.

"Okay," he said, looking up from the notebook, "so, while you guys are poking around the truck, we'll handle those interrogations. After that, I'll have a little heart-to-heart with Miss Jane Smith while the rest of you do your thing."

"Sounds like a fair division of labor to me," Grissom said, then turned to Catherine. "What do you think?"

"Give me a difficult crime scene and a shredded corpse over a bunch of arrogant and pissed-off undercovers anytime," she replied with a glacial-eyed shrug.

"Deal," Brass said with a satisfied smile as he turned and headed back to the parked Denalis, where the four CSIs were still engaged in their initial collection of evidence.

"Nice to know that our good captain still remembers the basic protocols," Grissom commented as he and Catherine turned their attention back to the shattered truck. "You think he's been one of those closet forensic types all this time?"

"I doubt it," Catherine said, shaking her head as she put her notebook back into her vest pocket. "I think he just likes to confront the bad guys, whoever and whatever they might be; and he doesn't seem to mind if he has to get a little dirty in the process."

During the next twenty minutes, which Grissom and Catherine spent carefully working their way around the perimeter of the scene in opposite directions—each taking a series of inward-facing overall scene photos and placing some of their locator flags next to potential evidence items or areas of interest as they progressed—Viktor Mialkovsky sat crouched beneath his protective canopy, carefully dividing his gear into two piles for what would probably end up being a strategic retreat down the western slope of the Sheep Range.

It was not a task that pleased him, but it had to be done.

The issue was weight and volume versus speed.

Mialkovsky was very much aware—because he'd reconnoitered the area a few days earlier—that a withdrawal down the back side of the Sheep Range, in the middle of the night, would involve two difficult elements: first, a strenuous climb over and around slick rocks and loose gravel; and then a hazardous descent through narrow, slippery, and often plunging gaps in the mountain's massive granite ledges, crags, and boulders, where a careless move could easily result in a hundred-foot drop and a potentially crippling—or even fatal—accident.

He'd included the route in his plans as a last resort, in spite of these obvious difficulties, because the detailed map he'd obtained from the U.S. Fish & Wildlife Service's Refuge Office had highlighted it as one of several paths on the high mountain range used by generations of mule deer and Desert Bighorns to escape their human and nonhuman predators. And the physically demanding aspects of the trail—those close-knit ledges, crags, and boulders—appealed to him in terms of concealment and egress from searching helicopters.

And that was the crucial thing—to successfully escape what was rapidly becoming a potential trap, Mialkovsky simply could not allow himself to be seen.

But in selecting this path as his emergency escape route, he'd been careful to account for the fact that a large, muscular human, encased in thick winter clothing, with a nightscoped and silenced rifle in one hand, a folded thermal canopy in the other, night-vision goggles strapped to his head, and eighty pounds of equipment and supplies slung on his back would be a far different creature among those narrow rocky gaps than a slender mule deer or agile Bighorn.

From the first moment he'd stood at the summit of the Sheep Range and stared down into the pathway marked on his map, Mialkovsky knew it would be impossible to descend the route quickly and evasively with all the equipment and supplies he'd be taking on the mission.

And that didn't even count the added problem of avoiding the night-vision and thermal sights of two helicopters conducting random search patterns overhead.

The only solution was to bury all of his nonessential equipment and supplies under some nearby boulders—and then abandon the dune buggy where it was now hidden, knowing that the night-camouflaged vehicle would be easily discovered by a daytime search team.

This was not how he had wanted to leave his carefully rigged scene.

But the unexpected arrival of the young Hispanic, the subsequent shooting at the campsite, and the rapid response of the Metro backup units had forced him to progressively alter his initial withdrawal plans. And now, the ever-expanding sweeps of the circling helicopters were forcing him to resort to an emergency escape route that he'd never intended to use unless his life was actually in danger, a possibility that had seemed so unlikely, that he'd actually chuckled to himself as he'd finalized his plans.

He wasn't laughing now.

It wasn't because he minded caching the equipment items and supplies at the scene. The likelihood of their discovery was remote, at best, even if the CSIs made a determined search of the area. He knew he could always retrieve the more expensive and difficult-to-replace items at a later date.

Nor was he concerned about abandoning the dune buggy at the kill site. He'd hot-wired and stolen the titanium-tube vehicle for this mission from a local auto mechanic—who'd been foolish enough to use a cheap and thus easily picked lock to secure his back storage lot—with the expectation that it would be found.

In fact, his initial plans specifically assumed the Las Vegas PD would eventually locate and track the stolen dune buggy back to the auto shop. And when they did so, they would find a blue tarp protecting a carefully arranged pile of empty boxes from the sun, instead of a twenty-thousand-dollar ATV, but nothing whatsoever to link him to the theft. The black recon clothing, hairnet, hood, and gloves he'd worn that night were very effective in retaining hair, fiber, and latent print evidence; and he'd had plenty of time to make sure that all of the prints left in the dirt by his soon-to-be-disposed-of boots were thoroughly eradicated.

The problem Mialkovsky was now deeply concerned about, as he began to transfer the small pile of essential equipment to his backpack, had little to do with abandoned items of evidence, and very much to do with the rapid passage of time.

Right now, time was his true nemesis.

Mialkovsky had counted on being back in Las Vegas—carefully and methodically cleansing his hotel room of any latent or genetic evidence of his presence—long before the body of his target was discovered and the CSI teams arrived at the scene. But that initial plan, long since abandoned, hadn't accounted for an unexpected third party arriving on the scene in a noisy red truck.

Withdrawal Plan Bravo had died in a blaze of gunfire, along with the driver of that truck.

And his alternate Withdrawal Plan Charlie had quickly evaporated in the rotor-wash of the Black Hawk helicopter as it came roaring overhead in a wide loop across the eastern face of the Sheep Range.

So that left Mialkovsky with the one remaining emergency escape plan he'd never really expected to use: an estimated one-hour climb and two-hour descent in complete—albeit night-vision-enhanced—darkness, followed by another half-hour trek across mostly open desert to reach a small motorcycle he'd prudently concealed as a backup for just such a situation.

Three and a half hours would still give him plenty of time to sanitize his hotel room and be well on his way to Los Angeles before the Las Vegas PD picked up the scent of a professional assassination. But he knew all too well that his earlier estimate had been based on "reasonably expected" conditions that had certainly not included helicopters that might happen upon him at any moment.

If the searching pilots did come this way, and he

was forced to take a more circuitous route down the mountain and out to the hidden motorcycle, Mialkovsky knew he could easily find himself on foot—and openly exposed to anyone who happened to glance in his direction—when the sun began to rise in the eastern sky.

That would be a terribly bad situation, one almost certain to result in his surrender, or a fight to the death that he would inevitably lose if the responding Metro officers recognized the non-civilian-like tactics of their adversary and possibly called for military backup.

The rules of *posse comitatus* supposedly forbade the military from ever interceding in civilian law enforcement affairs; but Mialkovsky knew from experience that a clever police scene commander could always get an extremely competent and heavily armed response if he claimed the suspect was operating in military uniform and with military equipment. He'd been a member of one of those special response teams on three separate occasions.

Nothing I can do it about that until it happens, he shrugged to himself as he hoisted the now much smaller and lighter pack over his shoulders, and then leaned down to pick up his nightscoped rifle and folded canopy, vaguely aware as he did so that his survival instincts were responding to some unseen and unheard stimulus, and beginning to demand attention.

Five minutes later, he understood why.

Tightly encased in a mountain-camouflaged winter survival parka that effectively retained his body heat, but necessarily limited his hearing, Mialkovsky was carefully working his way around the clearing where his target and the hapless mule deer lay crumpled and still on the ice-cold dirt and rocks, when the suddenly echoing roar of an approaching helicopter sent him scrambling for the shelter of another nearby juniper.

5

AFTER SEPARATELY AND METHODICALLY working their way around the circumference of the perimeter tape in opposite directions, Grissom and Catherine finally met back where they had started and briefly compared notes.

Then they entered the scene at the point where the patrol car illuminating the right side of the devastated truck was parked. They did so carefully, one at a time, gently holding the tape up for each other, and then started toward the truck; hesitating before each step to scan the ground with their flashlights, making sure they didn't step in or on any potential evidence.

Fifteen minutes later, the two CSIs finally stood at the passenger-side door of the bullet-pocked truck, having taken a total of sixty-three medium-ranged and close-up photos to document their progress. In their wake, a scattered field of bright-colored flags—sticking up out of the sand on long wire stems—marked the location of numerous expended pistol, rifle, and shotgun casings, and the few boot prints in the soft sand and dirt that offered some promise of a match back to one of the UCs or Jane Smith.

Around their boots, the light from the two flashlight beams reflected off thousands of glass shards—both slivered and cubic—scattered across the hood of the truck and the surrounding sand, dirt, and rocks out to a radius of approximately ten feet.

As Grissom and Catherine slowly swept the flashlight beams up the side panel of the truck . . . over the crackled surface of the mostly broken-out side window . . . and then finally into the truck cab, the waves of intense white light reflected colorfully off a similar collection of laminated and tempered glass fragments and widely splattered patterns of coagulating blood, splintered bone, and brain tissue that covered the seat and the entire rear window.

The body of the suspect lay twisted across the seat with the right arm extended toward the passenger door and the left dangling over the floor-mounted shift, as if he was looking under the dash for something he'd misplaced.

"Pretty obvious why Jane Smith couldn't positively ID this guy," Catherine commented as she swept the beam of her flashlight across the suspect's shattered skull, barely recognizable as human.

"Not much to go on visually," Grissom agreed as he turned on a small tape recorder attached to his vest, and then began to talk his way through the cab interior. "Subject is sprawled sideways across the single front seat of a red Ford pickup truck of undetermined age. He appears to be a muscular Hispanic male of uncertain age—possibly in his late twenties or early thirties—wearing what appears to be black nylon ski clothes and cheap work boots with broken leather laces. His facial features appear to have been destroyed by multiple high-velocity projectile impacts. His exposed wrists and neck are bare; no watch, no jewelry, no visible tattoos . . . but some very distinct scarring present on both sets of knuckles."

"Bare-knuckle brawler?" Catherine suggested.

"Or professional thug," Grissom replied with a shrug as he continued his visual inventory. "A set of keys are in the ignition switch. There's a bolt-action rifle lying on the passenger-side floor . . . and what appears to be powder burns on the exterior web of the subject's right hand." The CSI supervisor briefly painted the blood-splattered hand in question with his flashlight beam, and then switched the recorder to the OFF position.

"Not what you would call an auto-firing weapon," Catherine said as she panned her flashlight beam across the rifle's rusted bolt action.

"Definitely a slow rate of fire, not to mention a pretty poor choice in general if you're planning on taking on a team of armed drug buyers or undercovers single-handed," Grissom said as he continued to examine the blood and brain splatters on and around the body. "Odd, don't you think? I got the impression that in addition to being armed, tough, and violent, this Ricardo Paz Lamos had to be a reasonably smart and successful drug dealer if he's managed to frustrate the DEA all these years."

"You wouldn't know it from his apparent taste in clothes, weapons, and vehicles," Catherine responded as she too continued to examine the cab's shabby and splattered interior. "This truck has to be at least thirty years old—probably older than he is . . . or was."

"Maybe that's how he's managed to sell drugs and evade the narcs all these years: maintain a poor migrant worker cover that puts everyone at ease . . . until it's too late."

"It would have definitely fooled me," Catherine replied. "Do you see any other weapons?"

"I'll take a look from the driver's side in just a second, as soon as I finish . . . this," Grissom said as he knelt down next to the truck's flattened right front tire and used a small spray can to create a bright perpendicular line of green paint from the rusted hub to the ground, and then outward at a ninety-degree angle along the sand for about twelve inches.

Next, he placed three self-adhesive three-inch-diameter white dots—smaller versions of the photo-locator dots on the red traffic cones, each bearing an identical crosshaired grid of thick and thin reference lines and shapes—in a random triangular pattern on the external right side of the truck cab and bed, and then marked them sequentially as "1", "2," and "3" with a broad-tipped permanent ink marker.

Finally, he attached an identical bright-yellow-colored photo-locator dot in the exact center of the tire hub, and marked that dot "R-F" with the same broad-tipped marker.

"Okay, now for the other three."

After noting with satisfaction that Brass, Warrick, Nick, Sara, and Greg were engaged in placing pairs of traffic cones into position with the assistance of the five UCs, Grissom worked his way around the truck, painting identical green reference lines on the remaining three flattened tires, and placing randomly triangulated sets of three white photo-locator dots on the top of the cab, the cab bed, the hood, and the rear, left, and front exterior sides of the truck cab and bed, along with the three bright yellow photo-locator dots on the other three tire hubs, all of which he numbered or lettered with the broad-tipped marker.

The white dots were uniquely and visibly identified as photo-locators "1" through "18," and the yellow dots properly designated the four—right, left, front, and back—tire hubs.

"I'm surprised you could find enough nonpunctured space to set the front locators," Catherine commented, shaking her head in amazement at the amount of projectile-impact damage the grill of the truck had absorbed as she watched Grissom hesitate and then place the last two white photo-locator dots on the far opposite ends of the rusted front bumper. "How many shotguns are we talking about?"

"I saw two leaning up against their truck, both equipped with extended magazines, and what looked like an M-four carbine with a thirty-round magazine," Grissom replied as he continued to search the ground underneath the truck engine compartment with his flashlight, noting the presence of numerous torn and/or partially flattened lead pellets.

"With this many impact points, it's going to be really tough to map out the individual shot patterns, and then work out the timing sequence," Catherine said.

Grissom grunted in agreement.

"You do know that Greg's been hot to work a puzzle like this in like forever, don't you?" Catherine offered with an air of casualness, suggesting she really didn't care who got assigned the mind-numbing impact-pattern segment of the reconstruction.

"Really?" Grissom looked up at his senior CSI.

"I could be wrong, but this one would certainly be character-building; and Greg could certainly use some help in that area . . . maybe an extra dimension beyond cool and cocky," Catherine added with a grin that was part teasing and part hopeful.

Grissom hesitated. He knew from years of experience how difficult it was to try to identify and sequence these multiple-shot and overlapping pattern puzzles when only three or four shotgun rounds had been fired at a single target. So far, he'd counted seven expended shotgun hulls, and there could easily be at least three to five others he hadn't seen yet, depending on how the shotguns had been loaded. He wondered if it would even to possible to sort out and sequence the patterns formed by eighty-four individual buckshot pellets—much less a hundred and forty-four—in such a small impact site.

Greg's brilliant, but I'm not sure he's really ready for something like this, he mused.

The sound of another arriving vehicle caught Grissom's and Catherine's attention.

"Looks like Phillips is here," Catherine said,

motioning with her head in the direction of the approaching coroner's van.

"Good," Grissom replied. "We're going to need him to get that body out of the truck before we can start the reconstruction; but he'll have to be very careful doing it." He slowly stood up, wincing as his long-abused knees cracked, and looked around with a satisfied smile. "Okay, I'm checking out the cab from the driver's side."

As Catherine waited patiently, Grissom slowly worked his way toward the driver's side of the truck. He paused halfway there to examine the ground around his feet out to a radius of approximately six feet, and briefly frowned before walking up to the truck and aiming his flashlight through the partially blown-out side window and into the blood-splattered cab.

For almost half a minute, Grissom remained silent, an intently thoughtful expression on his face.

"See anything?" Catherine finally asked.

"Yes, I do," Grissom acknowledged, the flickering beam of his flashlight illuminating the bloodied and hammerless stainless steel revolver that was just barely visible under the front passenger seat.

"And?"

"As unlikely as it would seem at this point . . . I think our reconstruction job just got a little bit more complicated," Grissom replied with a sigh.

Assistant Coroner David Phillips and his morgue technician driver were standing beside the opened rear door of the brightly marked coroner's van, talking casually with the other four CSIs, when Grissom and Catherine finally ducked back under the scene perimeter tape and headed their way.

As the two senior CSIs approached the waiting group, they noted with approval that the five UCs were back in their camp chairs—now set approximately six feet apart from one another—and sitting quietly under the watchful eyes of the uniformed patrol sergeant.

"David, glad to see you made it," Grissom said, genuinely pleased to see the skilled and hardworking body-handler.

"I understand you've got a pretty messy situation out there," Phillips commented. "Are you ready for us to start things?"

"Not quite yet," Grissom replied as he gestured with his head at Warrick and Nick, who were standing next to each other with diametrically opposed sets of surveying equipment. "Warrick and Nick need to do a little work to stabilize and document the scene first."

Requiring no further instruction, Warrick walked over to the section of perimeter tape directly across from the truck's right-side door, a heavy-duty tripod in one gloved hand and a black twelve-inch-square Pelican case in the other. Kneeling down in the sand, he began to set up the tripod about three feet outside of the perimeter tape, utilizing a dozen ten-to-twenty-pound rocks that he'd already collected and positioned nearby to keep the three base-connected legs solidly in place.

"Any preference?" Nick asked, holding up a five-foot metal spike in one gloved hand and a twenty-pound sledgehammer in the other.

"I think directly in front of the truck, just inside the perimeter tape, should do fine," Grissom suggested with a slight shrug of his shoulders. "The ground looks pretty stable there."

"In front of the truck it is," Nick replied as he walked over to the perimeter line, ducked under the tape, placed the sharp end of the spike into the ground, and made a few light taps with the sledge to set the stake more or less upright. Then he began to drive the spike into the hard ground with grunting swings of the heavy hammer until a little less than three feet of the solid half-inch-diameter metal spike remained aboveground.

After tapping the top of the spike with his gloved hand to see if it would move, and nodding in satisfaction, Nick used a permanent marker to inscribe a red "X" across the slightly smashed spike-head surface, then returned to the group.

"Our triple-zero is set," Nick commented as he placed the sledgehammer in the back of his SUV, then picked up a second identical tripod and Pelican case set and a six-foot-by-two-inch-diameter plastic-pipe carrying case. "That stake is not going anywhere."

As the group around the coroner's van watched and waited patiently, Warrick helped Nick set up and secure the second tripod on the opposite side of the perimeter, directly across from the truck's left door. The two CSIs then proceeded to remove a pair of multifunctional rotating laser heads from the Pelican cases, secured them to the top of the tripod platforms, and used the built-in bubble-gauges to carefully level the platforms—both of which were now extended to a height of five feet from the ground.

"Reading true from your end?" Warrick inquired.

"On the bubble," Nick replied.

"Okay," Warrick said, "time for a little computer magic."

Moving over to the hood of the first patrol car, Warrick opened up a laptop computer and began to activate the first of his crime scene surveying programs. As he did so, Nick slowly pulled a six-foot-long-by-one-inch-diameter aluminum pole out of the plastic-tube case. The pole had a tapering ice-pick-like pointer-tip at one end and a multifaceted receiver/reflector on the other.

After pausing to connect the reflector/receiver at the end of the pole to a palm-sized Pocket PC, Nick carefully placed the pointer-tip in the exact middle of the "X" he'd drawn on the hammered spike-head, and examined the small PC screen to confirm that the pole receiver was picking up a signal from both rotating lasers.

"Computer acknowledges our triple-zero, and is waiting for data," Nick announced.

Humming to himself, Nick slowly approached the left side of the truck, placed the pointer-tip in the exact center of the white photo-locator dot marked "1," moved the top of the pole around in the air— keeping the pointer-tip firmly centered on the locator dot—until the Pocket PC confirmed that both rotating lasers had been detected.

"What's he doing?" Phillips asked Grissom, curious because he'd never seen any of the CSIs use this particular array of locator equipment at a crime scene.

"The pointer-tip and the receiver on the opposite ends of that pole, and the position of the two rotating lasers establish an interlinked pair of invisible triangles with one common side—the pole itself—that gives us an extremely accurate, three-dimensional position of that pointer-tip relative to the top of that stake Nick pounded into the ground. That's now our zero-zero-zero reference point," Grissom explained, happy as usual to provide a bit more scientific detail than his questioner really wanted.

"But what if the top of the pole moves?" Phillips asked, clearly confused.

"It really doesn't matter; in fact, we would expect it to move," Catherine said. "As long as the pointer-tip remains in the exact same location, the receiver at the top of the pole can move freely around to any location where it can pick up a signal from both lasers. No matter where it moves to, the pole itself will form new—but still cross-linked—pairs of triangles with one common side that the receiver will use to calculate the position of the pointer-tip. And as long as that receiver continues to receive a signal from both lasers, it'll continue to transmit the exact same to Nick's Pocket PC."

"Wow. Cool," Phillips whispered, and then blinked in confusion again. "But why do you need to do that?"

"We need to figure out exactly where that truck was located, three-dimensionally, every time one of our shooters pulled the trigger on their firearm," Grissom said. "And if we can do that, we may be able to figure out the sequence of who shot when, and what they hit, and—most important—if that particular shot was justified."

"You can really do that?" Phillips was clearly impressed.

"No, Warrick can do that, using his crime scene reconstruction programs, once he enters all of our digital-locator, photo, and laser-scanner data sets," Grissom replied. "Of course, it would be a lot easier for him and Nick to work all those details out if the surface that the truck and the shooters were on had actually been a flat plane; but as you can see"— Grissom gestured in the direction of the irregular landscape—"it wasn't . . . and isn't."

"And it would be a lot easier to do if the tires hadn't instantly deflated—significantly altering the three-dimensional position of the truck—when each of them got hit, but they did," Sara pointed out.

"And it would be even easier still if we could quickly distinguish each twelve-pellet shotgun pattern from the others where they overlap, helping us to determine distances; but that's going to take Greg quite a while to figure out," Grissom finished.

"*Me?*" The young CSI looked taken aback.

"An experience I can assure you you'll never forget," Catherine promised with a smile.

"And while Greg is doing that," Grissom went on, as if Greg and Catherine hadn't spoken, "we've got our work cut out for us. Sara will test-fire all of the weapons. Catherine will collect a grid-set of trace evidence swabs from the entire vehicle. Warrick's going to take a set of photos of the truck from all sides, and Nick is using the new cherry picker and laser scanner mounted on his van to create a set of

3-D images of the entire scene. I'm going to be collecting—"

The crackle of the radio in Brass's hand interrupted Grissom.

"Air One to Brass."

"This is Brass, go ahead."

"Hate to tell you this, guys, but it looks like we've got more bodies up here."

Brass, Phillips, his morgue tech, and the six CSIs all turned their heads westward and stared up at the top of the Sheep Range, where both visibly blinking helicopters were now circling.

A look of dismay and frustration crossed Grissom's face as he held out his hand to Brass. "May I?"

Brass handed Grissom the radio.

"CSI Grissom to Air One. Did you say 'bodies,' as in plural?"

"Yes, sir, that's correct," the LVPD helicopter pilot responded quickly. *"Do you want us to come pick you guys up?"*

"Yes," Grissom spoke into the radio mike as he and Brass and the other CSIs all met one another's gaze. "Please come get us, right now." Grissom looked around at the complex scene that was going to take his entire team several hours to reconstruct. Or at least that had been the plan. Things had just gotten a lot more complicated . . . again.

6

"CAN YOU SEE THEM?" the pilot asked, keeping a wary eye on the surrounding mountain ledges and crags as he maintained the LVPD Search and Rescue helicopter in a stable position. It was hovering one hundred feet over the clearing below while Grissom—wearing one of the communications-system-connected passenger helmets and sitting in the copilot's seat—peered through the shielded eyepieces of the thermal viewer.

"Yes, I can," Grissom answered. "Only one of them doesn't look all that human."

"Might be a deer or a sheep," the pilot responded. "You see a lot of wildlife in these mountains: deer, big-horned sheep, coyotes, even a cougar every now and then."

"Cougar?" Jim Brass's eyes opened widely.

"Don't worry, you hardly ever run across the big cats this high up, especially at this time of the year," the pilot said reassuringly.

Brass eyed the helicopter pilot suspiciously, and then spoke to Grissom through his passenger helmet mike. "Gil, does this guy sound like an expert in cougar behavior to you?"

"Not what I'd necessarily call an 'expert,' but you don't have to be a scientist to make useful observations," Grissom pointed out with a grimaced smile, much preferring to take his chances with the resident wildlife on the ground than stay up much longer in the intermittently bouncing and vibrating aircraft. He wasn't real fond of helicopters, and was already beginning to feel airsick.

"You guys ready to go down and take a closer look?" the pilot asked.

"You think you can set us down safely in that clearing?" Brass asked, all too aware of how close they already were to several million tons of very solid granite. "It doesn't look like you've got a lot of room to maneuver in there."

"Don't you worry, Captain, I'll get you both on the ground in one piece, one way or another. But I might have to drop you off a little distance away, or out on a ledge, or maybe even rope you down, if we can't find a big enough open space," the chopper pilot added.

"Great," Brass growled. "Give the damned cougars more time to see us coming."

"Don't worry, Jim," Grissom counseled, grateful for the distraction from his queasy stomach, "I'm sure they all know we're here by now."

Brass muttered something unintelligible.

Two minutes later, the pilot gently set the skids of the McDonnell Douglas MD500 helicopter down onto the widest surface they could find on the rocky clearing—about fifty yards from the point where the two bodies had appeared in the thermal scanner. There were several large boulders nearby, so he kept the rumbling airship in tight control, maintaining a steady flow of rotating power—but no lift—to the blades while Grissom and Brass scrambled out of their crew and cabin doors respectively, keeping their heads low as they ran to a safe position.

The pilot then waited while his search systems operator quickly hopped out of the backseat and returned to her normal front-seat station before he recontacted the two investigators on their portable radios.

"I'll put us back over the scene area at one hundred feet, and keep things lit up with the searchlight, while the DEA chopper makes a wider search with the thermal scope," the pilot said as he slowly and carefully brought the agile aircraft back up into the thin, cold air. "Let me know if we're getting too close with the downdraft."

"Will do," Brass said absentmindedly as he drew his semiautomatic pistol and nervously swept the nearby rocks with his flashlight.

"He was right, you know," Grissom said as he picked up his heavy CSI case and then used his own flashlight to start working his way toward the distant bodies. "It really is a little late in the season for cougars to be this high up in the mountains, especially when they could be down in the foothills where it's a lot warmer and there are plenty of rabbits and deer to eat."

"Yeah, but there's always that one oddball who

refuses to go along with the conventional thinking," Brass retorted, keeping the pistol out and ready in one gloved hand, continuing to sweep the surrounding area with his flashlight as he followed in Grissom's unsteady footsteps. "You ought to appreciate that more than most."

"Am I supposed to take that as a compliment?"

"Um, no, probably not," Brass conceded as he slowly made a three-hundred-sixty degree turn with his body and the flashlight beam, searching intently for the first sign of a stalking wildcat.

Four long minutes later, Grissom and Brass finally stood on opposite sides of an expensively outfitted obese human body sprawled facedown on a rocky ledge. The LVPD helicopter overhead provided a considerable amount of light on the scene, but the high-energy search beam also produced dark and concealing shadows.

Given the constantly shifting light situation, the two kept their flashlights on as they examined the coagulated blood on the ground around the upper portion of the body and the expensively silenced, night-vision-scoped, blood-splattered hunting rifle lying in the rocks a few feet away.

"Interesting," Brass said noncommittally as he watched Grissom kneel down and use a pressurized can to outline the positions of the body and the rifle with broad strokes of bright green iridescent paint.

"Let me guess," Grissom said, getting back up and placing the spray can back in his jacket. "You're thinking this guy might have been armed with some kind of auto-firing weapon, and got off a couple of bursts before some other guy armed with the silenced rifle shot him, switched weapons, and took off down the mountain . . . which would explain the shots the UCs heard, and the driver taking off in the big SUV right after the campsite shooting?"

"I *was* thinking that until I saw all the blood splattered on and around that rifle," Brass admitted. "It all looks like the same splatter pattern to me, but I'm not the expert."

"It does look like one distinct splatter pattern," Grissom agreed, "which would certainly eliminate the possibility of a weapon switch if the blood came from the victim at the time of impact. But that seems a little odd, because you'd expect a somewhat distant splattering like that to come from a fully ex-panded bullet tearing through an exit wound, and not from a bullet making an entry wound through a thick down jacket that would tend to hold the blood splattering in."

Grissom moved the focus of his flashlight beam across the rocky ground in a slow arc around the entire body, and then repeated the action once more at a three-foot radius from the body.

"All of that assumes, of course," he went on, "that this guy was shot, and not stabbed or cut, and that the bullet is still in the body. But if he was shot with an auto-firing weapon, I'd certainly expect to see a lot more blood splattering around here . . . and I don't."

"So we're talking at least one other shooter up here, armed with a single-shot-capable pistol or rifle, which might include our subject in the truck?"

"That's certainly a possibly," Grissom said. "Are

you thinking our victim here could be Ricardo Paz Lamos, instead of the fellow in the truck?"

"If the two deaths are related, that might help explain a few things down below," Brass acknowledged, "but from my perspective, and without a positive ID, to me this guy here doesn't look Hispanic. If anything, I'd say his visible features are more Mediterranean . . . maybe even Italian."

"And he doesn't look much like a drug dealer either," Grissom added. "Although I don't suppose there's a generally accepted dress code."

"Probably not for drug dealers," Brass agreed, "but you'd be surprised how much money some people are willing to spend on their hunting gear."

"Including nightscopes and silencers? That doesn't sound very sporting . . . or legal."

"It's neither, but I don't really think you'd be concerned about such minor details if you were wandering around the mountains in the middle of winter, and the middle of the night, searching for the Nevada hunting version of the Holy Grail."

"The Holy Grail?" Grissom's forehead frowned in confusion.

"Desert Bighorns," Brass clarified. "They're rapidly heading toward extinction, so the really dedicated trophy hunters—the ones who are going to do whatever it takes to get their Grand Slam before the possibility no longer exists—might be willing to go all-out in terms of equipment . . . not to mention unfair advantages."

Grissom nodded in understanding as he squatted down to examine the body and rifle more closely. "Such as state-of-the-art night-vision gear, a precision-machined silencer, fancy winter boots, cammo-covered down jacket and pants, and what looks like a very expensive hunting rifle that appears to be silver-engraved with the initials . . ."

Grissom focused his flashlight beam on the rifle's glistening receiver, blinked in surprise, and then looked back up at Brass with a bemused expression on his face, ". . . E.T."

"That's just . . . weird," Brass said with an odd catch to his voice as he went back to scanning the surrounding area with his flashlight.

Grissom stood up and let his own flashlight beam sweep slowly back and forth between the rifle and the facedown body. "You know, this *could* make for a very interesting breakfast presentation at the next American Academy of Forensic Sciences meeting," he said thoughtfully as he opened up his CSI kit and began to assemble his digital camera.

"A *breakfast* blood-and-gore show? You guys still do that at your meetings?" Brass asked as he reflexively reholstered his pistol, his mind clearly elsewhere now.

"Actually, the breakfast seminars are a long-standing tradition," Grissom acknowledged. "It's an honor, of sorts, to be selected as a presenter."

"I'm sure."

"I'd really have to work at coming up with something suitable," Grissom went on, ignoring Brass. "And the more photos the better, of course," he added as he knelt down, took a close-up photo of the rifle engraving, and then made a couple of quick adjustments to the strobe.

Brass started walking purposefully toward the

center of the clearing, using his flashlight beam properly now to scan the area in front of his boots for items of evidence. Then he kept on walking.

Grissom stood up and started to follow him across the clearing, curious as to what had distracted his ex-boss from the threat of stalking cougars. He had taken only a few steps when he suddenly remembered that more photos were always better than fewer.

In one smooth and seemingly instinctive movement, Grissom stopped, made a one-eighty-degree turn, triggered a quick overall photograph of the general area where the body and rifle lay sprawled, and then turned back and hurried to catch up with Brass.

Stunned by the events of the past ten minutes, Viktor Mialkovsky remained motionless under the protective cover of the drooping juniper, the surrounding rocks and boulders, and his camouflaged thermal blanket, watching the two men through the crosshaired and still-flickering screen of his night-scope walk past him—no more than twenty yards away at one point—toward the center of the clearing where he had spent so much time adjusting things to be just so.

Mialkovsky was finding it difficult to believe his eyes, much less his ears.

It didn't help that his retinas were still trying to recover from the blinding flash of green light that had briefly flared in his night-vision goggles and seared his eyes, an effect created by Grissom's sudden decision to turn around and take that single-scene photograph with a very powerful strobe. The directly aligned and unexpected burst of intense white light had instantly overwhelmed the extremely sensitive photoreceptors in the goggles Mialkovsky had been wearing, and the rifle scope he'd been about to raise to his eyes, receptors which had been specifically designed to work with tiny amounts of illumination. He was extremely fortunate that his night-vision gear had survived the unexpected assault. In his experience, earlier generations of the "star-scopes" abused in that manner had almost always flared out into permanently useless hunks of machined aluminum and glass, leaving their operators blind and vulnerable in the starlit darkness.

That was something Mialkovsky knew he could not afford at this point. A blind descent down his icy last-ditch escape route in complete darkness, and during what promised to be a fearsome winter storm, wouldn't be just difficult.

It would be suicide.

But you were the one who made that comment at the breakfast seminar, Grissom: that luck doesn't always work against the criminal, Mialkovsky remembered with a tight smile. *Which is ironic, because of all the Metro CSIs who could have possibly stepped out of that helicopter, it just had to be you. Why would I have ever thought otherwise?*

But, in point of fact, it was the timing of the events during the last half hour that Mialkovsky found truly ironic.

The sudden arrival of the LVPD helicopter directly

over the clearing, and the subsequent arrival of the much-wider-sweeping Black Hawk, had nailed him in place just as he was about to effect his escape. So he'd had no choice but to sit and watch and listen as Grissom and his companion performed their cursory examination of his target's body.

And it was Grissom's comment about the long-standing tradition of the American Academy of Forensic Sciences' bite-mark breakfasts that had nearly caused Mialkovsky to laugh out loud, and thereby reveal his presence to the two distracted and unsuspecting investigators, who undoubtedly thought they were alone on this five-thousand-foot mountain clearing.

It would have been a terrible blunder on his part, because his only viable options at that point would have been to immediately kill the two CSIs, try to quickly down or disable the LVPD chopper, and then make a desperate run for his escape route before the circling Black Hawk crew realized what was going on and called in overwhelming reinforcements.

I wonder what the going price would be for a hit on you, Grissom, Mialkovsky thought as he casually allowed the crosshairs of his still-restabilizing rifle scope to center on the CSI's head. *Possibly a great deal of money; but who would have the nerve to issue the contract? They'd have to know that the other CSIs would never stop looking for the killer . . . or the people who set it into motion.*

The idea of being known among his peers as the only assassin ballsy enough to take the internationally infamous Gil Grissom out with a single shot, and then successfully evade the subsequent all-points search by vengeful legions of detectives, CSIs, and forensic scientists, appealed to Mialkovsky in an oddly twisted Special Ops sort of way.

But he wasn't about to give in to the impulses that had once fueled his most outrageously risky and successful missions. He'd long since outgrown those youthful flashes of insanity. Or, at least, he assumed he had.

The truth was, Viktor really didn't know; and he only vaguely cared.

But of one thing he was certain: playing the odds with a clever and resourceful crime scene investigator like Gil Grissom was a Las Vegas long shot, indeed. Something he'd sworn not to do, but then accepted the Clark County contract anyway because the money had been too good to resist.

How long has it been, Grissom? Mialkovsky tried to remember. *Six, seven years since you and I sat at that table in San Antonio, listening to that nutso wildlife forensic scientist talking about conducting field necropsies on decomposing walruses? Would you even recognize me now?*

Mialkovsky didn't think it was likely because, years ago, he'd looked properly clean-cut and squared away in his Army Ranger uniform—a military CSI looking to expand his general knowledge of forensics, and to pick up a few practical pointers, just like all of the other two-thousand-plus AAFS attendees.

So that's what I'm going to do tonight, Grissom, the hunter-killer told himself as he continued to keep the CSI in the crosshairs of his scope, *watch how you*

approach this scene . . . and pick up a few practical point-
ers before I leave. Fair is fair, after all.

"And here's the deer you saw in the thermal scope,"
Brass said, illuminating the sprawled animal with
his flashlight as Grissom came up beside him. "Or
Mr. E.T.'s deer, depending on how you want to look
at it."

Grissom knelt down beside the sprawled carcass,
examined it briefly, and then looked back up at
Brass. "It's been shot," he said.

"That's generally what happens in a poaching
situation."

"But according to the blood-splatter pattern, the
shot came from somewhere over there"—Grissom
pointed to an area beyond the clearing—"ripped
through the deer's throat, and then continued on in
that direction," he finished, aiming his gloved hand
back in the direction of the sprawled human corpse.
"All of which suggests—"

"A hunting accident?"

"It certainly *looks* like a hunting accident," Grissom said. "Or, considering the high-tech rifle that
presumably belongs to our victim, and not the
shooter, maybe 'poaching accident' would be a better description?"

Brass looked skeptical. "I don't think I've ever
heard of a 'poaching accident,'" he said. "I've always
thought guys who did that sort of thing tended to be
loners. What I have trouble understanding is how a
hunter or a poacher aims at a deer, kills it, and with
the same bullet manages to hit and kill the only
other guy on the entire mountain. The odds against

that ever happening in real life would have to be awfully . . . I don't know . . . long?"

"Hold on just a second," Grissom said as he squatted down and lined up the deer body, the blood splatter, and the sprawled human body in the distance. Then he reached into his jacket pocket, pulled the can of iridescent green paint out again, quickly bracketed the position of the deer with four long strokes . . . and then continued to spray a bright green line heading away from the deer in the opposite direction for about ten feet, duck-walking backwards as he did so. Finally, he stood up, went back to the deer, stared along the green line for a moment, and then started walking in that direction.

"You really think you're going to find something out there?" Brass called to him as he watched Grissom walk a good hundred and fifty feet into the darkness, sweeping his flashlight beam in front of his boots the entire time, and then suddenly kneel down.

Moments later, the sound of a spray can, and then a bright strobe-flash that briefly illuminated the area where Grissom was kneeling, gave Brass his answer.

"Well?" he demanded as Grissom walked back to the deer with a grim smile on his face.

"One expended three-oh-eight Winchester rifle casing that hasn't been out in the weather very long." Grissom held up a six-inch piece of wood doweling with a shiny expended brass casing sitting on the end. "There's a spot back there where it looks like a hunter—or poacher—might have set himself into a prone observation position, waiting for his shot."

Brass pursed his lips, clearly unconvinced.

"Two poachers, independently working the same godforsaken piece of inaccessible mountain in the middle of a federal wildlife refuge, in the middle of the night, in the middle of winter no less, with a storm coming in; and neither of them realizing the other one was out there? And one guy ends up getting killed because the other one decides to shoot a malnourished mule deer instead of something actually worth making that five- or six-hundred-foot climb for? Is that what you're trying to telling me?"

"I'm trying to tell you what I *think* the evidence is saying," Grissom said patiently. "One rifle bullet ripping through a deer's neck and causing the tip to start expanding *before* it hit the victim, which would explain the blood-splatter pattern across the victim's rifle coming from an entry wound instead of an exit wound that doesn't seem to be there."

Brass started to say something, but then hesitated.

"And you're saying the lack of an exit wound in a human from a three-oh-eight rifle bullet could be explained by the fact that it hit the deer first, and slowed down from the impact and the expanding tip before it hit the human victim?"

Jim Brass appeared to be painfully conflicted by two sources of information he normally trusted implicitly: Gil Grissom's interpretation of physical evidence, and his own gut.

"That would be consistent with what we're seeing," Grissom agreed. "Based on the evidence we've found so far, it looks like at least two illegal hunters were up here trying to nail one of the last Desert Bighorns on the planet. Somebody decided to take a shot at this deer, for whatever reason, and accidentally shot their hunting partner . . . or their poaching partner . . . or maybe a complete stranger who just happened to be in the wrong place at the wrong time—which would still explain the character in the big SUV hightailing it down the mountain."

"What about the bursts of automatic gunfire the UCs all say they heard coming from roughly this direction?"

"We still haven't eliminated the testing range behind us as a possible source of that gunfire," Grissom reminded him. "Furthermore, I haven't seen any of the expended casings you'd expect to find from extended bursts of automatic gunfire; and I can't imagine anyone being able to find and pick them all up in a relatively few minutes, under pressure to leave the area, and in this kind of environment."

"But we haven't even started to make a detailed search of the area," Brass protested, seemingly unwilling to set his gut instincts aside.

"No, we haven't" Grissom said. "But we can't do a detailed search until daylight because we can't possibly get enough generator-powered lighting up here to do a decent job, and we'd go nuts trying to do it with those chopper searchlights. And it won't matter all that much if we wait until morning to look for casings, because they won't be impacted to any significant degree by the storm."

Brass stood quietly for a long moment, staring down at the sprawled deer, before he finally spoke.

"So what you're really saying is you think we're wasting our time up here. We're working what appears to be an unrelated hunting accident when we really ought to be down below at the campsite, trying to unravel a questioned shooting at a botched drug buy-bust before the storm hits and destroys all the evidence?"

Brass's vocal tones and body language made it clear that he didn't necessarily see things that way at all.

"This does look like a clear and simple accident, whereas the shooting situation down at the camp strikes me as being anything *but* clear and simple," Grissom said, standing his ground. "And that storm is coming—probably much sooner than later," he added as he glanced up at the sky. "So, yes, I do think we're wasting time up here."

Brass started to say something else, but then blinked as if he'd suddenly remembered something important.

Before Grissom could say or do anything else, Brass turned and started walking back toward the human corpse at a rapid pace, Grissom scrambling to keep up.

When they arrived at the body, Brass knelt down and examined the portion of the man's face that was exposed for a good five seconds with his flashlight beam. Then he stood up and turned to Grissom.

"Look, Gil, I'm really not disagreeing with your technical assessment of the evidence. I'm just trying to reconcile my 'right-sided' cop brain with your analytical 'left,' and it's driving me crazy, so just humor me for a moment. Take a picture of the body, right now. Take several, from all sides, like you usually do before the coroner's investigators move it."

"Why, what are you going to do?" Grissom asked suspiciously.

"When you're done taking the pictures, I'm going to try and turn the body over."

"Without a coroner's investigator being present?"

"Yes."

"Why would you do that?" Grissom demanded.

"Because I think you're absolutely right about one thing: if this *is* a hunting accident, it can definitely wait until after we've reconstructed the buy-bust shooting. But something about this entire situation stinks, and I'm not necessarily talking about this guy's corpse or that of the deer. I want to resolve this now, in my own mind, before we waste any more time; so yes, I'll assume responsibility for violating protocol."

Grissom considered Brass's statement for a moment, and then nodded in agreement.

"Okay, fine by me. You're the scene commander here, so it is your call."

As Brass waited impatiently, Grissom took a series of four overall, right-angle-to-the-body photos, and then a fifth of the man's partially exposed face.

"Okay," Grissom said, stepping back away from the body, "he's all yours."

Grunting something in the affirmative, Brass knelt down, struggled to slowly turn the heavy body over, directed the beam of his flashlight at the man's face, and then chuckled in satisfaction.

"You find this guy's death amusing?" Grissom

asked curiously. He hadn't seen this aspect of Brass's personality before.

"No, but I do find it very interesting that an extremely dangerous and paranoid mob boss like Enrico Toledano would allow himself to get himself killed on a remote mountain, in the middle of the night, by some idiot poacher shooting at a deer."

7

CATHERINE WILLOWS WAS BUSY overseeing the CSI efforts of four members of her team—while at the same time helping Coroner's Assistant David Phillips and his morgue technician gently move the bullet- and pellet-mangled subject out of the passenger-side door of the truck and into the waiting body bag— when her cell phone suddenly rang.

After carefully handing the hammerless Smith & Wesson pistol she'd removed from under the truck set to Sara—along with an admonition that the weapon was still loaded—Catherine stepped away from the truck and reached into her vest for her phone, snapping it open.

"Willows."

"Catherine, this is Gil. How are things going down there?"

Catherine looked around, taking in the entire scene for a few moments before framing her an- swer, knowing all too well that even when Gil posed his questions in a social manner, he was really asking for specific details.

"Things are progressing nicely," she finally said. "We have all six sets of the UCs' gloves, the gunshot-residue kits, my grid trace evidence samples from the truck, all the firearms and extra ammo, and all of the elimination print sets packaged, tagged, and locked up in our van. Their weapons consisted of one M-4 assault rifle, two twelve-gauge Remington pump shotguns with extended magazines, one Sig-Sauer pistol in forty-caliber, two Smith & Wesson MPs in forty-caliber, three nine-millimeter Glocks, and one hammerless thirty-eight Smith & Wesson from our Jane Smith. Interesting enough, that last weapon not only appears identical to the hammerless thirty-eight I just pulled out of the truck, but the serial numbers are within three last-digit numbers of each other."

"That *is* interesting," Grissom agreed. "Who's following up on that?"

"I was going to, but then I decided to wait until you and Jim got back. I don't think Jane Smith is going to appreciate the nature of my questions, nor will the rest of the narcs, Fairfax especially."

"Definitely hold off on that until we get back," Grissom said. "What else do you have?"

"We caught a little bit of a break on the ammo situation. All of the Glocks were loaded with identical nine-mil hollow-points from one case of ammunition from the UCs' truck; but Grayson and the two DEA agents carried different brands of forty-caliber hollow-points. And the state narcs loaded their shotguns from two boxes of buckshot that turn

out to be the same brand but different batches manufactured two years apart."

"That could be helpful."

"It could," Catherine agreed, "but not directly. It
turns out that both agents filled their jacket pockets
with buckshot rounds first, and then loaded their
shotguns . . . which probably resulted in a random
mix of rounds in both guns, based on the two
groupings of ejected hulls at the scene and the remaining live rounds in their pockets."

"Ouch. Poor Greg," Grissom remarked.

"Exactly," Catherine acknowledged, looking down
at the pair of coverall-encased legs sticking out from
under the front of the truck. "He's busy sifting sand
under the engine compartment right now, as we
speak, searching for deflected bullets and pellets.
When he gets done there, he and Sara are going to
follow the tow truck back to the station with the
firearms. She'll begin the test-firing while Greg gets
the truck onto the lift and then starts in on the
projectile-impact analysis."

"Excellent."

Catherine shifted her attention to Warrick and
Nick, who had positioned themselves out near the
"female-facilities" boulder and were busy manipu-
lating a laser scanner attached to the far end of a
thirty-foot-long double-elbowed "cherry picker"
mounted on the roof of their new CSI van.

"Warrick and Nick finished photographing the
shooting locations and the truck and then scene-
scanning the truck a few minutes ago," she went
on. "They're now in the process of repositioning the
scene scanner over the boulder and cones where

Jane Smith claims she was located when the truck arrived, and when she started shooting. We've got some conflicting information as to who was standing, kneeling, or prone when they were shooting specific rounds; but it's more a timing disagreement than anything else, and the knee and elbow prints in the sand should help sort things out. The guys are having a little trouble getting the scanning van positioned 'cause the sand is so soft, but they've only gotten stuck once so far. They say they'll be done in another couple of hours, but I'm thinking more like three or four at the outside. Some of the sand around here is pretty deep."

"The storm's going to hit long before then," Gil said. "It's already starting to get misty up here."

"I know," replied Catherine. "We're going after the most exposed and disputed locations first. And if nothing else, we've always got the location-point data to cross-link the digital photos with the truck scan."

Catherine looked over to her left, where Sara was kneeling down on a spread-out tarp in front of one of the parked LVPD patrol cars, using its illuminating headlights, an old-fashioned print brush, and fine white powder to dust the hammerless Smith & Wesson pistol for latent prints.

"Oh, and you'll be happy to hear that our new portable laser crapped out the moment we plugged it into the generator. Warrick thinks it's just the motherboard that probably got jarred loose on the road coming up here, but he doesn't want to open the case up out here because there's sand everywhere. He and Nick left the second laser back at the lab, because they needed the room for all the new scene-scanning gear; and our third unit is still in the shop, so we're stuck with brush and powder for latents. We'll wait on processing the UCs' weapons until we get back to the lab, but I've got Sara processing the rifle and pistol we found in the truck cab right now."

"What about—?"

"Sorry to interrupt, but I want to finish the scene-status report while I've still got it all in my head. David and I just finished getting our subject into a body bag. I'll let you talk with David separately, but I'll give you the basics: we didn't find any ID on the body or in the truck, and there were no externally visible tattoos on his hands, arms, neck, or what was left of his face. I swabbed both of his hands for gunshot residues, but we'll wait to fingerprint him back at the morgue."

"Sounds reasonable," Grissom agreed.

"Then, as soon as the morgue team heads back to the city," Catherine went on, "I'm going to start collecting the expended casings and look for whatever else I can find in the way of evidence—ideally before the storm hits; which means I could use some help down here ASAP . . . if you're not too busy up there, of course."

"Don't let David leave with the body yet," Grissom said quickly.

"Why not?" Catherine asked, immediately thinking, *Oh no.*

"What about the truck?" Grissom asked. "Any leads on it?"

"Not much. It looks like the license plates were

removed recently, and the VIN number comes back as a vehicle last registered to a local rancher, but he reported it stolen six months ago. There's a lot of dust and cobwebs in the cab and under the hood, so we're guessing it's probably been stashed away in some shed all this time and not taken out often."

"So our subject just appears, out of the blue without a discernible trail—a regular will-o'-the-wisp," Gil said.

"Wasn't that what Fairfax said about Ricardo Paz Lamos?"

"Yes, it was," Gil acknowledged. "Do you have anything on the make, model, and caliber of the rifle in the truck?"

Catherine quickly referenced her notebook. "It's an old bolt-action, Winchester Model Seventy, three-oh-eight caliber. We found an expended round in the chamber and two live rounds in the magazine."

"Excellent," Grissom replied. "That may help resolve things up here."

"Don't tell me—"

"We have what looks like an unrelated hunting accident, involving a well-known local. At least *I* think it's a hunting accident; but Jim isn't convinced, so I need the morgue guys to come up here in the DEA helicopter and pick up two more bodies before they leave. I've already contacted the DEA pilots and they're headed back your way now."

"Did you say *two* more—?"

"I'll come back to the campsite with the helicopter and explain it all when I get there," Grissom said. "Suffice it to say that our hunting victim may have been shot with a three-oh-eight rifle bullet."

"Oh" was all she could finally manage to get out at first. Then, after a couple of moments, she added: "Does that simplify things down here, or make everything a lot more complicated?"

"When you figure that out, please let me know."

Thirty minutes later, Grissom, Brass, Fairfax, and Holland were helping Assistant Coroner David Phillips and his morgue technician haul the heavy body of Enrico Toledano toward the distant DEA helicopter, each of the men struggling to hang on to one of the six looped straps sewn into the midsection and four corners of the extra-large rubberized body bag as they tried to move forward in some sort of coordinated manner without snapping their ankles on the now-very-slippery rocks.

It had started raining ten minutes ago, and the chilled drops were now coming down hard and fast, aided by a swirling wind that was starting to make the helicopter pilots—not to mention Fairfax and Holland—increasingly uneasy as they waited for the forensic team to hurry up and collect their bodies.

The two commanders hadn't been pleased when they learned the first smaller body bag contained the carcass of a small deer, but Brass had been in no mood to discuss the matter politely. He simply informed the pissed-off commanders and the storm-wary pilots that he had no intention of leaving the deer carcass or the body of Enrico Toledano up here to be chewed on by the local fauna; they were both coming off the mountain if he had to drag them down by himself.

As expected, mentioning the name of Enrico Toledano produced the desired effect: the two narcotics unit commanders had immediately scrambled out of the helicopter to lend a hand.

"Christ, how much does this guy weigh?" Fairfax demanded, gasping for breath as the six men took advantage of a sudden lull in the rainstorm to stop and recover their strength for their final run to the waiting helicopter. They still had another thirty yards to go, and it was all uphill.

"As a guess, I'd say at least three hundred and fifty pounds," Phillips said, looking decidedly pale in the light from the LVPD chopper high overhead. "Maybe closer to four hundred."

"We should have winched him up to the Black Hawk with the harness," Fairfax muttered as he shook the rain off his dripping head. "So what does all this mean, Brass? Are you telling me that Paz Lamos came up here and shot Enrico Toledano before he went after my team? God, if word of that gets out, we're going to have a mob-cartel war along the entire southern border."

"Ask Gil, I'm too tired to talk right now," Brass replied, looking around for something other than the body-bagged Toledano to use as a chair.

"Everything about this scene tells me that it was a hunting accident," Grissom offered, working to catch his breath. "And based on what we've found so far, it's easy to believe that Toledano was up here with his expensive gear trying to poach a Desert Bighorn—mostly because the evidence seems to fit, and the arrogance of it sounds in character for someone like him. We'll know a lot more once we get these bodies and everything else to the lab."

"So you really don't have any evidence that Paz Lamos was up here?" Holland pressed in a slightly wheezing voice. The state commander looked as pale as Phillips, but nowhere near as fit.

"We may be able to show that the subject in the car was up here, especially if the casing I found matches the rifle in the truck," Grissom said, amazed that his lungs were no longer burning in the cold, thin air. "But as for Paz Lamos himself, you're asking the wrong guy. At the moment, I don't have any evidence that he even exists. It's like trying to ID evidence on a Bigfoot case: we really need to start with a known comparison standard."

"Believe me, this guy exists," Fairfax growled. "I've got three dead snitches and two agents in a hospital recovering from near-fatal gunshot wounds who will vouch for that."

"And I've got a dead state officer who tried to help two Arizona troopers make a vehicle stop on the guy," Holland added, starting to look a little less pale now in the overhead chopper's sweeping search beam. "We found all three of them beside their vehicles, each shot in the head. And that was after he beat the crap out of a federal refuge officer who caught him crossing the border at the Cabeza Prieta National Wildlife Refuge with a load of coke. For whatever reason, he seems to like to make his big deals on federal refuges."

"So that's why you guys arranged the buy-bust out here," Brass said, nodding in understanding.

"Exactly."

"But do you have any kind of known specimen from this guy?" Grissom asked. "Blood, hair, saliva, fingerprints, footprints? Anything at all?"

"Nothing except for that one blurry photo. We took that off a videotape from one of the Arizona patrol cars," Holland replied. "According to everyone who's dealt with him, and survived, he always shows up separately at the drug deals, in dark clothes, mask, gloves, and hat, looking like a cross between Zorro and a ninja. He never goes near the drugs or the money, and he's always the first one to start shooting when things go wrong."

"Oh yeah, one other thing," Fairfax added. "Rumor has it that he used to be a much-sought-after contract killer . . . and that he's still perfectly willing to make a hit on anyone—Mexican and American cops definitely included—for the right price."

"Even a mob boss?" Grissom asked.

Fairfax shrugged. "You tell us."

"So, if Paz Lamos did shoot Enrico Toledano, it probably wasn't an accident," Brass concluded. "He doesn't sound like the type to waste his ammo on deer."

"There's always the possibility that one of Toledano's underbosses hired Paz Lamos to make the hit," Holland said. "We've heard word for months that his people are unhappy about their cuts of a declining revenue base, and that he's increasingly 'disengaged' from the daily operations, whatever that means."

"If that's what really happened up here, then the

shit is definitely going to hit the fan, big-time, because none of the other mob bosses want more federal attention on Las Vegas gambling; it's too
lucrative," Fairfax said. "They all know the focus of
federal law enforcement has dramatically shifted to
homeland security issues these last few years, but a
mob hit in Vegas could turn things around dramatically within twenty-four hours, especially if the
more or less independent families start going at each
other again."

"Which would probably reduce state and federal
emphasis on drugs coming in from Mexico even
more than it is right now," Holland added.

"Meaning Ricardo Paz Lamos and the cartels win
big-time—motive *and* opportunity—as long as he
isn't linked to the shooting," Fairfax said, looking up
as the rain started falling again, and then taking in a
deep steadying breath. "Oh man, it's starting to
come down again. Ready to make the last push,
guys?"

No one looked especially enthused about the
idea, but all six men bent down and picked up the
body bag again in a symphony of grunts and groans.

"Just one more question," Grissom said as he
staggered forward under his share of the load. "If
what you said is true, and a clever fellow like Paz
Lamos knows he and the cartels will only gain from
Toledano's death if they're not connected to it, then
why would he schedule the hit at the same time—
and pretty much at the same place—he was supposed to be selling ten kilos of cocaine to a bunch of
bikers?"

"That's the trouble with you linear-thinking

forensic types," Fairfax said half-jokingly as the six men began to lug the body bag uphill again toward the impatiently waiting helicopter crew. "You really don't appreciate the intricate and twisted workings of the devious criminal mind."

"Or the devious cop mind either," Grissom agreed amiably. "But that's okay; we really don't need to understand any of our adversaries, just so long as they keep on making helpful mistakes when it really counts."

From the shelter of a cavelike crevice in the rocks overlooking the helicopter landing site, Viktor Mialkovsky watched the six men load the second body bag into the Black Hawk with a mixture of unease and irritation.

He was uneasy because he didn't like the fact that Grissom and Brass had insisted on bringing the carcass of the deer down the mountain in an evidence-preserving body bag along with his target. It suggested Grissom might have spotted something that he'd overlooked when he was hurrying to set up the scene before the helicopters came back on another sweep.

Mialkovsky really didn't think he'd missed anything significant; but the shifting winds had carried Grissom's mildly sarcastic barb about "helpful mistakes" at the scene back to his hideout, and the words had rankled. He didn't like being reminded that luck invariably played a role in all cover-ups, and that mistakes—ideally small and inconsequential—were almost impossible to avoid.

These were principles that Mialkovsky had

depended upon in his earlier career to track down and expose deliberate violations of engagement rules by military combat teams.

But they were also the principles that Grissom and law enforcement would use to track him down if one of those inevitable mistakes turned out to be consequential.

Just have to hope that isn't the case, the hunter-killer mused, still thinking about the deer carcass as he stared glumly up at the sky.

He was irritated because, by hanging around the scene as long as they did before calling in the transport helicopter, Grissom and his companion (obviously a detective) had unwittingly managed to delay his retreat back down the mountain until the storm arrived.

And now that it was here, and growing rapidly, he was stuck in place until it abated, because the rain and cloud cover had the dual effect of making his planned escape route even more slippery and reducing the effectiveness of his night-vision goggles to almost zero.

That along with the wind and the near-total darkness virtually guaranteed that it would end very badly—at least one out-of-control fall or something far worse. He simply could not afford to risk it at this late stage of the operation, especially when he desperately needed to be skipping town—ideally in a completely inconspicuous manner—as quickly as possible.

The only saving grace was the likelihood that the storm would soon ground the two helicopters—or, at least, prevent them from flying too low—and thereby keep Grissom and his CSI team off the mountain until dawn.

He would need to remain hidden until the storm broke; quickly work his way down to the motor-cycle before everyone returned to the scene; and everything would work out fine.

Mialkovsky couldn't do much to influence the timing and luck factors at this point in his mission. But he did possess complete confidence in his military and survival expertise. Beyond that, he considered himself a very patient man.

8

DR. ALBERT ROBBINS and David Phillips both looked up from their work as Gil Grissom and Catherine Willows walked into the morgue wearing white lab coats.

"Gil, Catherine," the gruff pathologist said, briefly raising a bloodied scalpel in greeting. "I've come to the conclusion that it was a very good idea to start sending David out to your scenes. He's always coming back with something . . . different."

"I take it you're referring to the deer?" Grissom asked as he glanced over at the small mammal sprawled out on the third autopsy table. It was a different image indeed for the Clark County coroner's morgue: the thin and fragile-looking creature appearing very much out of place next to the shattered body of the truck driver on table two—where David was busily engaged with the contents of a GSR kit—and the much larger and visibly fat-laden body of Enrico Toledano on table one, where Robbins was finishing up his autopsy.

"Not your normal crime scene victim," Robbins said, his attention focused on the opened chest and partially dissected throat of Toledano, "unless the CSI teams have started working poaching cases in their spare time . . . and I didn't think you folks had any of that worth talking about."

"Actually, you might be working on a poacher right now," Catherine said as she came up beside Robbins and stared at the opened-up wound.

"Really?" Robbins looked at her in surprise. "I was under the impression that Mr. Toledano here was a—" He turned his head to stare over at Phillips for a moment, and then blinked in realization. "Well, yes," he said with a shrug as he went back to work with the scalpel, "I suppose you could always be both."

"Finding anything interesting, Al?" Grissom inquired.

"As a matter of fact, I did," Robbins said as he gestured at a small stainless steel pan next to Enrico Toledano's opened skull. "What do you think of that?"

Grissom and Catherine leaned forward and eyed the single object lying in a blooded piece of gauze in the middle of the pan.

"I'd say it appears to be a mushroomed rifle bullet, approximately thirty-caliber, with bits of tissue embedded under the peeled-back jacketing," Grissom responded.

"And?" Robbins prompted.

"There's more?" Grissom pulled a pair of plastic forceps out of his white lab coat and used them to carefully lift the bullet up to a point where he and Catherine could both see it clearly.

"It looks like the base of the bullet is slightly deformed on one side . . . like it hit some dense object a glancing blow?" Catherine suggested.

"Indeed, it did," Robbins said. "And the dense object it hit was the third cervical vertebra of our victim here."

Grissom and Catherine looked at each other in confusion, and then stood in thoughtful silence for a few moments.

"How does that work?" Catherine finally asked. "Don't rifle bullets usually hit their targets nose first?"

"They do if they don't tumble," Robbins replied. "For example, the relatively small and light 5.56-millimeter bullets used in our military assault rifles and several civilian knockoffs are infamous for deflecting off of relatively light objects and tumbling upon impact, thereby causing far more grievous wounds than expected."

"But this is a relatively large bullet, specifically designed for a high-powered rifle, so it shouldn't tumble at all," Grissom pointed out, pressing the pathologist to help flesh out his own theory about the single blood-splatter pattern he and Brass had observed around Toledano's rifle.

"No, it should not," Robbins agreed. "In fact, a high-powered rifle bullet like this really should have produced a fairly massive wound more like that"— the pathologist gestured with his scalpel over at the

shattered head of the truck driver on table two—
"instead of a relatively minor, albeit fatal, wound
like this." He gestured down at Enrico Toledano's
partially dissected neck. "Unless, of course, the bullet deflected against something fairly solid first, such
as a Kevlar vest with a ceramic or composite plate."

"Did it?" Catherine asked.

"Not as far as I can tell," Robbins said. "Our victim here was wearing that exceptionally large and
undoubtedly tailored Kevlar vest over there on the
table"—he nodded with his head over at a stainless
steel table in the corner of the morgue—"which, according to the label, is a first-stage protection model
designed to stop bullets up to and including .375
magnums."

"But not thirty-caliber, high-powered rifle bullets," Catherine said as she walked over and briefly
examined the blood-splattered vest.

"No, I'm sure a bullet like the one we have here
would have ripped right through that particular
vest, or any other similar vest that lacked a protective frontal plate," Robbins said. "But that wasn't
even an issue in our victim's case, because that bullet missed his vest entirely."

"You'd think Mr. Toledano's upper body and vest
would be fairly easy targets to hit—especially with a
rifle—if that was the shooter's intent," Grissom
commented.

"Undoubtedly true," Robbins said, "as demonstrated by the numerous bullet-wound scars we
found on his torso. It can't be much fun being an
exceptionally large mob boss with a long list of
enemies."

"But this bullet had to hit something substantial to mushroom like this, so what did it hit?" Catherine asked as she came back to the table.

"I have no idea," Robbins replied.

"What about a deer?" Grissom asked.

Robbins raised an eyebrow. "You mean like that one over there on table three."

"That's right."

Robbins walked over to the table with a thoughtful expression on his face, examined the deer for a few moments, and then came back to the group.

"My first inclination is to say no, probably not; because whatever projectile caused the wound on that deer appears to have missed the neck bones altogether and simply ripped through its relatively fragile throat. Death probably occurred instantly due to hydrostolic shock. I'll know more once I take some X-rays; but I wouldn't think the mushrooming characteristics or the trajectory of a high-powered rifle and large-caliber bullet like this would have been impacted to any significant degree by such a small amount of thin tissue. But then, too, I'm not an expert on the physics of mushrooming bullets; so that's why I'm giving it to you, along with the vest," he said with a smile.

Grissom looked at Catherine, who reached into her lab coat pocket and pulled out a small manila envelope. She waited for Grissom to slip on a pair of plastic gloves, and then held it open as he carefully folded the bullet back into the piece of gauze and slipped the entire packet into the envelope.

"I'm going to get this bullet to Bobby right away, along with the vest, the three-oh-eight rifles from the two scenes, and that cartridge case you collected," Catherine said as she walked over to the stainless steel cart where David was now waiting with a clipboard in hand. "Then I'll check in on Greg and Sara."

"Check on Warrick and Nick too, if you don't mind, and don't forget to get Wendy looking at the tissue under that bullet," Grissom said. "I've got to get to a meeting with Brass, as soon as I pick up the rest of the evidence."

"No problem," Catherine responded as she took the clipboard from Phillips, quickly signed the chain-of-custody form, picked up the tagged vest, and disappeared out the door.

"Everything that's ready to go is right here," David said, motioning at the tagged gunshot-residue kit and freshly inked fingerprint card that he'd laid down on the cart surface next to an identical set of materials tagged as being from Enrico Toledano. "I'll send all the tox samples over to the lab, along with whatever we find in our John Doe victim, as soon as we finish his autopsy."

"Fine." Grissom turned back to Robbins. "Anything else you can tell us at this point?"

"Not really." The pathologist shrugged. "We'll try to get direction-of-impact measurements on as many of the bullet and pellet impact points as possible, but I don't think we're going to be able to tell you much about the direction or sequence of the head wounds on our John Doe."

"No, I suppose not," Grissom said as he took a last look at the man's shattered facial features. "It looks like we may have to depend on a little electronic magic . . . and possibly even some high school trigonometry, if you can believe it."

"How's it going?" Catherine asked as she walked into the crime lab's primary garage examination area. She observed Sara sitting on a stool in front of the red truck, which was now raised up about a foot off the lab floor on the garage lift. Sara was carefully swabbing the edges of an indented hole in the exterior truck grill immediately adjacent to a long wooden dowel that had been fed through another such hole in the grill and a supposedly matching one in the radiator. A bundle of the four-foot-long dowels lay on the concrete in front of her knees.

From her position some ten feet away from the truck, Catherine could see at least fifteen to twenty other dowels sticking out of the grill, and an equivalent number of used trace metal swab vials on a torn square of butcher paper on the cement floor to the young CSI's right. It appeared to Catherine that Sara still had several dozen holes to go.

At a deep sink on the opposite side of the garage, Nick was busy scrubbing grease and oil off his hands.

"I think Nick's made the most progress so far," Sara said with a sigh as she quickly referenced a crude sketch lying on the concrete floor to her left, marked the swab vial, set it down on the butcher paper next to the others, and then reached down and picked up another dowel. "He managed to get our John Doe's vehicle off the tow truck, onto the lift, and jacked up to proper inflated-tire height while Greg and I were still reading the manual on the new crane-hoist."

"Nick volunteered to unload the truck?" Catherine raised a curious eyebrow. Grissom had assigned Nick to far more challenging and much less dirty work.

"I came by to see how badly shot up the front tires were, and heard Greg and Sara in here arguing with the tow truck driver about whose responsibility it was to get the vic's truck off his rig and onto the lift," Nick explained, looking up from the sink with a grin on his face. "I did some summer work at a neighborhood garage when I was a kid, so I know how to work a hoist. And besides, Warrick and I need the front-end impact data to work out our trajectories, and I didn't want Sara and Greg to end up smushing themselves with the crane and leaving me to clean up the mess."

"Normally, I'd be insulted by that remark. But right now, I'll happily trade you one massively perforated grill-slash-radiator, and a dirty job to be negotiated at a later date, for anything *you've* got," Sara said hopefully as she stretched out what looked like a very sore right arm, and then reached for another dowel.

"I can definitely hear Warrick calling my name," Nick said cheerfully as he waved good-bye and hurried out the door.

"So how'd you get stuck with the front-end work?" Catherine asked. "I thought Gil assigned that fun job to Greg."

"He did, but while Nick was working on the truck, and Greg was working on the rough sketches, numbering all of the holes and impact points"—Sara pointed to three separate sketches of the truck grill, the radiator, and the front of the engine, all quickly drawn on pieces of butcher paper with a thick marker pen—"I was over at the indoor range, starting to test-fire the shotguns, and I let one slip off my shoulder."

"Ouch," Catherine said, wincing sympathetically. "You okay?"

"Just a bad bruise—those twelve-gauge rounds have a wicked recoil—but you know Greg: chivalrous to the core. He heard the range master put out a call over the intercom for an EMT response, came by the range to check on me, and then offered to switch jobs."

"Two white knights to the rescue within the span of one hour—probably a new record around here," Catherine commented with a grin.

"Yeah, except I now owe both of them big-time, which probably means I'll be working the next floater all by myself . . . and I still have this insane puzzle to figure out."

"Let me go check in on the others, make sure they're all doing okay, and then I'll see if I can give you a hand with this Rubik's Cube for a while," Catherine said.

"Which means I'll owe you, too, right?" Sara said suspiciously.

"Better believe it," Catherine said with a wink as she headed toward the door. "I'm not real fond of working those floater cases either."

"Making any progress, guys?" Catherine inquired as she walked into the lab's small conference room where Warrick and Nick had set up shop with a pair of laptop computers that they'd networked to the lab's central servers and the three ceiling-mounted projectors, all of which were now displaying replicas of the two laptop screens on the left and right sectors of the far white wall.

The middle sector remained blank.

Both CSIs were hunched over their machines, working quickly to enter data from the truck shooting scene into their linked but very different programs; but both looked up, seemingly grateful for the interruption.

"I'm entering the location-point data into the scene drafting program, and what you're seeing right now is the basic two-dimensional top view," Warrick said.

"Why does the truck look like it's made of building blocks?" Catherine asked.

"That's just a place-holder right now," Warrick explained. "I'll download a standard 3-D figure of an old Ford truck for where the shooters each made their crucial decisions to shoot or don't shoot; but, eventually, we'll substitute a 3-D image of the real thing from Nick's scene scanner."

"That's assuming I can get thirty separate image scans to interlock and agree with each other," Nick corrected. "Right now that's looking a little iffy because the program isn't recognizing all of the individual locator dots correctly."

"A program glitch . . . or data overload?" Catherine asked.

"I don't know," Nick said. "I've been using this version for almost two months now, and it's worked fine on simple scene situations. What we're asking it to do is a little more complicated in terms of locator points, but not beyond its specs."

"What about data volume?" Warrick asked, looking up from his laptop.

"That shouldn't be an issue because I'm actually running the program off the lab's mainframe, so we've got all the crunching power we need," Nick replied. "And the program seems to recognize non-dotted objects just fine. Here, look."

As Nick keyed additional information into his laptop, a replica of Warrick's still-crude scene sketch appeared on the middle sector of the far white wall.

"There's the basic campsite, showing Pine Nut Road, the turnoff, the location of the UCs' truck, their motorcycles, the fire ring, the camp chairs, and the two large boulders," Nick said. "Now watch this."

The CSI double-clicked on the overhead image of the big boulder that Jane Smith used as the "female facilities."

Instantly, the 2-D top-view image of the large boulder appeared in the middle-wall-sector image of the campsite sketch.

"Okay," Warrick said, "now I'm going to take a walk around that boulder."

The middle-wall-sector sketch image suddenly shifted to a 3-D view of the massive rock . . . and then continued to shift as Warrick took an electronic "tour" around the boulder from about twenty electronic feet away.

"Wow, that looks almost exactly the way it looked at the scene," Catherine whispered, impressed in spite of herself, "except that—"

"The boulder was actually over here a little more," Warrick finished as he quickly shifted to the 2-D overhead view, nudged the boulder image over a few electronic feet, and then returned to the 3-D view.

"Yes, exactly," Catherine nodded. "Wow."

"Not *exactly* exactly," Nick corrected. "But that rock will be located precisely where it belongs on the finished 3-D sketch—along with the truck, the major bullet and pellet impact points, and the position of the six shooters when they first saw the truck and when they shot their weapons—to a plus or minus accuracy of at least one-one-hundredth of an inch . . . if and when I can get this damned software to work."

"And that should be real interesting," Warrick added, "because each of those 'shooting-locator' cones has a pole sticking out of it with a locator at the more or less precise height that each weapon was at when the shooters fired—whether standing, kneeling, or prone."

"So we'll be able to figure out what the shooters could or could not have seen at the time they fired their weapons," Catherine said, nodding in understanding.

"Yes, we'll be able to do that, but only if we can determine one absolutely known reference point of time and vehicle position that we can use to register and correlate all of the other shooting times and places," Warrick noted.

"And that's going to be tricky," Nick added, "because the best data we'll have to go on will probably be the shotgun-distance determinations. And you know how rough those approximations are going to be, even if Greg and Sara can sort out and calculate the individual patterns in that grill and radiator."

"So, what are you saying?" Catherine asked, slightly alarmed. "That all the locator points on the sketch—and the truck itself—are going to be high-tech-accurate to a hundredth of an inch; but the actual truck *location* at any particular moment may only be accurate to plus or minus a few inches?"

"Or maybe only plus or minus a few feet," Warrick said, "depending on what kind of data Greg and Sara can tease out of that grill and radiator."

"According to my expended count," Catherine said, reading out of her field notebook, "we're looking at ten high-base double-ought buck rounds, thirty five-five-six-mil rifle rounds, and a combined total twenty nine-mil and forty-cal pistol rounds . . . and most likely three thirty-eight special rounds . . . which pretty well tallies with the remaining ammo in the UCs' magazines, chambers, and cylinders."

"Ten high-base buckshot rounds?" Nick winced.

"At least that, and maybe eleven," Catherine went on. "Mace kept a round in the chamber of his shotgun, but he can't remember if he put four or five in the magazine. In any case, that all adds up to a minimum of one hundred and seventy-three projectiles potentially hitting the tires, the grill, the windows, and the cab of the subject's truck . . . all of which measure between three-tenths and four-tenths of an inch in diameter . . . and all of which can be very difficult to tell apart—bullet-hole-wise—depending upon the angle of the shot, velocity of the round, vector direction of the ricochets off the frame and engine block, projectile distortions, overlapping impacts, and target-metal fatigue. And that is precisely the situation poor Sara is facing as we speak."

Nick looked stricken. "We're not going to be able to get accurate distance determinations from the shotguns, are we?"

"Probably not, unless we conduct trace metal analysis on the edges of each impact hole, to categorize the source projectile," Warrick predicted. "Sara's collecting the samples, just in case; but that amount of instrumental work is going to take hours."

"What's this 'we' stuff?" Nick said. "It's going to take me all night to resolve this software problem, and you're not even close to having the 3-D scene correlated with Catherine's images."

"What about David?" Catherine asked.

"Grissom's got him working the GSRs as a first priority," Warrick replied.

"But I'm sure if you asked, our clever Mr. Hodges would offer to work the trace metal samples with his other hand," Nick added sarcastically. None of the night-shift CSIs were especially fond of the ass-kissing lab technician.

"What about Wendy?" Catherine said, ignoring the nonserious suggestion. "I'm pretty sure she's cross-trained on the XRF."

"She is—she passed her proficiencies last week," Warrick confirmed, "but Grissom's got her working the tissue lodged in the bullet that Doc Robbins pulled out of that mob boss's neck, and all of those blood-splatter and trace swabs you pulled out of the cab and bed of that pickup."

Catherine frowned. "Wait a minute, what about Archie? Why can't he help out in here, so that we can kick one of you guys loose?"

"Archie called in sick right before shift change," Nick replied. "We've called him twice—home and cell—but no answer."

"So you're suggesting he may not be quite as sick as he proclaimed?"

"My guess is he's over at the residence of that gorgeous young lady he's been telling us about, the one who doesn't seem to be much interested in dating a computer geek, no matter how cute and lovable he might be," Warrick offered. "I remember him saying something about her having trouble with her computer, and how he might use that as an excuse to go over to her apartment and try to get to know her better."

"You mean better than that supposedly steady girlfriend he's always bragging about?" Nick inquired. "Since when do geeks try to expand their horizons with women?"

Warrick shrugged noncommittally.

"Ever the optimist," Catherine commented, shaking her head. "Do we know this new young lady's address?"

"No, but I put in a request to patrol to keep an eye out for his car," Nick said with a smile. "There's nothing quite like an ornery uniform pounding on the door to put the kibosh on a blossoming relationship."

"Spoken like a man with sad but relevant experience?" Warrick smiled sympathetically.

"CSI call-outs can definitely put a damper on a guy's love life," Nick agreed as he looked up at Willows with a mischievous gleam in his eye. "On the other hand, not all of us—"

"Please. Don't even think about commenting on *my* love life *or* my free time," Catherine warned.

The conference room went silent for a long moment.

"This is all going to take hours, if not days. Brass isn't going to like this . . . and neither will Gris," Warrick finally said.

Catherine and Nick nodded glumly in agreement.

"So who's going to tell them?" Nick finally asked.

The two Level-3 CSIs stared directly at their nominal supervisor.

"Are you suggesting those very few extra dollars that occasionally get added to my paycheck make me the sacrificial messenger?"

The two slightly-lower-paid CSIs looked at each other, then both shrugged and nodded agreeably.

"Thanks, guys," Catherine muttered, glaring at her cheerfully smiling teammates as she headed for the door. *Dammit,* she thought. *I'm never going to have a day off again, am I?*

9

"I UNDERSTAND YOU GUYS WANTED to see me?" DEA Assistant Special Agent in Charge William Fairfax said as he stepped inside the open doorway to Gil Grissom's gruesomely appointed office, and observed Grissom and Brass sitting around a small stainless steel examination table.

"Yes, please come in—oh, and you might want to shut the door," Brass added as he pushed a third chair in the ASAC's direction.

Fairfax closed the door behind him, sat down in the offered chair, took one look at the two tagged hammerless Smith & Wesson revolvers lying on the exam table, and cocked his head at the two LVPD investigators.

"Am I to assume that one of those weapons belongs to Jane?" he asked.

"At least one," Brass replied.

"What do you mean by that?" Fairfax demanded, his eyes narrowing dangerously.

"One of those pistols was taken from Jane Smith at the scene; the other was removed from the cab of the subject's pickup truck," Grissom said. "Both weapons have been fired recently, but only one of them—the one we took from Smith—bears any latent fingerprints at all: on the weapon itself and the cartridges. And, curiously enough, the two pistols happen to have serial numbers with the last digit only three numbers apart."

"Interesting," Fairfax said noncommittally.

"Even more interesting," Brass added, "those two weapons have been identified by ATF as being stolen from a gun shop in Yuma, Arizona, approximately eight months ago."

"Excellent," Fairfax said, nodding in visible satisfaction. "Exactly the kind of confirming evidence we've been looking for."

"Oh? Why do you say that?" Brass inquired.

"Because Jane told Russell that the hammerless Smith she was carrying was a gift from Ricardo Paz Lamos," Fairfax replied matter-of-factly. "Obviously, from what you've just said, that pistol was one of a matched pair that was ripped off from that gun shop in Yuma, which is exactly where we're told he likes to cross the border into Mexico. And that tells me the guy in the truck has to be either Paz Lamos or one of his associates."

"That's certainly one interpretation," Brass said, nodding his head slowly.

"But you knew Jane Smith was carrying a concealed weapon, one that she'd gotten from a drug dealer . . . and that didn't bother you?" Grissom asked.

"She's an informant who—for reasons we won't go into here—is more or less willing to testify against active members of a very dangerous Mexican drug cartel, specifically and including Ricardo Paz Lamos," Fairfax said with a shrug. "That means her life expectancy out on her own is essentially zilch."

"Nice to hear that you're concerned," Brass commented dryly.

"Hey, I'm just trying to keep her alive until we can get Paz Lamos and a few of his main guys behind bars. What happens after that depends on her degree of cooperation," Fairfax responded firmly. "You know how the system works."

"Yes, I do," Brass said. "Go on."

"When Russell told me about the gun gift angle," Fairfax continued, shifting with seemingly little or no mental effort back into his relaxed and confident demeanor, "I had him issue her a Glock and a temporary permit. The idea has always been to keep her alive, and useful, as long as we possibly can; but I figured it probably wouldn't look too good in court if she ended up shooting a major drug dealer in self-defense with one of his own guns."

"No, I suppose not," Grissom said, "but there's one more problem."

"What would that be?" Fairfax asked calmly.

"These." Grissom reached under the table, brought out a pair of speed-loaders—each fully loaded with six .38 special cartridges—and set them gently on the exam table surface. "As you may recall, we removed them from Jane's left and right jacket pockets at the scene."

"Yeah, so?"

"It just so happens that the cartridges in these two speed-loaders—Federal thirty-eight specials—correspond with the cartridges in both of those pistols."

"I'm assuming that can't mean much," Fairfax said. "Federal is a very widely available brand of ammunition."

"That's true," Grissom agreed. "We would have to consider it circumstantial evidence at best."

"Much in the way we would view the fact that we found no similar speed-loaders, or any other supply of extra thirty-eight special ammo, in the truck," Brass added.

Fairfax started to say something, and then hesitated. "You're suggesting Jane might have been in possession of both hammerless Smiths at the campsite, and dumped one of them into the truck cab to cover the shooting?"

"It's a thought," Brass said, "either to cover the shooting, or her own actions at the scene. It's hard to understand why she would be carrying two speed-loaders in different pockets, while the truck driver—supposedly a very dangerous drug dealer who likes to shoot at cops—is carrying nothing in the way of backup ammo for a weapon he's wiped completely clean of prints."

"What about the rifle in the truck?" Fairfax asked.

"One expended casing in the chamber and two live rounds in the magazine," Grissom replied. "There was no other ammo of any kind in the truck or on his person."

"Okay, I see your point," Fairfax said, a thoughtful expression crossing his face.

"And, as I recall, every one of the UCs at the campsite agreed they heard Jane yell 'Oh shit, he's here!' the moment the truck came into view . . . which may well turn out to be the instigating act for the entire shooting incident," Brass said. "So she could have been in a position of believing she had to protect herself—especially if getting into some kind of witness protection program was contingent on her 'cooperating' with the DEA. As you said, her chances of surviving on her own, without you guys, is probably close to zero."

"But being the instigator of the shooting wouldn't necessarily be her fault, if she truly believed Paz Lamos was driving that truck," Fairfax said. "That's just her survival instincts kicking in—perfectly understandable with a guy like Paz Lamos."

"That's true, an instinctive scream on her part would be understandable . . . and justifiable," Brass said, "but not necessarily the barrage of shooting that followed, depending on—"

A sharp knock on the door interrupted them. Before the three could say or do anything, lab tech David Hodges opened the door wide enough to stick his head in.

"Pardon the interruption, Gil, but you said you wanted to know about the GSR results on the subject in the truck as soon as they were available."

Grissom started to say something that would have undoubtedly matched the exasperated look in his eyes, but the ever-aggressive lab tech went on quickly.

"I just wanted you to know that I did find gunshot residues on the subject's right hand that were definitely deposited within moments of his being shot." David then smiled brightly, as if waiting for the applause that would surely follow.

"And how would you know the time of deposition?" Grissom asked curiously.

"Actually, it was pretty obvious under the microscope that the GSR spheres were still forming and solidifying when they got hit with the blood splatters," David explained, the self-satisfied smile growing—if possible—even wider. "When you got right down at the surface, you could see where—"

"Thank you, David," Grissom said as he got up and walked over to the door. "I'll want to see your photo documentation as soon as we're done here," he added as he started to close the door on Hodges.

"One more thing," Hodges said quickly, seemingly reluctant to give up his place on stage until he was physically yanked off. "Wendy just finished working the tissue trapped under the edges of that mushroomed bullet Doc Robbins dug out of the mob boss, and it definitely turned out to be, uh, mule deer."

"Really?"

Hodges nodded. "I was right there when she got the results off the MALDI. What a great technique—using mass spec analysis of hemoglobin to identify species. I'm surprised I hadn't thought of doing it myself. Oh, and Bobby confirmed that the casing you found up on the mountain doesn't match the rifle in the victim's truck," Hodges added as he realized Grissom was gently moving him through the doorway. "And I almost forgot: I found unburned powder grains from the tape-liftings of the subject's hands that were visually and chemically identical to unburned grains on the pistol you and Catherine found in the truck. I guess that pretty much settles things . . . about the subject shooting at the UCs, I mean."

Grissom blinked and then paused to consider this last bit of information.

"Thank you, David," he finally said as he closed the door firmly on the lab tech and turned back to the two men in his office—who had clearly listened to the verbal lab analysis report from very different perspectives.

"Well, I must say, that's exactly what I expected to hear from your crack lab team: scientific proof that the man in that pickup was shooting at our UCs . . . and that our snitch didn't plant a weapon on our suspect," Fairfax said with a pleasant smile on his face as he walked up beside Grissom and casually grasped the door handle. "I'm looking forward to receiving a copy of your final report: the one that justifies the shooting and completely exonerates *my* team." Fairfax opened the door and walked out of the office.

"Well, that certainly wasn't what *I* expected to hear at all," Brass remarked from his chair. He was staring morosely at the pair of hammerless Smith & Wesson pistols on the exam table that no longer seemed to be of much significance.

"No, it wasn't," Grissom agreed, looking decidedly unpleased.

"If I understand things correctly," Brass went on

gloomily, "it would appear, from the initial evidence exams, that Enrico Toledano was, in fact, killed in a hunting accident; the subject in the truck did shoot at the UCs; and the two scenes are not related. It seems my gut instincts were wrong. Dammit. Maybe I'm getting too old for this job."

"I'm sure you're right—the evidence is definitely trying to tell us something. But I don't think we're paying close enough attention to what it's actually saying. Not just yet. You might want to hold off for a few hours before you start filling out those retirement papers."

Grissom and Brass were even less pleased fifteen minutes later, as they listened to Catherine finish her case status report.

"So, do you think the distance determinations on the pellet patterns are doable *without* the trace metal analysis to categorize the holes in the grill and radiator?" Grissom asked.

"No, I don't think so," Catherine said. "Sara's trying her best, but it looks like at least five of the shotgun patterns hit the grill and radiator directly. And the guys with the shotguns—the two state agents—were both going for the carburetor and spark-plug wires, to shut the engine down completely, just like they'd been taught; so those five patterns pretty much overlapped. Also, one of the state guys—I'm pretty sure it was Mace—fired two more rounds, one on either side of the engine block, going for the engine compartment firewall and anybody on the floor of the cab. So you've got to figure that at least a few of those pellets hit the grill and radiator. And that doesn't even count the Glock rounds and the bullets from that M-4 assault rifle that punched through the front of the truck, ricocheted off the engine block, and ripped right back into the radiator."

"How many rounds are we talking about?" Grissom asked.

"According to Agent Tallfeather's statement, he fired two three-round bursts at the front tires, and then at least two more into the engine compartment—and possibly three, he's not really sure—before he opened up on the left side of the cab with the rest of the magazine. I'm guessing that maybe a third of the incoming engine compartment bullets in total—the nine-mil and the five-five-sixes—ricocheted back into the radiator. It's kind of hard to tell the holes apart at this point. And without the ability to distinguish lead versus copper smearing at the edges, I think it's going to be impossible."

"Were they using ball ammo?"

"Yes, and the nine-mils were all jacketed hollow-points."

"How bad was the radiator torn up?"

"Pretty bad," Catherine said. "I didn't get a real close look, but there's an awful lot of damage that looks like mushrooming hollow-points or tumbling ricochet effects—mostly a lot of torn-up metal. If those heat-disseminating plates were as badly compressed or distorted as they appeared, we're going to have a real hard time isolating those individual shotgun patterns."

"No doubt," Grissom said, seemingly distracted by something.

"But if we don't isolate at least two or three of

those patterns, and determine that absolute reference point, I don't think we can position the truck at each shooting point . . . which means we can't reconstruct the shooting," Catherine went on.

"So you'd recommend we reprioritize our resources, put the Toledano shooting on the back burner, and focus our efforts on the trajectory-distance determinations at the campsite? Grissom asked.

Catherine hesitated, and then said firmly: "Yes, I would."

"And I agree," Brass added.

Grissom turned and stared curiously at the still-gloomy LVPD captain.

"Really? Since when?"

"A hunter *or* a poacher *or* an assassin aims at a deer, kills it, and with the same bullet manages to hit and kill a local mob boss—a guy who has a whole lot more enemies than friends, and who happens to be wandering around a mountaintop, in the middle of the night, with a night-scoped and silenced rifle," Brass replied. "I told you earlier that the chances of something like that actually happening in real life seemed extremely unlikely, to put it mildly."

"Yes, you did," Grissom said.

"Well, I haven't changed my opinion on that," Brass said. "But the problem is, the odds of an *assassin* waiting around for a jumpy little deer to put itself in the line of fire of his target—just so he can make the hit look accidental, have to be astronomical, mostly because it doesn't even begin to make sense. What kind of idiot would even think about trying to make something like that work?"

"No shooter I've ever heard of," Catherine agreed, "and God knows we've run across some really dumb ones."

Grissom nodded silently in agreement.

"And we know the bullet that killed Toledano hit a deer first, and that deer was lying right in the line of fire, relative to that casing location, so what can I say?" Brass shrugged. "Given all that, it seems to me a hunting accident makes a whole lot more sense than some kind of miracle-working assassin."

"What are you doing, Jim?" Grissom asked. "Standing up for the evidence now, instead of your cop gut?"

"I'm listening to what the evidence is telling me," Brass grudgingly replied. "You have a problem with that?"

"Yes, I do," Grissom said evenly, "because my forensic gut is telling me that there's something very wrong going on around here."

10

VIKTOR MIALKOVSKY WATCHED THE WATER pour off the narrow overhead ledge a few inches in front of his eyes with a sense of vague curiosity that might have led a casual observer to think he didn't care how long it would take for the rain to stop—which wasn't true at all.

He certainly did care, for reasons that had everything to do with the dwindling number of hours before daybreak, when his chances of being observed during his escape down the mountain would increase dramatically.

But the weather was something a man like Mialkovsky had long ago learned to accept for what it was: an independent variable that he could do little or nothing to change.

What he could change, however, was his capacity to adapt his surroundings to maximize his chances of success. In this particular case, change had necessitated two separate trips in the raging downpour to retrieve the portion of equipment and supplies he'd earlier deemed expendable to his escape.

Forced to rely on his own biological night vision, such as it was, to negotiate the rugged pathway back to his cache points, Mialkovsky had gotten lost twice, and had to resort to his compass and the distant—and barely visible—glow of the Las Vegas lights to realign himself. But that had turned out to be a good thing, because in working his way back to his ledge hideout, he'd located a small cave that had obviously once served as a den for a presumably very small bear.

The width ranged from three to five feet, the height barely two at the entrance, but rising up to as much as six at the visibly clawed out hollow in the back that was a good twelve feet from the entrance. All told, the irregular doglegged space—really more an expansive crevice created by some long-ago landslide of granite slabs and boulders than an actual cave—served the hunter-killer's needs perfectly.

It allowed him to strip down in the chilled night air, dry off, change into his one set of dry clothes, and then build a small fire with a handful of the Special Ops fuel sticks that produced a maximum of heat with a minimum of CO_2 discharge . . . which, in turn, allowed him to prepare a perfectly satisfying meal with the packs of freeze-dried trail food he'd brought along in his supply kit.

An hour later, he was back into his somewhat drier desert-camouflage Ghillie suit—with a full stomach and all of his gear and supplies repacked for a hasty recaching and escape—stretched out across the irregular crevice floor on some moder-

ately comfortable pine branches, watching for approaching lights, and waiting for the rain to stop so
he could begin his descent.

All things considered, Mialkovsky was reasonably
satisfied with his situation. The only thing that
bothered him was a lack of answers to some very
basic questions, such as:

Who was the Hispanic male who had shown up
at his scene at such a goddamned inopportune
moment?

What was that unknown element doing on this
mountaintop with an old Vietnam War–era nightscope?

When would the storm break?

Where would the helicopters go when it did?

Why had the cops at the campsite opened up on
the Hispanic with such a massive barrage of gunfire?

Finally, how would the investigation of that
crime scene impact the evaluation of his own carefully rigged scene?

But the thing that Mialkovsky wanted to know
more than anything else was what Gil Grissom and
his team were up to, right now, with God-only-
knew what collected evidence, down at the LVPD
crime lab.

11

FIREARMS EXAMINER BOBBY DAWSON and DNA expert Wendy Simms both looked up when Gil Grissom walked purposefully into the traditionally misnamed ballistics comparison lab.

"Hi, boss," Bobby said, pulling his stool aside from the comparison scope so that Grissom could get a good view of the evidence. Two expended brass cartridge cases were brightly visible under the reflecting lights of the dual stage mounts. "I was just getting ready to set the bullet from the Toledano shooting up on the scope. Sorry it's taking so long, but we had to be real careful in peeling back those mushroomed edges to get at the tissue; and I wanted to do that first, with Wendy here, so that she could get working on the ID."

"Which is great," the DNA technician said, "because it gave me plenty of time to set up some other tests while the MALDI was warming up."

"Yes, David told me about your results," Grissom said.

"He did?" A brief look of disappointment flashed across Wendy's pretty face as she glanced over Grissom's shoulder and saw Hodges at his workstation, grinning.

"Yes, and I want you to know that I really appreciate your effort in getting the results out so quickly," Grissom said, oblivious to the young tech's brief emotional response. "You may have enabled us to reprioritize our resources over to another case that's turning out to be far more consequential."

"Oh, well, uh . . . good, I'm glad I was able to help."

"You'll help us a lot more if you can take a quick look at all of those grid trace evidence samples and blood swabs Catherine collected from the cab and bed of the pickup," Grissom added. "I'm specifically interested in knowing if there's even the slightest trace of cocaine anywhere in or on that truck . . . and if there's any other blood in the truck that didn't come from our dead subject."

"Sure, of course," Wendy said, managing a reasonable facsimile of a cheerful smile. "I'll get right on it." She hurried out the door of the ballistics room in the direction of her DNA lab, pausing only briefly to give Hodges a dirty look.

Bobby Dawson, a hardened veteran of the internecine relationships and conflicts that seemed to intermittently plague the LVPD crime lab, had grimly observed the entire Wendy-and-David scene without comment.

"I'm about ready to compare the bullet from Toledano and the one I test-fired through the rifle found in that pickup," he said calmly. "But before I do that, I want to tell you a few things about that cartridge case you found on the Sheep Range."

"Actually, you may want to put that Toledano bullet comparison off until sometime later," Grissom suggested. "David said you'd already eliminated that casing as not coming from the rifle we found in the truck."

"Quite the town crier, isn't he?" Bobby responded, rolling his eyes. He'd expected nothing less from the self-aggrandizing trace expert once he'd heard what happened with Wendy's preliminary analysis results; but then, too, he was far less interested in sucking up to Grissom than either of the two younger lab techs.

"I'm sure he was just trying to be efficient, on behalf of the lab in general," Grissom offered, finally picking up on the not-so-subtle undertones.

"Don't doubt it for a minute," Bobby said, smiling and shrugging his shoulders agreeably. "But did he tell you what I discovered about that particular cartridge?"

"Uh, no, actually, he didn't."

"It may not mean much," Bobby went on, maintaining a professionally calm voice, "but the fact that a three-oh-eight Winchester cartridge is *almost* identical to a seven-point-six-two-millimeter NATO round might have some bearing on this case."

"How is that?" Grissom asked, genuinely curious.

"It's actually a pretty old topic among firearms experts that rattles around the Internet on a pretty regular basis. The chambers of military rifles made for the NATO round are exactly one-point-six-four-five inches long, whereas the chambers of civilian rifles using the three-oh-eight Winchester round are one-point-six-three-two inches long."

"And this means something?"

"It might in this case." Bobby said. "We're only talking about a difference of thirteen-thousandths of an inch. But if you were to fire a three-oh-eight Winchester round—especially one that had been re-loaded with a different grade of gunpowder than normal—in a rifle chambered for the slightly longer seven-point-six-two NATO round, you could easily get excessive stress on the civilian brass casing, which could result in early head separation of the bullet and some interesting deformation of the cartridge."

"And you saw all of that on the casing I found up on the mountain?"

"That's correct. The reloaded and thereby up-graded three-oh-eight cartridge you found was al-most certainly fired through a seven-point-six-two military rifle. And based on the ejector marks, I'm guessing a specific military sniper rifle; I'll know more about that after I do a little more research," Bobby explained. "In general, that would be a fool-ish thing for an amateur reloader to do, depending upon the age and reliability of the rifle in question. But it might actually be a clever trick for a ballistics expert to play—depending on what he or she wanted the bullet to do, of course."

"Are you suggesting a military sniper might have shot Toledano, accidentally or otherwise, on a fed-eral wildlife refuge?"

"I'm saying it's an interesting although remote possibility," Bobby said. "The Army testing range is right next door to the refuge, and it wouldn't surprise me a whole lot if an exceptionally ballsy trainee—or, who knows, maybe even an instructor—happened to wander out to the Sheep Range in the middle of the night when no one was supposedly looking. It would be a nice place to practice your, uh, ambush techniques, shall we say? Get in a little illicit hunting on the side . . . maybe something extra to supplement the field MREs?"

"But why go to the trouble of using a reloaded civilian round when—?" Grissom blinked in sudden understanding. "Ah."

"Getting caught shooting off base like that with an Army weapon would be a major no-no, regardless of your intended target, even if informal permission had been given by your sergeant or commander," Bobby said. "Probably find yourself walking guard duty on the Korean DMZ for the rest of your career, if there wasn't a nice war zone available where you could be walking point. So, you really wouldn't want to advertise your illicit activities out on the Sheep Range, whatever they might be, by using Army-issued ammo."

"No, I suppose not," Grissom agreed.

"But there could be another reason to use a specifically reloaded civilian round—one that was very practical. The shooter might have wanted this bullet to act in a very specific manner," Bobby said, tapping his gloved finger against the now-unmushroomed projectile lying in the wad of bloodied gauze on his microscope bench.

"Go on."

"I can't say for sure right at the moment, because I'm still collecting the comparison data, but I'm guessing this bullet is a Nosler Ballistic Tip. It's specifically designed for deep penetration and maximum stopping power—the kind of projectile you'd want to mount on a high-energy cartridge for serious big-game hunting, if you knew what you were doing. But that doesn't make much sense in this case."

"Why not?"

"Well, first of all, because a reloader who knew his stuff would never use a three-oh-eight high-energy cartridge to take down a little mule deer. It would be a complete overkill . . . and nothing a reloader would want to talk about with his buddies. And believe me, these reloaders like nothing better than to talk about what they did with one of their hot cartridges."

"So you're not expecting this particular cartridge to be the topic of any fireside chats?" Grissom queried.

"Absolutely not," Bobby said firmly. "Either because the load didn't work as planned, or because it did . . . That deer in the morgue? Doc Robbins showed me the wound on its neck, and photos of Toledano's wound they took before the autopsy."

"And?"

"If Toledano's death was the result of a normal hunting accident that occurred at the relatively short-range distances you and Brass described in your report, this bullet"—Bobby pointed at the peeled-open rifle bullet resting in a bed of bloody gauze next to his comparison scope—"should have either taken the guy's head off or, at the very least, done a whole lot more damage than I saw in those photos. Something slowed this bullet down and caused it to tumble; but it wasn't Toledano's vest, and I really doubt it was just the throat of that deer . . . unless this bullet was really going slow to begin with."

"So what are you suggesting?"

"Maybe another silencer," Bobby replied. "But I'm not talking about a half-baked rig put together by some wannabe gunsmith—like a suppressor that starts coming apart internally after the first shot, like the one Toledano had mounted on his rifle."

"Enrico Toledano was using a cheap silencer on his rifle? Why would he want to do something like that?"

"Probably didn't know enough about suppressors to realize the one he had was a piece of crap; or, at least, that would be my guess. Do you really want to let a firearms guy start talking about one of his favorite topics?"

"I'll take my chances," Grissom said. "Go on."

"Don't say I didn't warn you," Bobby said mischievously. "Okay. First of all, the suppressor on Toledano's rifle was only attached to the barrel at one point—by a little bit of threading at the end of the muzzle. Any professionally made suppressor is attached to the rifle barrel at *two* points. The usual method is to slip the suppressor down the barrel with some kind of snug O-ring mechanism, and then screw it into place at the end of the barrel. That gives you stable alignment all along the bullet path."

"Okay . . . ," Grissom said.

"And there's another thing about Toledano's suppressor system that tells me his manufacturers or suppliers didn't know what they were doing," Bobby went on. "The threading on the end of his rifle barrel was machined in the wrong direction."

"Are you serious?"

"Very much so," Bobby said, nodding solemnly. "When the spinning bullet leaves the rifle barrel and enters the suppressor baffling, its mass and rotation put a certain degree of torque on the suppressor— only a little bit if the suppressor is properly aligned, but a great deal if it's not. That is critical for one simple reason: if the muzzle threading is machined in a direction opposite to the spin of the bullet, the torque will tighten the suppressor onto the rifle barrel. But if the threading is machined in the same direction as the bullet spin, each successive shot loosens the suppressor."

"That doesn't sound like a good thing."

"No, it's not," Bobby said, "especially if the suppressor starts wobbling out of alignment just as the next shot is fired. That's how you get yourself a faceful of shrapnel. But that wouldn't have happened in Toledano's case, because his piece-of-shit suppressor would have come apart internally long before it fell off the end of his rifle."

"So where does this leave us?" Grissom asked, truly curious now.

"I think it's important to note that this bullet, the one that killed Toledano"—he pointed again at the bullet wrapped in the bloodied gauze—"has no visible damage that you'd expect to see from anything unsymmetrical or poorly aligned. If that bullet was slowed down by a suppressor, it had to have been one that was very carefully machined and crafted; like the ones the Navy SEALS or DELTA teams use."

"So we're back to a military shooter again—somebody from the Army test range wandering into the refuge, and not wanting to get caught by a trophy-hunting poacher?"

"Hey, I couldn't even begin to answer that one," Bobby said, opening his gloved hands out in mock surrender. "But I'll tell you what: from a ballistics *and* a hunting point of view, I think this whole 'accidental-shooting' theory is garbage. I don't necessarily know why, or how, but it is."

"Would you be able to tell if this bullet went through a sound suppressor before it hit the deer *and* Toledano?"

"I don't know," Bobby admitted truthfully. "I'd need to put some serious time in with the SEM to determine something like that."

"So, basically, you'd like to do more work on the Toledano shooting . . . is that what I'm hearing?"

"Yes, sir, it is," Bobby said, nodding.

Grissom sighed. "This really doesn't help in the sense of reprioritizing our resources."

"No, I suppose not."

"What about all those bullet and casing matches

we're going to need in order to reconstruct the truck shooting?"

"Well, all of the shooters are pretty much in agreement as to which weapon each of them used, and the number of rounds they fired. So, presumably, the purpose of the reconstruction will be to determine their relative positions and the timing of the shots. That being the case, tentative breech and firing pin impression IDs made by just one examiner will probably tell you all you need to know at the onset; and two of us can always get together to resolve any questioned IDs. I know Catherine's heading this way with all of the casing and hull evidence. She and I—and maybe Nick, too, if he's free—could whip those tentatives out pretty quickly if we're left alone for a while."

"I'll see what I can do," Grissom promised, looking distracted again as he headed out the door.

Bobby Dawson followed Gil Grissom out, coming to a halt beside lab tech David Hodges, who seemed to be making a very determined effort to look busy and distracted as well.

"How's it going, bud?" Bobby inquired, slapping his thick hand on David's thin shoulder.

"Oh, uh—hey, you're firearms," David said, his eyes widening anxiously. "You probably just contaminated my lab coat with GSRs. Now I'm going have to change into a new one."

"Tell you what, sport," Bobby said, leaning down to whisper in the now visibly nervous lab tech's ear, "you ever try to report my findings—or Wendy's—

to Grissom or any other of the CSIs again, and I'll personally see to it that you have to change your shorts too."

Grissom literally ran into Catherine in the hallway, almost knocking the box of test-fired casings and shotgun hulls out of her hand.

"What's the matter?" Catherine asked, staring into her supervisor's glassy eyes. "You look . . . distressed . . . or something?"

"I just had a ten-minute seminar on sound suppressors from Bobby," Grissom said quietly, the better part of his mind still clearly elsewhere.

"Really?" The look on Catherine's face ranged somewhere between sympathy and dismay—she didn't think she ever wanted to know that much about anything involving firearms; that was why the crime lab employed technical specialists. "Did you find it . . . useful?"

"Actually, I think it was," Grissom replied, "but now I'm more confused than I was when I went in there, and I'm not really sure I know why."

"That's not very encouraging," Catherine said, looking down at the box of test-fires in her hands with a sense of impending doom.

"No, it's not," Grissom agreed. "Everything seems to be in flux with these two cases, starting with the very basic question of whether or not they're related by a common suspect, victim, or evidence."

"I suppose, then," Catherine said cautiously, "what we need is a starting point . . . one that we can all agree on?"

A smile of understanding slowly slid across Grissom's face. "You're right. That's *precisely* what we need." He looked around the hallway as if he couldn't quite remember where anyone or anything was. "Where's Nick?"

"I, uh, think he's still in the conference room with Warrick."

"Good," Grissom said. "I think it's about time we made better use of his talents."

12

When Gil Grissom entered the conference room, he found the crime lab's computer and audiovisual technician, Archie Johnson, sitting in front of what looked like Nick's laptop, while Warrick watched over his shoulder.

"What happened to Nick?" Grissom asked, looking around the room in frustration. "And what are you doing here, Archie? I thought you called in sick."

"Well, uh—"

"Apparently Archie started feeling a whole lot better when he finally realized that young lady we were discussing earlier really didn't need *her* computer worked on after all," Warrick interjected. "Which meant he was off the hook, so to speak."

"Oh?" Grissom's eyebrow rose curiously.

"It seems the young woman has an even younger brother who does have a computer problem, and apparently wouldn't mind dating a cute and lovable computer geek," Warrick added helpfully as he patted Archie on the shoulder.

'Oh," Grissom said again, only with a much different inflection.

"*Complete* misunderstanding," the computer tech said firmly, finally looking up at Grissom. "Not that I have anything whatsoever against whatever people . . . uh . . . want to do with each other," he added hurriedly. "I was just trying to be . . . uh . . . polite and sensitive in my approach, and I guess I wasn't—"

"Impolite and insensitive enough?" Grissom's eyebrow rose again.

"Next time, try the almost-housebroken Neanderthal approach," Warrick advised. "It actually works every now and then, with those really special women; and it's definitely a crowd-pleaser when it doesn't."

"I think we need to have a staff meeting at some point about improper absences," Grissom remarked.

"Sorry, Gil. Won't happen again . . . but speaking of things working," Archie said, desperate to get off the current topic, "I did manage to get Nick's program to respond to the locator dots."

"Oh, really? How did you do that?"

"You're going to love this, Gil," Warrick promised as he patted the computer tech's shoulder again. "Go ahead, Archie, tell him."

"I . . . uh . . . got the sensor module to . . . recognize each one of the locator dots on the vehicle and cones, and remember their relative positioning with each other by . . . changing their color," Archie said, his face now a bright shade of red.

"Take a look," Warrick said as he reached past Archie's shoulder and hit one of the function keys.

Instantly, the middle sector of the far wall lit up with a 3-D laser scan image of the scene facing the left side of the truck.

"Hot pink?" Grissom was not quite sure what else to say.

"I tried all of the primary colors first," Archie said quickly, "and there's no good reason—or at least none that I can figure—why the sensor module would need to see the dots in color anyway. But it was the vendor who made the suggestion, so I tried the primaries, just to see what would happen. And when nothing much did, I ran the entire spectrum through the module on the second pass, just on a hunch, and the bright pink seemed to . . . work."

"Clearly another sensitivity issue," Warrick said, trying to keep a straight face. "I don't know what it is about you, Arch, but you do have a knack for getting things to work."

"And Nick?" Grissom asked, deciding that the young computer technician had suffered enough; or at least enough for the time being, he amended.

He'd also remembered, finally, that he'd come into the conference room for a specific purpose.

"Nick was heading back over to the garage, to give Sara a hand," Archie said. "And I'm really sorry about the call-in earlier. It won't happen again, I promise. And I will try to get the sensor module to acknowledge another . . . uh . . . color. I do realize that bright pink locator dots on a shooting reconstruction layout could be a little . . . much for a courtroom presentation."

"Or, maybe just not quite . . . enough?" Grissom suggested with a shrug as he turned and headed toward the door.

He was halfway out the doorway, deep in thought again, when he suddenly stopped and turned back.

"Thanks for getting us back on track, Archie," he said firmly. "I'm grateful for that."

"I'm glad I could—," the computer tech started to say when Grissom interrupted.

"And when you and Warrick get all of those laser scans and digital photos loaded into the program, I want you to take a look at some of the photos I took up on the mountain. I have another 3-D trajectory problem that I'm going to need you to help me figure out."

Grissom was heading toward the garage, the germ of an idea beginning to take solid root in the back of his mind, when he glanced over at the analytical chemistry lab and saw Sara sitting in front of the X-ray fluorescence spectrometer with a pair of sample vials in her hand.

"Hi, how are you doing?" he asked, coming up beside her and gently patting her shoulder.

"Worn down, hungry, grinchy . . . and a few other things that are best discussed outside the office," Sara replied, looking back over her shoulder and giving Grissom a tired but affectionate smile.

"I thought you'd taken over Greg's work because you'd hurt your arm," Grissom commented uneasily as he quickly looked around the instrument room to confirm they were alone, wondering as he did so if he had any idea at all of who was working where on this case anymore.

"I did," Sara said as she set the vials on the lab bench. "But all the test-firing went real fast once Catherine got Sergeant Gallager to do the shooting. So, I gave Greg back his original job on the grill and radiator so that I could run all these trace metal swabs I took from the impact holes through the XRF. If I can figure out which holes are from the mostly lead pellets and which are from the copper-jacketed bullets, I think we've got a fighting chance to isolate the individual shotgun patterns."

"Really?"

"I think so," Sara said as she picked up another pair of vials, each of which contained three gray pellets. "We caught another break with the shotgun ammo. You remember those two boxes of buckshot rounds the state narcs used to fill their pockets before they loaded their shotguns . . . the ones that had two different batch dates?"

"Yes?"

"Well, it turns out that the pellets in the later-dated box contain almost four percent antimony—which is a new buckshot composition the company put out strictly for law enforcement, to harden the pellets—whereas the pellets in the earlier box have only trace amounts of antimony."

"And you've tested how many standard knowns so far?"

"Three pellets each from three rounds selected randomly from the remaining ammo in both boxes."

Grissom thought for a moment. "And what's your standard deviation so far?"

"Point-oh-two percent."

"Let's go with it," Grissom said with a smile. "How long will it take to run all the swabs?"

Sara winced. "Maybe another three hours, if everything goes okay. Simple work, but slow. We sure could use that auto-sampler."

"I'll remind Ecklie that he's been sitting on our requisition for three months now," the CSI supervisor promised. "But you know what he thinks about auto-samplers in general."

"How can we trust a machine to never make a mistake when they're programmed by humans," Sara repeated from memory. "Is he ever going to get over that?"

"Probably not," Grissom said. "But then, too, maybe he shouldn't. There's a lot to be said for going back to the basics."

13

WHEN GRISSOM FINALLY GOT to the garage, he found Greg on his knees in front of the truck grill, facing what now looked like a porcupine array of dowels, and Nick setting up a digital camera on a tripod.

"Do you and Warrick need more photos of the truck?" Grissom asked.

"Actually, what we need are better photos taken under controlled lighting conditions," Nick said. "Warrick and I are pretty well convinced it's the uneven lighting from the strobes and headlights out at the scene—mostly the reflective glaring—that's causing the program to either mismatch the reference dots, or ignore them completely."

"And you'd just as soon not have to resort to Archie's color scheme, if you can find a way around it?"

"That too," Nick admitted with a smile. "But for me, simple usually works out being better."

"That's what I said to Sara," Grissom replied absentmindedly as he stood behind Greg for a few moments, watching the young CSI try to figure out which of the many holes in the radiator matched the one in the grill that he'd already run a dowel through.

"Did she tell you about the positioning mistake we discovered on Officer Grayson?" Greg asked, looking up from his work and blinking as if he'd just realized that Grissom had walked into the room.

"No, she didn't." Grissom replied. "What kind of mistake?"

"Well, I guess it wasn't so much a mistake; more like the guy just didn't realize where he was when he started shooting. It wasn't all that clear in the dirt and sand impressions around that rock, and I guess no one else really saw where he was at because of that big boulder being in the way."

"So, there was no confirmation on Grayson's position from anyone else?"

"No, just his recollection, which seemed okay at the time because he was being so cooperative," Greg said. "But when I gave Catherine the ejection pattern results from all the weapons, she said that Grayson couldn't have been where he said he was during the shooting, because the four ejected casings from his Sig wouldn't have ended up where they did."

"And where was that?" Grissom asked.

Greg thought for a moment. "He was out in the open and moving back toward the 'guy facilities' boulder the entire time he was shooting."

"Instead of immediately taking a barricade position, which would have seemed a much more logical option if he was expecting the arrival of a dangerous drug dealer," Grissom pointed out.

"I called him on his cell a few minutes ago and asked him about that," Greg replied. "He said it all happened real fast, and his memory is a little fuzzy. But he definitely remembers quickly zipping his pants up when he heard the truck coming, and walking toward the dirt road to see what was going on . . . and then grabbing for his pistol when he got caught in the truck's headlights . . . and starting to shoot at the tires when the truck swerved away and headed straight for the camp."

"Which would make sense—about not barricading himself—because he wouldn't have felt as directly threatened as the others, once the truck swerved away from his position," Grissom said, mostly to himself, as he stared at the hoisted truck's flattened tires. "Instead, his movements suggest he was upset at having been caught off guard, and was trying to make up for it."

"And because the truck was already past him when he started shooting," Nick said softly, starting to understand where Grissom was going, "he had to have been very limited in what he could shoot at. Otherwise, from his position, he'd have been putting rounds directly into the camp."

"Which probably limited his targeting to the rear tires, and only for a short time period," Grissom added.

"That would have been roughly when he and the truck were lined up with the 'female facilities' boulder . . . which also means Grayson could have been the source of the bullet that hit Jane Smith," Nick finished with a smile of growing awareness.

"Exactly," Grissom said. "Can you reinflate these tires?"

"Not the front ones," Nick replied. "They're too shredded. I'd never be able to get the patches to hold at anything like standard tire pressures. But the back ones only have a few holes in them. Yeah, sure, I can get them patched and reinflated. But how are we—?"

"I'm going to need a 2-D overhead scan of the campsite that includes where the truck first came off the main road and turned toward the camp, and where it came to a stop," Grissom said, his mind racing, "as well as the starting and ending positions of all six shooters . . . all projected up on this wall," he added, pointing to the bare white wall on the opposite side of the garage.

"Only the 2-D scan?" Nick asked as he reached for his cell phone.

"That's all we'll need right now," Grissom said; "that and a calculator or laptop computer we can use to run some trig functions."

Nick paused. "We're going to use *trigonometry* to solve this?"

"Going back to the basics," Grissom said. "Do you remember how to use the functions?"

"I—uh, think I'm going to get Warrick over here," Nick said as he returned his attention to his cell phone. "I'm a lot better working with a tire iron than I am with high school math."

"While you're doing that, I'm going back to the

lab. There's something about the results we've been getting that just doesn't add up."

When Grissom walked into the ballistics comparison lab, he saw Catherine and Bobby Dawson—both garbed in white lab coats—hunched over a pair of comparison microscopes mounted a few feet apart on a low lab bench. The rest of the bench surface was covered with rows of marked envelopes and vials, and their individual notepads.

"Do I dare ask how things are going?" Grissom probed.

"Did you come in here to help?" Catherine asked, her eyes staying fixed to the eyepieces of the expensive scope.

"No, not really," Grissom admitted.

"In that case, things are going painfully slow," Catherine said with a sigh as she continued to adjust the three-dimensional position of the bullet mounted on the left ocular stage of the microscope.

"I wanted to ask both of you something," Grissom said, perfectly comfortable with the fact that he was being visually ignored. "Did either of you swab the pistol we found in the truck for GSRs?"

"I didn't," Catherine said.

"Me neither," Bobby echoed.

"So that means David probably took the swabs," Grissom concluded, sounding not exactly pleased by the revelation.

"Is that a problem?" Catherine asked, finally turning away from the scope to stare curiously at Grissom.

"I'm not sure," Grissom replied. "He came into

my office when I was talking with Brass and Fairfax, and proceeded to tell all of us that he'd confirmed the subject in the truck had fired a weapon just before being shot, based on the interaction of blood droplets with cooling GSRs."

"Sounds like an impressive piece of work," Catherine said.

"That's what I thought too." Grissom nodded. "But then he went on to say that he'd identified unburned grains of gunpowder from the subject's hands as being visually and chemically identical to unburned grains found on the Smith & Wesson hammerless pistol in the truck. So now Fairfax is convinced that we've exonerated his buy-bust team."

"Kinda jumping the gun a bit, isn't he?" Bobby asked.

"Who, Fairfax?"

"Well, yeah, him too; but I'm talking about David. 'Visually identical' doesn't mean a whole lot when you consider that most of the smokeless gunpowders in the world are made up of only a half-dozen possible kernel shapes. And 'chemically identical' doesn't necessarily mean much either, depending on how far he went with his analysis. Hell, you could say the same thing about a couple of Twinkies—they might be visually and chemically 'identical,' but that doesn't mean they came from the same bakery, or even the same state, much less the same package."

"So you're saying he had to be talking about class—as opposed to individual—characteristics?" Grissom asked, clearly seeking confirmation for something he'd already suspected.

"Unless you guys have got some fancy new gunpowder analysis instrument I don't know about," Bobby replied.

Grissom closed his eyes and sighed.

Wendy Simms looked up from the gas chromatograph/mass spectrogram when Grissom entered the analytical chemistry lab.

"How are you coming with those swabs?" Grissom asked.

Wendy checked her notebook.

"I've got results on thirty of the swabs so far, which is less than half of the samples that Catherine collected; but I placed them into the auto-sampler in a random order, thinking that might give us a general location in or on the truck to focus on."

"And?"

"Nada," Wendy replied. "And I've got the detector ratcheted up to three times normal sensitivity. If there was ever so much as a bindle of cocaine in that truck—much less several kilos—I ought to be seeing something in the way of trace evidence . . . but I'm not."

"But then again, it's always difficult to prove a negative."

The unmistakable voice of David Hodges. Grissom and Wendy both looked up as the lab tech came into the room.

"What can I say?" David went on as he walked over to the X-ray fluorescence instrument. "It's not every day that one of us techs gets to solve a puzzle that has the entire graveyard CSI team stymied."

"No, it isn't," Grissom agreed, staring thoughtfully at Hodges. "And that's exactly why I stopped by. I wanted to take a look at your photo documentation. That GSR–blood droplet interaction might be worth publishing . . . and maybe even presenting at the next Academy meeting."

"Do you really think so?" In spite of his thin stature, David managed to look as if his chest was about to explode out of his lab coat.

"Very possibly; let's take a look."

David hurried over to his computer and quickly sat down at the keyboard. Moments later, a 50,000x scanning electron microscope image of a still-solidifying GSR particle—looking like a drab and slightly flattened pumpkin at the edge where it had apparently been hit by a microscopic spray of blood—appeared on the flat screen.

"What do you think?" David asked, moving out of the way so that Grissom could get an unimpeded view of the telltale image.

"Very impressive, indeed," Grissom said. "Have you proven that the impact material is, in fact, blood?"

"Well, actually, no . . . not yet," David hedged uneasily. "It seemed pretty obvious that—"

"You'll want to make that confirmation before you write that paper . . . and certainly before you write your report," Grissom said firmly. "Now, what about that unburned gunpowder you found on the pistol and the truck driver's hands?"

"Oh, uh, yes . . . of course." Visibly flustered, David quickly tapped the keyboard again. Moments later, a pair of 20x-magnified images of what looked like identically thick, short, and partially melted segments of black licorice appeared on the screen.

"There they are," he said. "The grains on the left came from the pistol, and the ones on the right are from the subject's right hand."

"Actually, what you have there are unburned *granules* of smokeless gunpowder," Bobby corrected from the doorway; "or, to put it in more technical terms, unburned extruded tubular kernels."

"Grains, granules, kernels—what's the difference?" David asked uneasily as he and Wendy and Grissom watched Bobby walk over to a nearby lab bench, sit down in front of a 20-40x dissection microscope, pull a vial out of his pocket, and pour something into a small plastic tray. He slid the tray underneath the lens of the low-powered scope, made a quick focusing adjustment, then pointed to the adjacent flat-screen monitor.

"That's the difference," Bobby said calmly, as he stepped away from the lab bench, allowing David, Wendy, and Grissom to gather around the screen curiously.

"I don't understand," David said, looking perplexed.

"Yes, exactly," Bobby agreed. "What you are looking at on this screen are some of the cut round *flakes* of smokeless gunpowder that I just pulled out of one of the live thirty-eight-special cartridges taken from the Smith & Wesson that Gil and Catherine found in the subject's truck."

"But those . . . granules . . . aren't even close to—" David started to say.

"No, they're not. 'Cut round flakes' are fast-burning granules of smokeless gunpowder that you would typically find in pistol ammunition; whereas 'extruded tubular kernels' are slower burning granules"—Bobby walked over to David's computer screen—"that are typically found in rifle ammunition."

"But how can that be—?" David protested. "I—"

"I'm guessing you swabbed the outside of the pistol, probably somewhere near the grip . . . correct?"

"Yes, of course; that's what the protocol says to do."

"It does say that," Bobby went on. "But it also says to swab *both* sides of the weapon *separately,* and the inside of the barrel and chamber as well. *Had* you done that, you would have probably found unburned *flakes* of smokeless gunpowder that do not match the swabs from the subject's hands."

"But that means—" David looked horrified.

"Based on your SEM work, it appears that the subject—or someone very near to his location—did discharge a firearm just before he was killed, but that firearm was almost certainly a rifle," Bobby completed.

"Well, David," Grissom said with a tight grin after a long moment of silence that filled the analytical chemistry lab, "*that* certainly changes the situation a bit, no?"

14

"IT WAS MY FAULT," Catherine said glumly.

As she addressed Grissom, she was in the process of taking a new swab out of her right lab coat pocket, and gently ran the white fibrous tip across the blood-splattered dash of the truck. She then snapped the protective plastic cap closed, broke off the thin wooden stick, and marked the cap with the next "located item number" in order. After making a couple of quick notations in her notebook, Catherine dropped the collected swab into her left lab coat pocket . . . where it joined the other twelve swabs that she'd taken from the interior of the truck cab.

"Not necessarily," Grissom demurred.

"Of course it was! I could have swabbed the pistol right there at the scene, or at the very least made sure that David swabbed both exterior sides, the barrel, *and* the chamber before he gave it to Brass," Catherine replied. "So now we don't know if the pistol was in the vehicle before the shooting started or dumped there afterwards."

"There are a lot of things we don't know yet," Grissom said, "but I think we're starting to make some significant progress."

The entire graveyard CSI team was now assembled in the lab's spacious two-bay garage. Sara was helping Catherine by documenting the interior truck cab with her strobe-mounted digital camera, while Warrick sat at a small portable table between the two bays and adjusted the laptop-projected 2-D image of the campsite scene on the far garage wall. At the front end of the still-hoisted truck, Greg was on his knees, using some of the data that Sara had generated to reposition some of the wooden dowels through the now correctly matched holes. Approximately half of the dowel-ends were now also marked with colored pieces of tape to indicate the impact path of a lead pellet or a copper-jacketed bullet.

Satisfied with the work in progress, Grissom walked over to the adjacent garage bay, where Nick was busy adjusting the lab's portable laser scanner—once again attached to the cherry picker mounted on the roof of one of the lab's black Denali SUVs—over the successfully patched and reinflated left and right rear tires from the bullet-riddled red truck. The exterior points where bullets had penetrated the walls and treads of the now-patched and reinflated tires were visually marked with small bright pink dots.

"Okay, I'm ready to scan," Nick called out to Warrick, who quickly brought up another window on his laptop.

"Do it," Warrick said, and then watched approvingly as the digital images of the two tires slowly appeared on the laptop screen.

Once the scan was completed, Warrick said: "Okay, time to turn them over."

Nick quickly flipped the two tires over onto their opposite sides, and then set the scanning operation into motion a second time.

"Okay, that should do it," Warrick called out, watching with a satisfied smile as the second pair of tire images filled his laptop screen.

"I'm truly impressed by the new software, I really am; but I have to confess I still can't help thinking that you and Nick are cheating just a bit," Grissom commented as he stood over Warrick's left shoulder and watched him manipulate the two sets of two-dimensional images with a series of program tools that gradually turned the data into a pair of amazingly lifelike three-dimensional tires.

"You were really expecting us to run dowels through those four sets of bullet holes, patch the tires around the dowels, carefully inflate the tires to a few pounds of pressure, mount them back on the truck, and then use several hundred trig calculations to figure out where Grayson and the truck were in correct alignment for each shot?" Warrick was staring at his boss in disbelief.

"That's how it would have been done once," Grissom replied, a little self-consciously. "It's a solidly established protocol, going well back into the sixties. Criminalists like John Davidson from the San Bernardino Sheriff's Lab worked very similar scenes using a slide rule to do all the math."

"A slide rule, to do 3-D trig? Jesus, how long did *that* take?" Warrick asked, looking horrified.

"Several weeks, as I recall," Grissom said. "And granted, it would have taken us a while to make all of the relevant calculations, but—"

"Well, that's pretty much how I'm going to do it, too," Warrick said cheerily as Nick approached the portable table and stood over his right shoulder, watching his partner continue to manipulate the pair of 3-D tire images until they finally appeared mounted on a digital rear axle assembly, "except I'm not going to make my head hurt in the process. I say let the computer do all of the hard work."

As Warrick continued to work, the laptop screen split into two sections, each showing one of the digital tires mounted on the axle with a screen-wide pair of coordinate lines crossing at ninety-degree angles at the precise center of each hub.

"There," Warrick said with evident satisfaction. "Now watch this."

As Grissom and Nick looked on, Warrick caused four digital dowels to appear, and then transected them—one at a time—through the sixteen pink dots on the digital tires that the scanner program seemed to have no trouble locating.

"How do you know which holes each of those dowels go through?" Grissom asked.

"I don't know . . . yet," Warrick answered as he expanded the screen image out so that it now included a graphical 2-D version of the scanned campsite—the two large boulders, the twelve shooter-position cones, a dotted outline where the truck had come to a stop, and a pair of roughly parallel dotted lines leading to the campsite that represented the truck's tire tracks.

"But there are only two entry and exit holes on each tire—looks like Grayson was a pretty decent shot. That means there are only four possible combinations of the two dowel-vectors, entering and then exiting each tire," Warrick explained. "I'm going to try each possible combination, one at a time, and see what we get in the way of correlation."

"What are those four red circles to the left of that upper boulder?" Grissom asked.

"Those are rough position estimates of where Grayson was standing when he fired each of his four shots, based on his boot prints in the sand and the location of the four casings from his weapon," Warrick said. "The height of the end of his pistol barrel from the ground when he was shooting at the tires is approximately sixty inches."

"How accurate are the x and y position estimates?"

"Plus or minus two feet. Not all that accurate, because Grayson was running and shooting, which would pretty seriously impact the landing-points of the ejected casings," Warrick replied, "but good enough for what we're doing here.

"We'll start with the first possible combination of dowel-vectors as I've got it shown here," Warrick went on, "then I'm going to move the rear axle assembly—I'm really moving the entire truck, but I only care about the rear tires, so that's all I'm going to show on the screen—back along the tire track . . . like so."

"Wow," Greg said.

Grissom looked up, observing that Catherine, Sara, and Greg had stopped what they were doing and were all now watching the digital show being displayed on the far garage wall.

"Okay," Warrick explained, "what you're seeing is the rear axle assembly reversing its path from its position where we found it at the campsite back to the road, the two tires traveling approximately eight feet every full revolution. And as that happens you can see that each of the two dowel-vectors is moving also; but at different rotational angles because of their different orientations to the moving center axis of the axle itself."

"But you can't really see that from an overhead view," Nick pointed out.

"No, you can't," Warrick said, "but if you look at it from a 3-D side view"—he made a couple of selections and the view shifted accordingly—"you can see how the dowels and their extended vectors rotate differently, narrowly or widely—depending on the angle the bullets entered and exited the tires. If you can imagine the truck jacked up slightly, so that the tires rotate but don't move forward, like this"—another mouse click brought the rotating tires up off the electronic road—"you can see that one dowel-vector forms a cone with a *wide* base and the other dowel-vector forms a cone with a much *narrower* base."

"Ah, I see. But if you allow the tires to drop back down to the road and move forward," Nick said as he reached over Warrick's shoulder and clicked the mouse again, "you can see that the imaginary end of the two dowel-vectors form a pair of arcs—one large and one small frog hop—that disappear underground for two different time intervals . . . and then continue to reappear and disappear, forming either a few large hops or a large number of much smaller hops as the truck continues to move."

"Sweet," Greg commented enthusiastically.

"But this might not be the correct combination of vectors," Grissom said.

"And, in fact, it's not," Warrick agreed, "because when you shift the 3-D side view to include the four approximate locations of Grayson when he fired those four shots"—the computer screen view shifted again, and now showed four sticklike figures standing in the four circles aiming a stick gun at a slightly downward angle—"there's no 3-D alignment with the two left rear tire dowel-vectors and the first two gun-barrel-aligned shooting positions for Grayson. In fact, it's not even close."

Warrick shifted the screen view again to show that the two dowel-vector lines from the left rear tire missed the linear-bullet-path from the "stick-figure-gun"—a thin red line drawn from the gun toward the general location of the passing truck—by several feet in each case.

"And that can't be right," Warrick went on, "because the barrel of Grayson's pistol had to be lined up on one of the dowel-vectors coming out of those tires at the precise moment of each shot; that's just basic physics, not to mention common sense."

"Hey, wait a minute, how do you know Grayson fired the first two bullets at the left rear tire, and not the right one . . . or maybe one at the left tire and *then* one at the right?" Sara protested.

"Well, first of all, because that's what he said he did," Warrick replied, "and secondly, from his vantage point at those first two circles, he couldn't possibly see and hit the truck's right rear tire, because it was being blocked out by the left rear tire and the truck bed."

"Oh . . . okay, that makes sense," Sara agreed as she examined the scene diagram displayed on the wall more closely.

"But we always want to hear what the evidence has to say, rather than the suspects and cops," Warrick said, "so now we'll go back to the final resting position of the truck again"—the computer screen shifted accordingly—"change the dowel-vectors to the second possible set of connected-bullet-hole combinations, backtrack again all the way to Grayson's first shooting position, and—"

"Oh my God, it matches," Catherine whispered.

"And then we move forward again to his second shooting position," Warrick went on.

"And you have an almost perfect alignment with the second left rear tire dowel-vector," Nick said, the awe evident in his voice.

"And continuing on to the third and fourth dowel-vectors," Warrick finished, and then said nothing else as all six CSIs watched the slowly moving and rotating dowel-vectors line up almost perfectly with Grayson's third and fourth shooting positions.

"And there we have it," Warrick finally said after several seconds of silence, "the starting point we need to reconstruct the shooting scene: four precisely known positions of the truck when Grayson fired his four shots . . . because that's where the truck *had to have been* at those four specific moments in time."

"I take back my comment about you and Nick cheating," Grissom said breathlessly. "You've clarified the initial events at our scene in a way that can only be described as elegant. I think John Davidson would have been proud . . . not to mention more than a little envious of your technological advantages."

"Here, here," Catherine added her congratulations.

"Actually, I hate to be the one to rain on our parade," Nick said hesitantly, "but I think we just made one aspect of our reconstruction a lot more confusing."

"Why do you say that?" Grissom demanded, his forehead and eyebrows furrowing into a painful-looking expression.

"If we assume Grayson's four shooting positions are accurate, as they almost have to be, based on the path of the truck," Nick explained, reaching over Warrick's shoulder to hit a function key and then pointing up at the 2-D overhead scene image displayed on the far garage wall, "he has no possible line of sight on Jane Smith during any of his shots, because she's completely blocked out by the 'female facilities' boulder; so Grayson *couldn't* have been the one who shot her."

"You're right," Grissom acknowledged. "So where does that take us . . . back to a rifle shot from the subject in the truck?"

"I guess that would be possible." Warrick created a pair of direct lines from two of the truck positions—based on Grayson's third and fourth shooting positions—to the position where Jane Smith claimed to have been crouching when the truck first roared into the campsite. "The driver of the truck clearly would have had a line of sight on her at the onset— at least for a brief moment before the boulder blocks her out. But a one-handed, high-powered rifle shot through the passenger-side window, while he's driving at high speed through sand with the other hand, and heading directly toward five other well-armed narcs? That really doesn't make a lot of sense."

"Not unless he was willing to commit suicide just to nail her," Nick added, "which really doesn't sound like the guy Fairfax and Holland were describing."

"I suppose you never want to underestimate the illogical behavior of a psychotic killer," Grissom said softly, "but I agree: it doesn't make sense . . . which means we need to take another look inside that truck."

"Again?" The expression on Catherine's face was pained. "I must have collected at least a hundred swabs from that cab by now, and those chunks of brain splattered across that back window and seat are definitely starting to get ripe. What else can we do in there?"

"You've all heard me say, many times I'm sure, that a well-performed crime scene investigation is always comprised of a mechanical process and a thinking process," Grissom replied. "And how easy is it—when you're facing a huge amount of evidence, as we certainly are on this case—to fall into the trap of collecting evidence mechanically without really thinking about what you're seeing and smelling and otherwise sensing?"

"So?" Catherine said uneasily.

Grissom smiled sympathetically, remembering that he'd observed his senior CSI swabbing by rote several times while working the truck, visibly forcing herself to ignore the surrounding gray-white splatterings of brains. He guessed she was now wondering what she might have missed while going through the motions.

"So I think we need to do a little more thinking about what we're seeing . . . or, more to the point, what we're *not* seeing," Grissom replied carefully. "Which means I think we need to do something that John Davidson would have almost certainly done before he ever considered pulling out his slide rule," he added as he removed a folding knife from his lab coat pocket and flicked open the sharp blade.

"Cut his wrists?" Greg said.

"No," Grissom replied. "This time, we really *are* going back to the basics."

15

TWENTY MINUTES LATER, in the chemistry section of the laboratory, Gil Grissom and the other CSIs watched as Greg Sanders carefully placed an irregular piece of bloodstained fabric—cloth that Grissom and Catherine, a few minutes earlier, had cut out of the right interior door panel of the truck—onto a large chemically treated piece of smooth-surfaced filter paper.

Working quickly now, Greg removed a large swatch of cheesecloth—cut roughly the same size as the piece of bloodied fabric and the filter paper—from a beaker filled with 15 percent acetic acid, and then gently arranged the dripping cloth over the piece of fabric. Finally, he picked up a hot steam iron, pressing it across the entire surface of the cheesecloth . . . and then immediately recoiled as the hot acetic acid vapors rose around his face once again, ripping into his now extremely sensitive sinuses.

"Very nicely done, Greg," Grissom said approvingly. "Your technique is definitely improving."

"You couldn't prove it by me," the young CSI said, looking thoroughly miserable as tears rolled down his cheeks. "What did you call this test again?"

"The modified Greiss test for nitrite residues," Grissom said. "When smokeless gunpowder in a cartridge is detonated, a great deal of nitrites are produced that would normally be very distinct and visible as powder burns or powder pattern residues on a nearby surface. But if those burns or pattern residues happen to get deposited on a dark or discolored surface—such as the bloody seat fabric, door panel, and roof panel fabrics of our subject's truck—then these burns and patterns may not be distinctly visible." Grissom paused. "Surely you learned this in class?"

"I'm pretty sure that was the lab a couple of us skipped out on to go see Marilyn Manson," Greg said. "I seem to remember we all agreed that we wouldn't be missing much, because there had to be a more modern test for nitrites."

"Oh, there is," Grissom said. "But old-fashioned as it may be, the Greiss test has certain advantages—the primary one being range and density of the color reaction. When the hot acetic acid vapors penetrate the fabric in question, bright orange spots are produced on the paper that indicate a significant buildup of nitrites."

"You mean like this?" Greg asked, holding up the large piece of photo paper, which was now visibly covered with a fine spray of light orange dots.

"No," Grissom said, shaking his head, "not like that at all. We're looking for *significant* deposits of nitrates that would give us an indication of a rifle shot going in a specific direction. What you see there is almost certainly the result of a cloud of gunshot residue flying around the inside of the truck cab, and coming to rest on varying surfaces in a generally random and even manner."

"You mean like the seat cover I just tested?" Greg asked.

"Yes, exactly like the seat cover . . . which means you've got one more piece of cloth left to process," Grissom said. "Consider this a makeup class."

Greg sighed. "I think I'm beginning to believe in karma . . . it really wasn't one of Manson's better shows," he said as he reached for the crude rectangle of faded, worn, and torn fabric that Grissom and Catherine had cut and pulled from the interior roof of the truck cab.

In a series of motions that appeared far more hurried than methodical, Greg repeated the steps of the modified Greiss test, finally picked up the resulting piece of vapor-impacted filter paper, and said: "Wow, look at that."

"Yes, look at that, indeed," Grissom said, staring thoughtfully at the bright burst of orange color that seemed to erupt from the lower left corner of the filter paper like a small rising sun.

"Isn't that—?" Greg started to say, blinking at the glowing image with his watering eyes.

"The forward-right-hand corner of the cab roof, suggesting that a shot was fired through the upper-right-hand corner of the windshield from inside the cab," Grissom finished. "Not where you'd expect the average psychotic drug dealer to be aiming if he was trying to hit someone standing or kneeling on the ground in front of his oncoming truck."

"Maybe the truck bounced at the wrong moment . . ."

"Possible," Grissom agreed. "Or we may be seeing evidence of a completely different series of events. I think we need to revisit the truck."

Back in the garage bay, the five members of the graveyard CSI team stood in a semicircle around the still-hoisted truck, watching attentively as Grissom hand-sprayed a large piece of chemically impregnated filter paper with a solution of 15 percent acetic acid and then carefully placed the slightly moist paper on the passenger-side floor of the cab interior.

Then, after placing several layers of dry cheesecloth over the filter paper and adding a few plastic-coated weights to press the entire paper-cloth mass firmly against the cab floor surface, Grissom stepped away from the truck and checked his watch.

"I think three minutes ought to do it," he said.

"Aren't you going to steam it?" Greg asked. Grissom was making no effort to reach for the plugged-in steam iron sitting on the garage floor next to the opened passenger-side door of the truck.

"No, I don't think that's going to be necessary," Grissom said. "We can't force hot acetic acid vapors through the floor, and the chemical reaction works almost as well without the heat if you give it enough time."

"Isn't that sort of . . . uh . . . cheating?" the young CSI asked cautiously.

"Yes and no," Grissom replied with an amused shrug. "I want you to know how to use the Greiss properly; but I also want you to feel free to consider necessary modifications to the protocols. Modifications, of course, which you would only use after proper and intensive research . . . and my final approval. Basically, I want you to be thinking like a scientist when you work your scenes, not just collecting and processing evidence like a technician— you don't need a protocol to function as a forensic scientist. We're talking about attitude and approach as much as anything else. Sometimes, all you have to do is look at your problem from a different point of view."

"Like I should have done about an hour ago," Catherine interrupted with a distinct edge to her voice. She was now staring at the back side of the damaged rear window with an irritated expression on her face.

"See something interesting?" Grissom inquired, his right eyebrow rising curiously.

"Yes, I do," Catherine responded. "Come back here and take a look."

Grissom walked over and stood beside his senior CSI.

"Oh," he said, after staring at the rear window-pane for less than thirty seconds.

"I was all over the bed of this damned truck," Catherine muttered. "All I had to do was look up . . . and, of course, think."

"Unfortunately, I did precisely the same thing

when I was placing the scanner-location circles," Grissom confessed.

"What are you two talking about?" Warrick asked.

"I think Catherine and I just demonstrated that, every now and then, attitude and approach can actually be the source of the problem as opposed to the solution," Grissom responded with a vaguely amused smile as he checked his watch again, "but first . . ."

He walked back over to the open door of the truck, reached in, pulled out the still-moist piece of filter paper, and then held it out for all to see.

"It looks just like the first ones I did," Greg said. "Just a mist of falling GSRs, right? No actual pattern?"

"Yes, that's exactly right," Grissom said. "Go over to where Catherine is standing and tell me what you see."

As Greg did so, the other three CSIs looked at one another, then got up from the table and walked over to join the assembled group.

Greg stared at the back side of the cracked pane of glass for a good minute before he said: "I'm staring at a piece of plate glass that's been hit by . . . uh . . . lots of projectiles: a whole bunch around the left—the driver's—side and the one over here in the lower right behind where a passenger would have been sitting."

"How do you know it's plate glass as opposed to tempered glass?"

"Tempered glass is designed to fracture into small cubic chunks when it breaks, instead of sharp and pointed shards that can be really dangerous in a vehicle accident," Greg replied. "Come to think of it, aren't the side *and* the rear windows of automobiles all supposed to be made out of tempered glass?"

"Yes, they are," Nick interjected, "but it's real easy to break a rear window in a truck when you're using it on a farm to haul tools with long handles, and plate glass is a lot cheaper substitute. Not really a smart thing to do, but farmers tend to be pretty conservative with their money."

"And fortunately for us, the owner of this truck seems to have been more concerned about his wallet than his safety," Grissom added.

"Okay, I can tell that all the projectiles traveled from the front of the truck toward the back . . . hey, wait a minute—!"

Greg stared at the multiply cracked pane for a good thirty seconds.

"Yeah, look, you can see that the projectile that made the hole over here to the right"—he pointed at the irregular inch-sized hole in the lower right side of the windowpane—"*had* to have hit the glass panel before all of the other projectiles on the left side . . . because that first projectile sent out all of those long radial fracture lines . . . and when the other projectiles hit, you can see where their radial lines *stopped dead* when they hit one of those first-projectile radial cracks."

"And what else can you tell me about that specific first-projectile hole?"

"Well . . . I'm guessing you and Catherine couldn't see that from inside the cab because the inside surface is almost completely covered with blood and splattered brain tissue?"

"Sadly correct," Grissom agreed, "but that's not telling me anything about the hole . . . or the projectile that made it."

"We probably can't tell much about angle of impact because the front windshield is pretty much destroyed," Greg said. "I don't think we could ever put it all back together again, in order to figure out which impact hole was made first."

"Probably not, but we shouldn't need the windshield data anyway, because there is something else we can infer from that hole. I trust you and your friends did attend the lecture on velocity of impact?"

Greg stared at the punctured window for a long moment. Finally he said, "A relatively smaller and higher-velocity bullet produces more radial cracks— but shorter ones—than a relatively larger and slower-velocity bullet, which produces fewer but *longer* cracks."

"Excellent." Grissom nodded in approval.

"Which means"—Greg leaned forward to make a closer examination of the single hole in the glass pane—"this hole was probably made by a pretty high-velocity bullet instead of by a slower one."

"It certainly appears that way," Grissom agreed, "but that's curious because . . ." He paused and looked over to the middle of the garage. "Warrick, can you put the 2-D overhead scan of the scene back up on the wall, showing the final position of the truck and all six shooters?

"Will do."

Warrick hurried over to the table and began working his laptop. Moments later, the requested image glowed on the far garage wall.

"Okay," Grissom said, pulling a laser pointer out of his lab coat pocket and aiming it at the wall image, "as you can see here, we have all six shooters positioned relative to the truck's final stopping point, which we'll designate the twelve-o'clock position—precisely where state officer Boyington is standing with his shotgun. We also have Refuge Officer Grayson positioned way behind the truck at the seven-o'clock position with his SIG pistol, DEA agent Jackson close up and even with the left-side window of the truck at the nine-o'clock position with another SIG, state officer Mace close up with another twelve-gauge at the eleven-o'clock position, and our dear Miss Smith behind that big boulder with her Glock at the two-o'clock position."

"You forgot DEA agent Tallfeather, farther out, at the . . . oh . . . roughly ten-thirty position," Sara pointed out.

"Oh no, I didn't forget Agent Tallfeather," Grissom said, "because he's the most interesting member of the team right now."

"You mean because he was armed with a high-powered rifle?" Nick asked. "What about Grayson, Jackson, and Smith? They all had high-velocity ammo in their pistols."

"Yes, they did," Grissom agreed. "But we can account for all of Officer Grayson's shots—and he was at the wrong angle, so that probably eliminates him as a possible source for this window shot. And the other two pistol shooters would have had to have been firing at the windshield to make this particular hole in the rear pane. But given the fact that they were all using *hollow-point ammo*, it's pretty likely that the initial impact against the windshield—or even the side window—would have slowed the mushrooming bullets down considerably before they stuck the rear window."

"Which basically makes them slower and bigger bullets." Catherine nodded with a satisfied smile.

"Yes, which leaves us with Agent Tallfeather as the most likely source of this bullet hole, and possibly the bullet that blew the subject's head apart—except for one thing." Grissom turned to observe Greg, who was rapidly thumbing through his scene and evidence examination notes.

"Except for the accounting of his shots," Greg said, looking up. "According to his statement, Agent Tallfeather fired six rifle rounds at the tires of the truck—almost immediately after Officers Grayson and Boyington fired their first shots—from the eleven-o'clock position . . . moved around to his right, where he fired nine rounds at the truck's engine block . . . and then emptied the magazine at the driver's-side door, because by then the subject had disappeared from view."

Greg checked his notes again.

"I don't know where the bullets went that he shot at the tires," he went on, "but I did find six expended casings in one general location that was consistent with his reported first shooting position . . . nine expended casings consistent with his second position . . . and fifteen expended casings consistent with his third position."

"That doesn't mean the bullets all went in the same direction," Sara pointed out.

"No, it doesn't," Greg said, nodding in agreement,

"but I also found nine bullets, all dented and smashed at the tip, on the ground underneath the engine compartment, looking like they'd all hit something really hard, like an engine block—and there are fifteen bullet holes aligned in one continuous sweep in the driver's-side door," he added with a smile as he pointed over to the nearby truck. "See."

"Devil's advocate," Catherine said. "What if he already had one round in the chamber when he loaded that magazine?"

Greg frowned. "Why would he carry an automatic rifle with one in the chamber? Wouldn't that be against the rules?"

Catherine chuckled.

"You're suggesting federal agents don't have to follow basic rules?" Greg asked.

"It may be a matter of using conjecture instead of the evidence at hand," Grissom commented.

"Wait. Hang on—the M-4 was empty when we took it from Agent Tallfeather, and we only found *thirty* expended casings, not thirty-one."

The CSIs all looked at one another.

Catherine finally voiced what everyone was thinking: "Another rifle at the scene, one they didn't tell us about?"

"When I interviewed Officer Mace," Warrick said, "he claimed he felt a bullet whip past his head right after he fired two rounds at roughly the eleven-o'clock position and was moving over to the ten-o'clock position, where he would fire three more rounds."

"Which side of his head?" Grissom asked.

Warrick quickly pulled out his field notebook. "Right side."

"That could have been one of Tallfeather's bullets," Nick pointed out. "He was behind Mace and to his right when he claims he started shooting at the truck tires."

"But didn't someone say—or at least imply—that Tallfeather fired all six rounds in one burst?" Sara asked.

"I found those six expended casings in one pretty tight group—the smallest possible containing circle was something like two feet," Greg said. "I guess he could have been standing there firing them, one at a time, but I got the impression that all of this shooting happened and then ended pretty quickly . . . like in a matter of seconds."

"So, what do you think, Gil?" Catherine asked. "Are we on the right track?"

"I think," Grissom said slowly, "that Brass, Fairfax, and I need to have a serious talk."

16

". . . ALL OF WHICH EXPLAINS why we now believe there was at least one other shooter at the scene who fired at the truck with a high-powered rifle," Grissom said as he set the green whiteboard marker down and turned to face the two men seated in his closed office.

For very different reasons, both Captain Jim Brass and Assistant Special Agent in Charge William Fairfax looked decidedly displeased with this latest evidence briefing.

"Did you recover that specific bullet?" Fairfax asked after a long moment of silence.

"No, we haven't . . . or, at least, not yet," Grissom amended.

"What do you think your chances are?"

"Probably remote, at best," Grissom said with a shrug. "We'll give it a try, after the storm clears; but it's an awfully big desert out there."

"Based on your descriptions, I would think it's

likely that shot came from one of Paz Lamos's men, dug into a sniper position some distance away from the campsite, trying to protect his boss," Fairfax offered. "Pretty damned ironic if it turns out that bastard got nailed by one of his own men. And, of course, it also explains the bullet Officer Mace said he felt whip past his head," he added after a contemplative pause.

"Yes, it could have been one of Paz Lamos's men," Brass agreed. "But during the interviews, I got the distinct impression that none of the UCs were especially concerned about watching their backs during the shooting. I'm not sure I would have felt the same way if a bullet whizzed by *my* head."

Fairfax started to say something else, and then hesitated. It was clear to Grissom that Fairfax's mind was churning furiously. The belated discovery by the CSI team that the subject in the truck had almost certainly fired his rifle only once—through the roof of the truck, and immediately after getting hit by an incoming round—was turning out to be an inconvenient fact.

"On the other hand," Brass went on calmly, "I also distinctly remember that every time I worked a major buy-bust with a team of DEA agents, they *always* put a protective sniper team out on the perimeter to monitor the agents making the exchange."

After a few more seconds of silence, Fairfax sighed deeply and then met Brass's gaze with a sense of ease that jarred Grissom. He was a strong believer in the idea that people—cops especially—

ought to look and feel guilty when they got caught lying.

"I did assign a protective two-man SWAT team to Agent Jackson for his operations," Fairfax conceded. "But Jackson said they were a considerable distance from the campsite—still working their way toward a good oversight spot, and very much out of position—when the shooting started."

"What? You didn't think that was worth mentioning—you had four DEA agents at a questioned-shooting scene, instead of two?!" Brass demanded, his eyes glaring.

"Jackson told me these agents were nowhere near the campsite when the shooting occurred, so I never considered them as being 'at the shooting scene' or a relevant part of the reconstruction," Fairfax answered matter-of-factly.

"Oh, come on," Brass retorted.

"Immediately after the shooting ended—when Jackson discovered the coke was not in truck, and he realized that Smith couldn't make a positive ID on the body—he radioed instructions to the protection team to immediately begin searching the outer perimeter for Paz Lamos and the drugs. Given the time of night, and Lamos's reputation for extremely violent assaults against law enforcement officers in general, I felt this was a perfectly reasonable precaution."

"But also something that Agent Jackson failed to mention during our interview," Brass said, raising his voice.

"An unfortunate omission," Fairfax said, "but not quite the same thing as falsifying a report. Agent

Jackson had a lot of issues to deal with during a very short time period immediately following the shooting, not the least of which was the possibility that Paz Lamos was still alive and in the general vicinity of the campsite. All things considered, I think he handled the situation in a satisfactory manner."

"So your sniper team—wherever they *were* actually located—didn't fire at the subject in the truck once the shooting commenced? Is that what you're saying?" Brass pressed.

"That's my understanding from Agent Jackson," Fairfax said, nodding his head firmly. "Given the distance involved—I believe he said they were about four or five hundred yards away—I'm sure it would have been a very dangerous shot to take in the best of conditions, which hardly describes the situation these men were facing. Any one of our UCs could have been hit by an off-target round, and they were well on their way to controlling the situation anyway; so, I really do think Jackson *and* the protection team made the right calls."

"Five hundred yards isn't all that long of a shot for an expert marksman," Brass said, seething.

"Not if the weather and visibility conditions are favorable," Fairfax agreed. "In this situation, I gather they were not."

"When can we expect to receive their weapons for examination?" Grissom asked.

"I . . . uh, don't see any reason why they should—"

"Actually," Brass interrupted, "given the still-open question as to whether or not your SWAT team *did* fire one or more shots in the direction of the campsite, I believe it's *imperative* that you order the immediate delivery of any firearms in their possession to our lab."

"But the search—," Fairfax started to protest.

"I don't think it will be necessary to pull them off the ongoing search for the drugs and Paz Lamos's men," Brass said. "Assuming that the search is still ongoing?"

"Yes, of course it is," Fairfax said heatedly. "I'm not about to miss out on an opportunity to take these bastards down on account of some poor weather conditions."

"Then it should be a simple matter to collect their weapons and issue them new ones—from that reserve arsenal I saw stored in your helicopter—right out in the field," Brass said. "Five minutes of paperwork and they're back in business. Simple."

Fairfax hesitated.

"Listen, I do realize this is going to undoubtedly piss them off thoroughly. But I also think it's critical to this reconstruction that we eliminate those SWAT weapons as being the possible source of *any* ballistics evidence related to the subject in the truck," Brass went on firmly. "I'm sure you wouldn't want the question to still be dangling in the wind during the hearing, any more than I do. And that's likely to be an issue after our pathologist testifies as to his findings and conclusions."

Fairfax frowned. "I wasn't aware that your pathologist found any actual physical evidence of a high-velocity rifle bullet hitting the body. I thought the evidence was basically circumstantial."

"I'm not aware of any *direct* physical evidence either," Grissom said, getting up and heading toward the door, "but knowing Doc Robbins . . ."

Dr. Albert Robbins muttered something under his breath as he reached for his ever-present cane, and then hobbled over to a pair of flat-screen monitors mounted on the far wall of the pathology lab, just above a biohazard-protected computer, keyboard, and mouse pad.

Grissom and Brass followed the annoyed pathologist at what they presumed was a safe distance.

"There's nothing wrong with your hearing, or my eyesight," Robbins replied as he manipulated a rubberized mouse to bring a menu up on the left screen. "And I distinctly remember indicating in my report that there were no discernible bullet fragments in the head wound of your John Doe."

"I realize that, Al," Grissom said with a vaguely apologetic smile. "I was just hoping there might be some barely discernible—or even microscopic—fragments that you hadn't bothered to report . . . perhaps because you knew we wouldn't be able to do anything with them."

Robbins favored Grissom with an unimpressed glare. "Is that the best you can do?" he demanded grumpily.

"It's been a long night," Grissom said with a shrug.

"Yes, it has," the pathologist agreed as he clicked the mouse twice, and then waited as the digital X-ray appeared on the left flat screen. "And *that* is one of the reasons *why* it's been a long night."

The three men stared at the crisp X-ray image of a terribly shattered human skull.

"As you can see—*for yourselves,*" Robbins said with emphasis, gesturing at the vivid 3-D skull image that displayed varying bones, tissues, and depths with distinct shades of black, gray, and white, "there are no discernable metal fragments in that wound path at all. You can see the three lead pellets in the lower jaw and neck, but no bullet fragments."

"Is that . . . normal?" Brass asked, starting to look just as irritable and frustrated as Robbins now.

"With a hollow-pointed and copper-jacketed bullet, no, that's not what I would expect," Robbins said. "With that kind of bullet, you can almost always find a little bit of a trail . . . usually small copper-jacketing fragments coming off the peeled-back and spinning edges. It doesn't take much in the way of resistance to tear thin bits of sharp-edged copper loose. Even in that little mule deer"—Robbins manipulated the mouse again, causing a pair of deer-skeleton images to appear on the right flat screen—"you can see a couple of fragments near the exit point of the wound . . . and *that* bullet didn't hit bone at all."

"What about a hardened round?" Brass asked.

Robbins turned to Brass. "What do you mean by 'hardened'?"

"I remember seeing our SWAT team out on the range shooting rifle ammunition with green tips a few months ago," Brass replied. "When I asked the team commander about them, he said they were 'hardened' rounds designed to penetrate body armor and barricade materials. The idea was that you wanted the suspect to go down hard and fast if he had a weapon on a hostage."

"Presumably meaning he was willing to risk a lot of collateral damage among the general population—and, of course, do without the enhanced hydrostatic-shock effects of a hollow-point round—knowing he had a marksman capable of putting a bullet in the ten-ring every time. Makes sense, I suppose," the pathologist said, nodding his head as he stared intently at the left-hand flat screen again.

"Thank God something around here does," Brass muttered.

"So, yes, I'd say that a hardened high-velocity bullet such as the one you described could easily create a wound like we have here," Robbins went on. "But then my question to you is, how would you prove it . . . especially if the bullet remained entirely intact after exiting the target?" he asked, turning to stare quizzically at Grissom.

"We'd have to find the bullet, and work backwards from there," Grissom replied, "which may not be as impossible as it sounds if . . ." He paused as he continued to stare at the right flat screen. "What's this?" he finally asked, pointing to what looked like an enlarged image of an oddly shattered arm bone.

"Something I haven't gotten around to putting in a report yet," Robbins responded. "Thought you might be interested to know that pathologists can make clever interpretations of fracture lines also . . . just like criminalists."

"Fracture lines in a bone?" Brass moved in closer to stare around Grissom's shoulder at the digital X-ray image.

"A lone bone is very much like a pane of glass in many respects," Robbins said. "Here, you can see it better in this image." A new image appeared on the right screen. "What we have here is a beautiful longitudinal fracture in the right ulna of our John Doe subject—initiated by the impact of a buckshot pellet at the distal end of the bone—that suddenly comes to a halt when it hits a very nicely defined compound fracture right . . . here." Robbins pointed a gloved finger at a jagged break located midway down the length of the forearm bone.

"And this is interesting because . . . ?" Grissom prodded.

"It's interesting, *I think*, because this particular compound fracture had to have occurred at least ten to fifteen minutes prior to the impact of that buckshot pellet . . . which, as I recall from your time line of the shooting, is probably a significant event. It takes at least that long for bruising of this nature"—Robbins manipulated the mouse again, and a color photo of the visibly bruised underportion of John Doe's right forearm appeared on the screen—"to develop. There are ambient temperature and protective-clothing issues involved in the timing, of course, but the underlying process is very simple. This fellow's heart had to be pumping pretty seriously for bruises like this to form in the area of a tissue-crushing and capillary-rupturing impact. And, if I have the shooting time line correct on this case, his heart would have stopped permanently within a very few seconds of his being hit with double-ought buck pellets from a shotgun."

"So, ten to fifteen minutes *before* he drove wildly into the campsite and was shot by several apparently surprised undercover officers, our John Doe had some kind of accident . . . ?" Grissom asked.

"Perhaps he ran into something with the truck?" Robbins suggested.

"I don't think so," Grissom said. "That old pickup was thoroughly dinged and scratched, in addition to being shot full of holes; no question about it. But all of those impact damages—at least all the ones I saw—were clearly older than a few days . . . or even a few weeks. I saw nothing in the way of external damage to suggest a recent vehicular accident . . . or at least nothing violent enough to have broken his arm like that."

"I agree," Brass said.

"Well, that's good," Robbins said, "because it helps support my theory that John Doe fell hard against something very solid at least a couple of times right before he died."

"A couple of times?"

"In addition to this pretty clear bit of evidence, I found recent minor fractures—and directly related scrapes and bruising—on both knees, both femurs, and both elbows, as well as several phalangeal dislocations on both hands. It would be difficult to accomplish all of that with one fall—not impossible, but difficult. Oh, and I'm pretty sure his nose was broken, too; but given the massive facial damage he sustained from the bullet, I really can't prove that. Add all of that to the tears in his clothing, and the grit, dirt, and sand we found in the pockets of his clothing, and I'd say your John Doe fell down something pretty serious—like maybe a rocky cliff or even a significant portion of a mountain—very shortly before he drove off to his death."

"Really?" A look of pure satisfaction appeared on Brass's face, suggesting that his gut instincts were about to be vindicated once again.

"Sounds like he went through a pretty miserable final hour," Grissom said absentmindedly. He, too, had a sense that the two supposedly separate shooting scenes at the Desert National Wildlife Range were starting to come together into one strangely related series of events. But the critical connecting pieces hadn't shown themselves yet.

"Undoubtedly true," Robbins agreed, "but probably not as miserable as the last week or so of *this* poor critter's life." The pathologist used the mouse one more time to bring a pair of images up on the right screen.

"The mule deer from the Toledano case?" Grissom's eyebrows furrowed in confusion. "I was under the impression *his* life ended pretty abruptly with that bullet through his neck."

"As I recall, you're always the one reminding everybody else that things are not always as they seem," Robbins said.

"I . . . have said that on more than one occasion," Grissom agreed, "but hey, what's that?" he asked, pointing to a dark area on the hindquarter portion of the second X-ray.

"Something that I also found to be quite interesting," Robbins said as he hobbled over to a nearby table and picked up a stainless steel bowl. "Take a look for yourself."

Grissom stared down into the bowl. "Is that the broken-off end of an arrow?"

Dr. Al Robbins's grizzled face broke out into a beaming smile.

"No," he said with the air of a man who rarely got the best of Grissom, "that is not the broken-off end of an arrow; it's the broken-off end of a crossbow bolt."

"Doesn't look like any bolt I've ever seen," Brass commented, staring over Grissom's shoulder into the bowl.

"That's probably because neither of you have ever taken much interest in medieval weapons," Robbins said with a satisfied smirk. "You're missing out on some fascinating, albeit extremely violent and gruesome, history—most of it involving hand-to-hand combat with axes, maces, broadswords, and knives. One can only imagine what it would have been like to work as a pathologist during that era."

"I'd rather not," Brass replied with a wince.

"And in case you were wondering if we humans have improved much over the past centuries, you should know that poor little mule deer," Robbins went on, gesturing with his head at the small sheet-covered corpse on the distant table, "spent a thoroughly horrible week or two hobbling around the Sheep Range in a great deal of pain, because some idiot shot him in the behind with a crossbow bolt."

Brass wandered over to the table, lifted up the sheet, and casually examined the dissected left rear leg and hip of the deer.

Wendy Simms stopped halfway through the doorway into the pathology lab. "Should I come back later?"

"Not if you've got something for us," Grissom said, ushering her forward into the lab area as the door swung shut on its pneumatic hinges.

"Actually, I do have something," she said. "I finished analyzing all of those blood swabs that Catherine collected from the bed of the truck." Wendy paused to sort through her notes. "Four of the swabs taken from the right front section of the truck bed—relative to the cab—were definitely human blood. I'm running them through CODIS now, along with a sample from John Doe."

"And the other, uh"—Grissom checked his notebook—"twelve samples?"

"They were all deer . . . mule deer, specifically," Wendy replied.

"Just like the tissue sample you extracted from the bullet taken out of subject Toledano's neck, correct?"

"Well, yes and no," the young DNA technician hedged. "The twelve nonhuman blood swabs from the bed of the truck were all from male mule deer—in fact, three distinct and different deer," Wendy explained. "But the tissue in the bullet from Toledano's autopsy was definitely from a female mule deer."

"Oh," Grissom responded with a mild "okay" shrug, making some quick additions to his notebook as Brass walked back to the stainless steel table bearing the mule deer carcass, pulled aside the bloodied sheet, and lifted up one of the mule deer's rear legs. Then he looked over at Robbins and made a "come over here" gesture with his right hand.

"I never really cared much for biology as a class subject," Brass said, as first Robbins and then Grissom and Wendy scrutinized the hapless creature from a new perspective, "but the one useful thing I did learn was how to definitively separate the girls from the boys."

Minutes later, Catherine, Warrick, Nick, Sara, and Greg looked up from their work as Grissom burst into the crime lab's garage.

"Shut things down here right now, secure your evidence, and pack up your scene gear. We're leaving in ten minutes," Grissom directed in a no-nonsense manner that matched the infuriated gleam in his eyes.

"What's going on?" Catherine asked, realizing far better than the others that such an emotional outburst from their generally amiable supervisor was both rare and meaningful.

"We've been had," Grissom muttered, forcing the words through seemingly clenched teeth. "Or, to be more precise, *I've* been had."

"What do you mean?" asked Catherine.

"Somebody rigged the Toledano shooting scene up on the mountain to make it look like a hunting accident," Grissom explained, forcing himself to slow down, "so we're all going back out there and do the job that I should have done properly in the first place."

"Out there in the storm . . . now?" Greg stared at Grissom incredulously, unaware that Catherine,

Warrick, Nick, and Sara had all started to repack their crime scene equipment and secure their evidence.

"Yes, Greg, we're going out there right now," Grissom said with a degree of calm that didn't even begin to match the determined look in his eyes, "all of us except for you."

"Why not me?"

"Because I'm sending you back to basics one more time," Grissom responded with a brief smile.

"I'm not going to like this, am I?" Greg asked.

"No, you probably won't."

17

BRIGHTLY ILLUMINATED IN THE HEADLIGHTS of two CSI vehicles, four LVPD patrol cars, and one Fish & Wildlife Service Refuge truck, the churned-up and abandoned campsite-turned-shooting-scene looked even more eerie and forlorn than it had several hours earlier when a shot-up red pickup truck had been the central feature.

Without the truck or the UCs' vehicles and camping equipment for reference, the only recognizable elements that told the CSIs they were in the right place were the two huge boulders that had once served as isolated bathroom facilities for the UCs; the makeshift rock fire ring; and the metal stake Nick had pounded deep into the ground as a reference point for his laser scene scanner, and then forgotten to retrieve.

As Grissom waited with visible impatience, Catherine, Warrick, Nick, Sara, Refuge Officer Shanna Lakewell, and seven LVPD uniformed officers quickly assembled themselves in a loose circle around the fire ring, which now enclosed a stack of twelve red traffic cones and two tripod-mounted rotating lasers. All thirteen men and women wore heavy waterproof boots and insulated rain gear over their varying field uniforms and jackets. It was still pitch black and raining, but the storm seemed to be subsiding.

"So, what's the plan?" Officer Lakewell asked, somehow managing to look both energetic and enthusiastic in spite of the beads of water streaming down her face.

"Two plans," Grissom said as he considered his team assignments. "The first one involves Catherine and Warrick, who are going to conduct a grid search of this scene with the assistance of Sergeant Cooperson and five of her patrol officers. And to assist that search, Warrick will use the 3-D digital model of the shooting he generated earlier this morning to help all of you place the twelve shooter-location cones back into their previous positions."

"Remember, for all of that to work out correctly, we're going to need to use the same numbered cones for the same shooter positions," Warrick said.

"Okay," Grissom went on. "Once you all have those cones in place, Warrick is going to use that same model to establish a laser-illuminated corridor along a line that includes two specific points: the high-velocity bullet hole we found in the corner of the truck's rear windowpane—when the truck was halfway to its final stopping point from where Officer Grayson hit the first rear tire—and a second point roughly two feet to the right of the spot where

Officer Mace was standing when he felt a bullet whiz past his head."

"How accurate is that going to be?" Catherine asked.

"Not very," Warrick admitted. "The uncertainty of that second point is definitely going to give us an increasingly large error factor as we move farther out along the corridor from the truck, but there's not much we can do about it. Those are the only two reference points we've got for this phantom bullet."

Grissom looked around at his assembled team.

"Once that search corridor is established," he said, "Catherine and Sergeant Cooperson will each take a metal detector and two uniformed officers with searchlights and conduct grid searches of areas specifically marked out by Warrick along that corridor. The two teams will continue these grid searches until someone finds a single hardened rifle bullet of unknown caliber that may or may not be bloody, and may or may not have a green tip."

Grissom paused, waiting for a reaction. But, to his amazement, no one commented on the immensity of the task, or the remote likelihood of success. "There's little or no evidence to suggest this bullet slowed down very much as it ripped through the skull of our John Doe; and the corresponding hole through the rear window of the truck was definitely made by a high-velocity bullet, so it could easily have landed some considerable distance away. But, on the positive side, a bullet is significantly bigger than a needle in a haystack . . . so it ought to be a lot easier to find."

"It's still a pretty big haystack out there," Sergeant Cooperson said.

"Yes, no question about that," Grissom acknowledged. "It's a huge task . . . and this weather isn't going to make things any easier."

"What about the rest of us?" Lakewell asked.

"The 'rest' of us—you, Nick, Sara, one of the uniformed officers, and I—will proceed up the mountain trail to the clearing where we earlier discovered the body of Toledano and a *male* mule deer. We'll then proceed to re-search and reevaluate the entire scene in an effort to determine why and how the hollow-tipped bullet that apparently ripped through our male mule deer's throat, before killing Mr. Toledano, managed to acquire *female* mule deer tissue along the way."

The flickering of headlights had warned Viktor Mialkovsky of the approaching CSI team long before the roar of the GMC Denali engines became audible on the high mountain clearing.

Thus by the time the two CSI vehicles, four LVPD patrol cars, and one Fish & Wildlife Refuge truck had parked at the abandoned campsite, and the thirteen distant figures were gathered around the fire ring, the hunter-killer had moved to a position at the edge of the high clearing—overlooking the valley below—where he could observe at least some of their activities through the crosshairs of his weather-impacted but still-functioning nightscope.

The storm that had forced him to stay tucked into the shelter of his small cave for the better part of the night seemed to be tapering off. Now, a little less than an hour and a half before dawn, the pounding rain had turned into a steady drizzle only intermittently swirled by gusts of ice-cold wind. Unfortunately, there was no way to tell if the storm was truly dying out . . . or just catching its proverbial second wind. In spite of the protection of the small cave, and his continued efforts to stay warm, fed, and hydrated, Mialkovsky realized that his extended high-altitude exposure to the elements was starting to have a significant impact on his strength, endurance, and concentration. He knew he couldn't wait much longer to begin his descent, even if the storm started back up again. But before he did that, he wanted to satisfy his curiosity about what was going on at the distant campsite.

Mialkovsky focused the nightscope on the one small and indistinct figure that appeared to be giving instructions to the others. It wasn't possible to distinguish one person from another at this distance, even if they hadn't all been dressed alike in foul-weather gear; but he was looking for some visual clue that would confirm his sense that Grissom had returned, once again, to haunt his waking hours as well as his dreams.

Yeah, it's you . . . has to be. So goddamned stubborn, aren't you? What did you find in all that evidence you collected? Had to be something significant to drag your entire team all the way back out here in this weather.

Fearless and self-confident in so many other ways, Viktor Mialkovsky found it ironic that the reappearance of a single forensic investigator at an abandoned shooting scene would make him uneasy. Part of it, he realized, was the fact that he still hadn't come up with answers to all the other wild-card factors in the whole mess.

The thing that truly frustrated Mialkovsky was his sense that Grissom and his investigators had either found the answers themselves or were about to do so. And if that was the case, the hunter-killer knew that the success of his mission—and even the necessary elements of his escape—could be undone by events that he could neither predict nor control.

He was still mulling over those frustrations when five of the distant figures suddenly broke away from the others and started walking toward the parked vehicles.

Moments later, Mialkovsky felt his heart tighten in his chest as he observed two of the vehicles—the USFWS Refuge truck and one of the dark Denalis belonging to the CSI team—pull away from the campsite and begin heading up the dirt road toward the base of the Sheep Range.

"You did find something, you bastard," he muttered to himself as he broke out of his hidden recon position and began to quickly scramble back across the clearing toward the cave, wondering as he did so if he would ultimately be forced to start shooting the CSIs in order to make his escape.

Not something I want to do, Mialkovsky thought as he carefully worked his way down a particularly steep and slippery section of rocks, forcing himself to execute slow and deliberate movements, *but these people may have pushed things too far this time.*

18

THE MULTIPLE SETS OF BLURRED TIRE TRACKS—all badly marred by the storm, but still distinctly visible in the headlights of the USFWS Refuge truck—caught Grissom's attention as the two climbing vehicles approached the base of the Sheep Range.

"Pull off the road, Shanna, over there," he said to the young refuge officer, pointing to a relatively flat section of dirt and gravel about fifty yards from the base of the mountain.

As soon as the truck came to a stop, Grissom was out the front passenger door with a high-intensity flashlight in his left hand, a canvas kit bag in his right, and a stuffed backpack over his shoulder. He moved toward the sets of interwoven tire tracks, rapidly followed by Nick, Sara, Lakewell, and uniformed LVPD officer Joe Carson, each of whom had their own flashlights, kit bags, and backpacks—all of which appeared to be stuffed full of equipment and supplies, except for Sara's.

For about two minutes, the three CSIs and two officers quickly ran the beams of their flashlights across the track sets as they spread out in five different directions.

"Anybody find a useful segment?" Grissom finally called out from his position next to a pair of large boulders about fifty yards from the base of the mountain.

"Nothing here," Nick replied. "Tire width at best; and even that's going to be an estimate. And, as far as I can tell, all of the tread patterns that should have been left in dirt or sand have been washed away."

"That's what I'm seeing too," Sara agreed. "But you can definitely tell there were two different vehicles up here, both of which went back down the road at pretty high speeds."

"And you can also tell that the vehicle with the narrower set of tires—which, I think, are consistent with the tires on the red pickup in terms of width— came up here after the first vehicle, and then left ahead of the first vehicle," Nick added as he started taking strobe-enhanced photos of the tracks with his digital camera, using a two-dimensional grid ruler as a scale.

"Which accounts for our red pickup and the big dark-painted SUV," Grissom said as he swept his flashlight beam across the relatively flat area that had clearly served as a parking lot for at least one of the two vehicles.

"And here's the trail where they went up . . . and apparently came down at a pretty fast clip," Lakewell called out, standing near the base of the mountain with Officer Carson and shining her light beam at a gap between a pair of graffiti-painted boulders.

"Where does it lead to?" Grissom asked as the three CSIs quickly gathered around Lakewell and Carson.

"It comes out on a pretty large rocky clearing about two hundred yards up," Lakewell replied. "Maybe two-fifty if you count all of the weaving back and forth."

"And that's the clearing where we found Toledano's body?" Grissom asked.

"Yes, I'm sure it must be," Lakewell replied. "It's the only large flat area on the southern portion of the range."

"Six hundred feet uphill, in the dark, and with a drizzling rain just to make things interesting," Sara said, sweeping her flashlight beam across the exposed rocks above her head. "Sounds like a great way to take a nasty fall. Maybe we ought to wait for the helicopters?"

Grissom consulted his watch. "It's going to be a while before they arrive, even if the weather stays reasonably calm," he said, "and we do need to get up there and conduct our search before dawn."

"We do?" Nick and Sara echoed, their eyebrows rising in unison.

"Yes, definitely," Grissom said without further explanation.

"It won't take us all that long to get up there, but it's not going to be an easy climb," Lakewell warned.

"That's okay, we're going to need to conduct a

thorough search of the trail as we go anyway," Grissom said as he started up the trail, his flashlight beam sweeping across the narrow pathway. "And besides, it'll be a lot easier coming back down."

"How do you figure that?" Lakewell asked. She'd made the trip at least a half-dozen times in the last few months while getting to know the refuge, and knew all too well how easy it was to slip and fall coming back down the treacherous trail.

"I've made arrangements for Greg to pick us up," Grissom said over his shoulder, his eyes already focused on the patch of ground illuminated by his flashlight beam.

It was LVPD Officer Carson—a competent and experienced climber, as he'd claimed, though nowhere near as agile and energetic as Lakewell—who found the helmet about a hundred and fifty feet up the trail. A dented and shattered nightscope was still attached by a single partially torn strip of duct tape.

"Isn't that one of those first-generation night-vision scopes? Those haven't been around for thirty years," Carson said as he handed the helmet to Grissom.

"Yes, I think so," Grissom said as he examined the helmet closely before handing it to Sara. "And it looks like we've got some blood inside the tube. Can you get a swab?"

"Sure, no problem."

Sara waited while Nick took a quick photo of the helmet-and-tube assembly, put away his camera, and then pulled a small folded tarp out of his backpack. With the help of Grissom, Lakewell, and Carson, he opened the tarp up and held it over Sara as a protective shelter as she removed a swab from her raincoat pocket and quickly collected a sample of the blood from inside the broken and bent tube. Then she slid the helmet and tube into a plastic bag, placed the bagged piece of evidence into her empty backpack, and looked up at the group. "Next?"

It was Lakewell—still moving about the rocks like one of her treasured Bighorns with her flashlight, kit bag, and backpack, while everyone else was starting to breathe heavily—who found the shattered pair of night vision binoculars . . . and then, a few feet away, a badly dented and scarred Uzi submachine gun, about halfway up the trail.

"Automatic gunfire, indeed," Nick commented.

"And very possibly the reason why our John Doe was so anxious to get away from this mountain," Grissom said, once again holding a corner of the unfolded tarp while Nick carefully unloaded the lethal assault weapon, placed it in a large paper bag, and then slid the parcel into Sara's backpack.

Three-quarters of the way up the trail, it was Lakewell, again, who found the next item of evidence while the rest of the CSI team were sitting on the most comfortable rocks they could find, trying to catch their breath.

"Do you think this could be relevant?" she asked as she handed the wooden contraption to Grissom.

"I do indeed," Grissom said as he used his flashlight to examine the crude weapon with reverence, as if he were a devout believer handling an ancient religious icon.

"What is it?" Nick asked as he forced himself to

his feet and walked over to examine the latest find.

"I believe it's a crossbow," Grissom replied with a slight smile.

"That thing? You've gotta be kidding."

"I don't think our good Doctor Robbins would call it a *classically constructed* crossbow," Grissom said, looking up at Nick with a smile, "but a rusted strip of truck-spring steel screwed to the end of a piece of two-by-four ought to create a considerable amount of tension on a wire bowstring. Granted, it doesn't look especially safe to operate, or even easy to cock; but if you were poor *and* hungry, and didn't mind bending the local rules a bit . . ."

"The deer blood in the back of the truck . . ." Nick stared down at the crudely made weapon in sudden realization. "Are you thinking our John Doe may just be a deer poacher, and not a drug dealer or an assassin?"

"It's certainly a possibility," Grissom said.

"Then . . . what happened up there?" Lakewell asked, staring at the trail.

"That," Grissom said as he looked at his watch, and then forced himself to stand on his aching legs, "is precisely what we need to figure out."

19

Captain Jim Brass entered the crime lab's expansive garage and saw Greg Sanders outside through an open bay door, loading a three-foot-tall stainless steel canister into the back of one the CSI team's Denalis. Two more canisters were lying on the ground next to his feet.

"Hey, Greg," he called out, "where's Gil?"

"Out at the crime scenes with the rest of the team, Captain," Greg said as he reached down for the second canister.

"You mean the UC shooting scene out by Sheep Range?"

"Yep, that one and the hunting accident up on the mountain too, I'm pretty sure."

"What's he doing back up there?" Brass demanded.

"I don't really know," Greg said, looking at his watch. "I think they went back to look for more evidence."

"More evidence of what?"

Greg shook his head. "He didn't say. All I know is, I have to be back out there, too . . . and I'm running late because we didn't have enough of the premix in the lab, and I had to go find more in the stockroom . . . and Grissom's going to be really upset if I don't—"

"Go, go," Brass said, waving his hand in dismissal, and then looking bemused as the young CSI bolted for the driver's-side door of the Denali. Moments later, the black CSI vehicle disappeared into the darkness and drizzling rain.

Rolling his eyes, Brass hit the button to close the garage bay door, and was starting to walk over to the shot-up red pickup when computer tech Archie Johnson burst into the garage.

"Sir, do you know where I can find Grissom?" the young tech asked, looking wide-eyed and—from Brass's perspective—possibly even a little scared.

"Greg just told me the entire team went back out to Sheep Range," Brass said. "Is there anything—?"

"Oh, great," Archie whispered.

"What's the matter?" Brass demanded.

"I—uh, think you'd better come with me."

When Brass entered the crime lab's conference room behind Archie Johnson, he found firearms examiner Bobby Dawson and an Army officer whom he didn't recognize and who was dressed in a field uniform sitting at the conference table. Both of them were staring intently at the screen of a laptop computer, but Bobby rose to his feet instantly.

"Captain Brass, this is Colonel Sanchez," Bobby

said, motioning with his hand to the rising Army officer.

"Colonel," Brass said warily, "what can I do for you?"

"Actually, it may be more a question of what I can do for you," the colonel responded, taking Brass's hand in a firm grip.

"I'm sorry, I don't understand—?"

"I'm the one who started it, sir," Archie said quickly, still looking wide-eyed and scared. "Grissom asked me to pull some digital photos off his flashcard and then help him determine some kind of trajectory on that hunting accident scene up on Sheep Range. So I downloaded all of the photos, and I was starting to go through them, to find the ones he described, when—"

"When I came into the conference room with Colonel Sanchez, whom I called and asked to come over as quickly as he could because I'm pretty sure I spotted what I *think* are the distinctive markings of a TX-twelve-twenty on the bullet Doc Robbins took out of Enrico Toledano's neck," Bobby interjected.

"The TX-twelve-twenty is an experimental sound suppressor being developed for our Special Ops teams," Colonel Sanchez explained. "It's very classified, top-secret—which means it's a device that even law enforcement firearms experts like Mr. Dawson here shouldn't know anything about—but it seems our development engineers have a difficult time learning to keep their traps shut."

"What?" If possible, Brass now looked even more confused.

"The incredible thing is, "Bobby said, "the design engineers must have figured out how to incorporate nanotube fibers in the baffle stacks—nobody thought it was possible to assemble ten billion of the damned things in a precise cylindrical alignment. You can only see them—or, actually, the tiny scraping marks against the copper jacketing of a bullet—with a scanning electron microscope. I'd heard about the concept, and when I saw those markings under the SEM—or at least what I was pretty sure were the markings, because nothing else I know of leaves markings *that* fine in copper—I called the colonel, because we've met before out at the range, and I figured he ought to know about this."

"And Mr. Dawson is correct: it's a damned good thing he did call, because of *this,*" Sanchez said as he reached down and pressed a key on the laptop.

Instantly, the slightly rain blurred image of a rock-and-boulder-strewn ridge appeared on the far wall.

"What's that?" Brass asked, thinking that the image looked familiar.

"That's an overall shot from the Toledano shooting scene up on the mountain that Gil took just before he followed you over to the place where you found the deer carcass," Archie explained.

"And that's the photo that was on the wall when the colonel and I came in here looking for you and Gil," Bobby continued. "Only none of us noticed what the colonel saw immediately."

"The upper left corner—where you see the two

small light reflections—if you will, please," Colonel Sanchez directed, and then waited patiently while Bobby quickly manipulated the image on the laptop screen. Moments later, the image on the far wall changed.

"What the hell is that?" Brass whispered, feeling a chill run down his neck.

"That is a TX-twelve-twenty sound suppressor— or silencer, if you prefer—mounted on a standard military M-24 bolt-action sniper rifle," Sanchez replied.

"No, I meant—"

"I know what you meant, Captain," Sanchez said. "The individual holding that weapon is wearing a standard Army sniper Ghillie suit and night-vision goggles, and he has placed himself in a classic position to observe . . . or to take action."

"By take action," Brass said softly, "you mean—?"

"Kill his target . . . or targets," Sanchez finished. "I understand there were two of you up on the mountain at the time this photograph was taken."

"What in the hell is a military sniper doing up there . . . on a federal refuge . . . aiming a rifle at us?" Brass demanded, barely able to get the words out through his constricted throat.

"First of all, the man in that photograph—if I'm correct as to his identity, which I believe I am—is no longer a U.S. Army sniper . . . or a military criminal investigator . . . or even a member of the military. In fact, we were under the impression that he had died in a rather violent accident six months ago."

"You can positively identify him based on that photo?" Brass asked, staring at the blurred image that he wouldn't have even recognized as including a human form had Sanchez not pointed out the specific pieces of equipment.

"I'm certain of the identity of that sound suppressor, because of its distinct shape, and because it's the only one missing from the very few we have in our inventory. The fact that it was checked out to First Sergeant Viktor Mialkovsky at the time he was supposedly run off a mountain road and into an extremely deep lake by an intoxicated truck driver leads me to believe that we are looking at a resurrected First Sergeant Mialkovsky. That and the fact that Mialkovsky lost the little finger of his left hand in Afghanistan—ironically, by his own knife, while he was busy cutting someone's throat—leads me to believe we have a positive identity. You can just barely make out the fact that the fourth finger is not present on the left-hand glove holding the stock of that rifle."

"Jesus," Brass whispered.

"Indeed," Sanchez responded, nodding his close-cropped head in agreement. "As you may have gathered from my comments, First Sergeant Mialkovsky was—and apparently still is—an extremely competent and extremely dangerous individual. The fact that your CSI happened to take that photograph at the very instant he was raising the rifle—thus generating the reflections off the night-vision scope and his night-vision goggles that I noticed in the photo Mr. Johnson was examining—was pure happenstance. Had it not been for that bit of bad luck on his part, I doubt you would have ever known he was up there."

"We *didn't* know," Brass whispered. "We had no idea—"

"Your problem, of course, is what he was actually *doing* up there," Sanchez said sympathetically. "I gather from talking with Mr. Dawson that a member of organized crime—a Mr. Enrico Toledano—was found shot and killed at that location earlier this evening?"

"Yes, that's correct," Brass said.

Sanchez frowned. "That's unfortunate, because it strongly suggests that First Sergeant Mialkovsky was somehow involved in that shooting . . . which also suggests that he's now making use of his considerable skills for less-than-honorable employment."

"As a professional assassin?" Brass whispered again, his face pale.

"That would seem to be the case," Sanchez said. "It's certainly not the first time we've had one of our soldiers go rogue, but the interesting question is: What was he still doing up there on the mountain when that picture was taken?"

"I don't understand."

"How long had Mr. Toledano been dead before you and Mr. Grissom were up there examining the scene?"

"I don't know." Brass shrugged. "At least an hour or two . . . probably more."

"Which makes very little sense," Sanchez said, "because a professional assassin with the shooting, recon, survival, and evasion skills of a man like First Sergeant Mialkovsky should have been long gone from the scene within minutes of his kill. There's absolutely no reason I can think of why he would have stayed around, unless . . .." Sanchez stared directly into Brass's widening eyes.

"Us?"

"It's a plausible explanation," Sanchez said, "except for one minor thing."

"You mean, why didn't he kill us when he had the chance?"

"No, I mean why didn't he kill you, period?" the colonel corrected. "It would have taken him two seconds with the rifle, at the most . . . or he could have used a knife . . . or a handy rock . . . or even his bare hands."

"But we were both armed," Brass protested.

"With pistols?"

"That's right."

"And I gather you weren't being . . . evasive or defensive?"

"We were standing up in open view, looking around the scene with flashlights," Brass rasped as awareness sunk in.

Sanchez smiled sympathetically.

"But there *were* helicopters overhead," Brass added.

The colonel's eyes narrowed. "Ours?"

"No, one of ours . . . and a Black Hawk from the DEA," Brass said.

"Then it wasn't you he was after—or, at least, not at that moment," Sanchez said after a brief hesitation. "He wouldn't have viewed those choppers as a significant threat or hindrance. Perhaps whoever he was waiting for hadn't shown up yet."

Brass suddenly blinked in shock. "You're saying he could still be up there?"

"If First Sergeant Mialkovsky *was* waiting for someone to arrive, or something to happen, it doesn't sound like your people have done anything to scare him off . . . and he certainly wouldn't be bothered by the inclement weather we're experiencing right now," Sanchez said with a slight smile. "Why, is that a concern?"

"Grissom's gone back up there with his entire team," Brass said, his eyes wide with realization.

Sanchez's head snapped up. "They're back on the mountain . . . where that picture was taken?" The colonel's dark eyes were flashing dangerously.

Brass nodded mutely.

"How long ago?" Sanchez demanded as he pulled a cell phone from his belt.

"I don't know," Brass admitted. "Forty-five minutes . . . maybe an hour. They've got to be climbing up the trail from the road, because our helicopters are still grounded." He fumbled for his own cell phone. "I'd better warn them—"

"Wait, do you have encrypted communications?" Sanchez asked as he quickly thumbed a pair of buttons on his phone.

"Not with these cell phones," Brass replied, hesitating.

"Then don't try to warn them. Mialkovsky will be monitoring your frequencies; you can count on that."

"But—"

"This is Colonel Sanchez," the military officer barked into his cell phone. "I'm calling an Echo-

Charlie-Romeo alert . . . repeat, Echo-Charlie-Romeo . . . full platoon—both squads—night-vision gear and live ammo. This is not a drill."

Sanchez paused for a moment, listening to whatever response he was getting from the duty officer.

"Furthermore, advise Captain Jambeau, Lieutenant Maddox, the two squad sergeants, and all insertion and support units that their designated target is First Sergeant Viktor Mialkovsky."

Sanchez paused again.

"That is affirmative; First Sergeant Mialkovsky is apparently alive and now functioning as an active enemy combatant in our immediate area. Metro police discovered one DOA on the east side of the Sheep Range linked to his activities, and there may be others in the area. Advise all units that Mialkovsky is armed with a Mike-twenty-four rifle, an Alpha-Tango-Nora nightscope, and a Tango-X-Ray-twelve-twenty suppressor, and that he appears fully equipped for night recon. I'll coordinate our access into the refuge. Advise all units also that a Metro CSI team is responding to that location now, and they are unaware of Mialkovsky's presence."

Another brief pause.

"Yes, put the Apaches up in support, but remind the crews there are armed police investigators in the immediate area who don't know we're coming . . . and we're not going to warn them because Mialkovsky is undoubtedly monitoring their radio traffic. We want zero collateral damage on this op; repeat, zero collateral damage. Advise all units they have a green light to shoot on confirmed sight, or in response to any hostile fire; my authorization. I'll confirm at the scene. Over."

Colonel Sanchez quickly returned the cell phone to his belt and then stared directly into Brass's eyes.

"Captain," he said, "I need to speak with your chief, immediately. We've got some very serious legal issues to resolve."

20

GIL GRISSOM, NICK STOKES, SARA SIDLE, and Officers Lakewell and Carson all stood at the top of the trail, working once more to catch their breaths as they looked out across the rocky clearing with their night-vision goggles.

From Grissom's perspective, in the cold and drizzling night air, the multihued green expanse of rocks and boulders looked even more eerie and foreboding than it had a few hours earlier.

Once he got his bearings, he shut off his night-vision goggles and flipped them up and away from his eyes, and directed the others to do the same. Then he turned on his high-intensity flashlight and began picking his way gingerly around the rocks and boulders to the ridge where he and Brass had first observed the sprawled body of Enrico Toledano.

"This is where we found his body and the silenced rifle," Grissom said as he pointed out the two sets of bright green outlines with his flashlight beam. "Over there—"

He redirected the glaring beam to a distant spot in the middle of the clearing that suddenly glowed a faint green.

"That's where we found the mule deer."

He shifted the beam one more time.

"And directly over there—in a straight-line path from here through the deer position—is where I found the expended casing, and what appeared to be a crudely arranged prone-shooting station."

For a few seconds, four more glaring flashlight beams played over the huge expanse of rocks and boulders.

Finally, it was Sara who spoke the words that all four investigators were thinking.

"Are you really expecting us to search this entire clearing with flashlights, before daybreak, and actually find something . . . without snapping our ankles in the process?" she demanded.

"No, I'm not," Grissom said as he reached into his jacket pocket and pulled out his cell phone.

"But I thought you said—?" she started to say, and then hesitated as Grissom briefly held up his hand for silence, quickly punched a series of buttons on his phone, and then held it up to his ear . . . spoke briefly to someone at the other end . . . checked his watch . . . and snapped the phone shut. Finally, he knelt down, opened up his kit bag, and removed five full-face-shield respirators and five fresh cans of bright fluorescent green spray paint. He handed masks and cans to each member of his team, and then stood up.

"I assume both of you are both qualified to wear a respirator?" he asked Lakewell and Carson. Both officers nodded.

"Good. The filters in these masks may clog up pretty quickly," Grissom went on, "but that shouldn't matter because the wind and rain will work in our favor . . . and we'll only have a few minutes to find something anyway."

"We're going to wear a respirator, in the rain, because we're worried about a little spray paint?" Carson asked.

"No, not exactly," Grissom said, as he stared up at the sky. "Ah, there they are."

Four sets of eyes followed his pointing hand, and they all saw the running lights of the LVPD helicopter climbing slowly and then finally hovering a hundred feet or so over the clearing where it connected to the trail. From their position, they could just barely make out the lone figure of Greg Sanders standing in the open doorway of the familiar aircraft.

"You've got to be kidding me," Nick said as he first stared out at the helicopter, then down at the mask and spray paint in his hand, and finally back at Grissom.

"It's a very sensitive test," Grissom said.

"Yeah, it is," Nick agreed. "But over a couple of acres of rocks and boulders, in drizzling rain, and after a pretty serious storm? Do you really think it's going to work?"

"It certainly should."

"Okay, so tell me, guys, what exactly are we going to be trying to avoid breathing by wearing these masks?" Carson pressed.

"Three-amino-phthalhydrazide," Nick replied as he began adjusting the straps on his mask.

"Luminol reagent," Sara added as she began to readjust the straps on her mask. "It reacts with the iron in hemoglobin to produce a cold chemical luminescence that can be detected with the human eye. The reagent's really not all that dangerous, but we're going to be applying it in a very nonstandard manner, and there's nothing wrong with being careful," she added.

"A luminol test for blood, sprayed from a helicopter, in the middle of a rainstorm?" Carson stared at Sidle as if she'd lost her mind.

"Don't look at me," she said, pointing at Grissom, "it's his idea."

Grissom gathered everyone in close. "What we're going to do is position ourselves as equidistant as possible over this clearing, crouch down, wait for the helicopter to make the first spray pass—and remember, they'll have to fly in pretty low or the luminol will disperse too far—and then quickly look for any sign of chemiluminescence on the ground or in the rocks."

"A bright bluish glow," Sara translated for Lakewell and Carson.

"Correct," Grissom said, "and it won't last long, especially considering the dilution factor of the rain, so we really will have to move quickly. The instant you see any sign of a bluish glow, run over and spray a circle around the area as fast as you can with your paint can. The green paint will fluoresce brightly in the visible spectrum for about an hour before it begins to fade, but—"

He quickly checked his wristwatch.

"—that should get us close enough to sunrise that we'll be able to relocate and search the marked areas for blood-related evidence with some degree of daylight."

"How many runs do we have?" Nick asked as he helped Lakewell adjust her mask.

"Greg was able to prepare four ten-gallon canisters with the supplies we had on hand. Each of the canisters will be valve-connected to a spray rig that Search and Rescue used to fertilize the lawn out at the heliport last year. I'm figuring one canister per pass, hitting roughly a quarter of the clearing each time with some overlap. And we'll have a little time in between passes, because Greg will have to wait until the last moment to add the sodium perborate to each canister."

"Probably a lot of overlap, with this wind," Sara predicted.

"Exactly," Grissom agreed, looking around. "Is everybody ready?"

Nick, Sara, Lakewell, and Carson all nodded.

"Okay," Grissom said as he pulled the respirator over his head, "let's go find ourselves some blood!"

Viktor Mialkovsky pulled the thin desert-patterned thermal blanket and camouflage net tight around his body and then settled comfortably into his new prone observation position at the far southwestern edge of the clearing, a little less than twenty-five yards from his planned escape point. He was watching the five indistinguishable figures through his nightscope as they pulled the respirator masks over their heads and then ran to five approximately equidistant positions across the clearing.

What in the hell are you doing? the hunter-killer wondered as he observed the figure closest to him—now less than a hundred yards away—suddenly crouch down amid the rocks and boulders.

Then, a moment later, the LVPD helicopter began its first pass, sending a whitish spray from six jets mounted on the landing skids directly beneath the chopper cabin, and Mialkovsky suddenly had a sense of what Grissom might be trying.

No way . . . not after this storm, he told himself, feeling the downdraft as the LVPD helicopter roared overhead and then made a sudden sharp turn to the south.

But then he saw one of the figures in the middle of the clearing suddenly run forward, kneel down, and spray a wide circle on the rocky ground, and his jaw dropped.

Christ, that's right where I—

At that instant, Mialkovsky heard the familiar distinct rumble of an Army MH-60G Pave Hawk helicopter coming in fast from the west, its four composite rotor blades clawing at the thin mountain air as it roared overhead, swooped down—disgorging two dark figures in the middle of the clearing, who instantly flattened to the rocky ground; two more a hundred yards farther to the south; and a final two at the eastern edge of the clearing—and then banked away sharply, roaring up into the darkness.

Instantly switching into combat mode, Mialkovsky reflexively fed a hollow-pointed round into the chamber of his rifle, vaguely aware that the CSI figure closest to him was now running frantically toward the far eastern edge of the clearing where it connected to the trail . . . followed a second later by another figure who lunged up and began running in the same direction.

Perfect. Keep on going. . . .

A half-second later, Mialkovsky had the first figure in the crosshairs of his nightscope, the better part of his mind aware—and methodically recording—that a second Pave Hawk was dropping three more shooter-spotter teams high into the rocky mountain some five hundred yards north, northwest, and east of his position. He was starting to squeeze the trigger—having already made the tactical decision that caring for five wounded CSIs would provide a useful distraction for the hunter-killer teams whose primary mission was undoubtedly to hunt and kill him—when the equally familiar but far more chilling roar of a very different helicopter caused him to instinctively flatten down into his boulder-protected enclave.

He sensed—but didn't dare look up to see—the pilot of the AH-64D Apache attack helicopter come in very low and not all that fast over the clearing, daring Mialkovsky to try for a shot at one of the armored aircraft's very few vulnerable points . . . and, in doing so, expose himself to boulder-shredding mayhem of the under-the-fuselage-mounted 30-mm chain gun manned by the Apache's undoubtedly smiling copilot-gunner.

Viktor Mialkovsky wasn't even remotely suicidal, so he stayed down for the four to five seconds it took the Apache to transverse the clearing. Then he brought his head back up, regained his target—and saw the face of Gil Grissom suddenly appear in a distant, billowing, and seemingly hallucinogenic flash of pale green light, like a hovering forensic conscience, in the background of his nightscope.

Mialkovsky recoiled in shock . . . recovered . . . and then squeezed the trigger at the very instant a dark camouflaged arm reached out and yanked the frantically running figure to the ground behind a large rock.

Rapidly feeding another round into his rifle, Mialkovsky brought the second running figure into his crosshairs, squeezed off a second round, instinctively reloaded . . . and then felt a sudden sense of eerie calm, as if the entire scene had gone deadly still the moment his first bullet ricocheted off the distant boulder in the middle of the clearing. He could easily imagine the excited words being exchanged between the hunter-killer teams:

Incoming fire . . . two shots . . . two civilians down.

Where's the shooter?

Don't know.

Anybody see him?

A series of single radio clicks signaled negative responses.

And then the platoon leader's terse order:

All teams, maintain radio discipline. Locate source of incoming fire, engage target, and pin him down, now.

Mialkovsky felt the rush of adrenaline coursing through his bloodstream as he waited for the first sign of movement, knowing that the directional vector of the first leapfrogging sniper team would reveal the platoon leader's chosen tactics. He had played this role countless times in his career, almost always to the chagrin of the opposing trainee-lieutenant. But that had been with simunitions—high-velocity paint bullets that had left the methodically outwitted and exposed hunter-killer teams with physical bruises to go along with their all-too-visible impact splotches and mental pain. Live 7.62 ball ammo was a different situation entirely.

And that was Mialkovsky's significant advantage: the fact that he'd perfected his tactical skills in the high mountains of Afghanistan, against men whose patience and expertise with long-range rifles easily matched his own. It had been arrogance as much as anything else—their sense of religious superiority, and their refusal to take their adversary seriously— that had doomed those Taliban snipers, one after the other; a mistake he was certain this particular platoon leader wouldn't make.

But even the best hunter-killer tactics will fail if the teams hesitate, Mialkovsky reminded himself, smiling as he imagined the young soldiers' responses to what was very likely their first exposure to incoming live fire from an unknown vector.

He remained completely immobile for another thirty seconds . . . watching and waiting . . . and then finally nodded in understanding.

Not moving in on me yet. Trying to gather up and protect the CSIs first. Lousy tactics. Understandable, but still lousy . . . leaving his teams vulnerable like that, just to protect a few civilians.

Mialkovsky smiled.

You're losing your advantage of surprise, Lieutenant.

It's still my playground, and you're giving me way too much time to maneuver out here.

Mialkovsky had already calculated his first series of moves, all designed to cut off and progressively harass and unnerve the three high-ground-located hunter-killer teams, all of whom had dropped awkwardly out of their Pave Hawk—*brand-new trainees, and I'm their first live rabbit, poor bastards*—when the familiar rumble of an Apache attack helicopter became audible again. Only this time, the sound was different . . . deeper . . . more guttural . . . and somehow more intense.

Two of them . . . and something else?

The two attack helicopters came in from opposite directions—north and south—and higher this time, the fearsome aircraft performing a lethal ballet turn over the clearing with deft twists of their composite rotor blades, and then hovering there, less than a hundred yards apart . . .

Daring me to engage again? Thanks, but I don't think so, Mialkovsky thought, vaguely amused—and, admittedly, impressed—by the typical Army-macho display of brute firepower that had been sent over the Sheep Range to deal with one man and one rifle.

. . . as the first Pave Hawk came back in low and very fast over the clearing from the west, swooping down suddenly like a talon-armed predator reaching out for its prey . . . but this time disgorging only a single dark figure from its side door—at a point approximately two hundred yards northwest of Mialkovsky's position—before it roared up and away under the protective lethality of the two hovering Apaches.

Unlike the three sniper teams, who had revealed with their hesitating movements their limited degree of training and experience, this lone dark figure had exited the helicopter fast, like a Navy rescue diver, and then seemed to disassemble or evaporate in midair before hitting the ground.

Shit, Mialkovsky cursed as he began to move backwards in quick, crablike movements until he was completely turned around and facing his escape route.

The series of cat-and-mouse games that Mialkovsky had envisioned with some amusement—utilizing his tactical advantages and expertise against the hunter-killer trainees based at the Nellis Test and Training Range for some undetermined time period before he finally broke off the lethal exercise and disappeared into the mountains—had completely vanished from his conscious mind . . . much like the fleeting image of the single rifle-armed figure who, he guessed, was probably now less than a hundred and eighty yards away, and likely closing in fast.

First Sergeant Viktor Mialkovsky realized that he'd been effectively outthought and outmaneuvered, not by a trainee sniper-platoon-leading lieutenant, but by a far more experienced and deadly man very much like himself.

Thought you'd have gone back home by now, you cold-hearted bastard, Mialkovsky mused as he quickly secured the thin desert-patterned thermal blanket and camouflage net tighter around his body, knowing that he didn't dare get caught on a protruding branch. Not with Major Ken Park out here in the darkness, homing in on his position like a top-of-the-food-chain predator. Park, the widely renowned and feared South Korean Army sniper instructor—on loan from the ROK—who disdained the use of spotters because he believed they got in his way. The only hunter-killer who had ever defeated First Sergeant Mialkovsky in the advanced sniper tactical exercises . . . not once, but twice.

But that had occurred within in the limited perimeter of the Nellis Test and Training Range, using simunition rounds in time-limited scenarios, and with vigilant referees to keep the all-too-real exercises from getting out of control.

No limits and no referees today, Major. Just you and . . . and the trainees you're honor-bound to protect because you deliberately put them at risk in order to save a handful of civilians, Mialkovsky thought with an oddly mixed sense of hope and fatalism as he first made a final survey of the equipment he would use to make his escape, and then checked his watch.

Time was the only weapon he now possessed that offered him any advantage against a master hunter-killer like Park . . . and he sensed it was rapidly ticking away.

Time to move . . . now.

21

FOCUSED ON THEIR DETERMINED HUNT for any sign of blue fluorescence among the thousands of rocks scattered across the mountainside clearing, and having grown accustomed to the rumbling drone of the LVPD Search and Rescue helicopter overhead, the arrival of the first military Pave Hawk helicopter—signaled by the thunderous roar of its powerful twin engines as it came in low, fast, and blacked-out from the west—caught Grissom, Nick, Sara, Lakewell, and Carson in their spaced-apart locations completely by surprise.

Had the five law enforcement investigators possessed the survival instincts and military training of Viktor Mialkovsky, or the hunter-killer teams who had come to deal with him, the sudden, terrifying arrival of the huge and nearly invisible helicopter would have immediately sent them diving to the ground and scrambling toward the biggest boulder they could find.

But lacking those instincts and training, the five investigators all simply squatted down, turned in the direction of the noise, and stared curiously up into the darkness, completely unaware that night-cammo-uniformed soldiers had been pouring out of the blacked-out airship . . . until urgent voices began yelling, "Get down!"

Nick, Sara, Lakewell, and Carson all obeyed instantly, the low-frequency *whump-whump* reverberations of the four military assault helicopters and the single LVPD airship now echoing crazily among the huge rocks and boulders—not to mention the terrifying images of lethal rotor blades slicing through the thin mountain air just over their heads—providing more than enough incentive to send them diving for the rocky ground and searching frantically for solid cover.

Gil Grissom was equally unnerved by the horrific noises and images, but as he flattened down and started to crawl toward the nearest large boulder, he saw—from his new position—a rapidly fading glow of blue fluorescence beneath a large flat rock about twenty feet away.

Determined not to lose what might turn out to be a critical piece of evidence, Grissom scurried toward the faint glow, trying to stay as low to the ground as possible, and then lunged forward with the spray can outstretched in his right hand, sending a burst of brightly fluorescing green paint into the air over the faint blue glow—and unknowingly illuminating himself in the process—as the powerful downdraft from the churning Army MH-60G Pave Hawk helicopter barely twenty feet overhead slammed him down hard onto the rocky ground.

Frightened by the eardrum-pounding air assault in the darkness overhead, Sara Sidle was still scrambling on her hands and knees toward what looked like the slightly less dark mass of a protective boulder when her night-blinded eyes were suddenly drawn to a small burst of fluorescent green light about seventy-five yards east of her position.

To her stunned amazement, the light from the brightly glowing—albeit wildly swirling and dissipating—aerosol cloud showed Gil Grissom being hammered to the ground by a huge, dark, and rapidly moving mass that appeared to be swooping down and across his sprawled body like some kind of monstrous raptor.

"Gil!" Sara screamed. And then, without pausing to think about the consequences, she leaped up and began running desperately in Grissom's direction, never seeing the dark camouflaged arm that suddenly lunged out and yanked her sideways off her feet.

About eight yards to the north of Sidle's position, Shanna Lakewell heard—and then vaguely saw—Sara Sidle sprinting toward the distant glowing cloud of bright green paint. Hesitating only a second, she, too, lunged to her feet and began running in the direction of the vaporous light that was rapidly dissipating into a widespread will-o'-the-wisp, the faint particles of light drifting to the ground like the remnants of a spent flare.

Like Sara Sidle, Lakewell never saw the hand that suddenly lunged out to grab her left arm . . . but she definitely felt the sharp explosion of pain as the high-powered and hollow-pointed rifle bullet ripped through her upper right shoulder, the savage impact wrenching her around and forcing a grunt of agonized shock from her lungs as the dark camouflaged figure dragged her behind a protective bounder.

Awash in pain from her torn and shattered nerves, Lakewell vaguely heard the young soldier cursing into his radio mike. She was trying to concentrate on the words—realizing they had something to do with her—when the pain was suddenly muted and then overwhelmed by a sense of soothing and all-encompassing darkness.

Still stunned and aching from the impact of the Pave Hawk helicopter's ferocious downwash, Grissom was in the process of pushing himself up off the rocky ground when a large human body suddenly landed on his back, slamming his upper torso once more into the bed of sharp-edged rocks and forcing the air out of his lungs for the second time in a very few seconds. Gasping in shock as his protesting lungs fought for air, Grissom tried unsuccessfully to twist himself out from under the crushing weight, and then yelled in surprise and pain when an incredibly strong gloved hand ripped the spray-paint can out of his grasp.

"Sorry, sir," a deep voice growled behind his right ear. "Didn't mean to hurt you, but I can't let you squirt that damned thing again. You lit up the neighborhood like a frigging bordello."

"What—?" Grissom rasped in confusion, relieved to feel his lungs expand again as the man quickly rolled away . . . but kept a second gloved hand pressed on his back.

"You need to keep your head down, sir," the deep voice ordered.

"Okay, I will," Grissom promised in a weak voice, wondering as he did so how many of his ribs were broken, "but—who are you, and what's happening out here?"

"Sergeant First Class Gardez, sir. Platoon sergeant, First Platoon, Sniper Training Company. We're here to evacuate your team from the area ASAP."

"You mean away from our crime scene?" Grissom wasn't sure he'd heard the soldier correctly.

"Roger that, sir; now just relax for a second and keep your head down," Gardez said as he reached out and physically dragged Grissom over to a nearby boulder where another soldier was busy talking on his radio mike. "This is Lieutenant Maddox, commander of First Platoon," Gardez added. "I'm sure he'll explain everything." With that, the platoon sergeant disappeared into the darkness.

Grissom reached up with shaky hands and readjusted his night-vision goggles over his eyes, allowing him to finally see the greenish shape of a camouflaged soldier who—in spite of the apparent weight of command on his haggard-looking face—looked all of twenty-two years old.

Grissom waited until the young officer stopped talking on his radio, and then cleared his throat.

"Excuse me, Lieutenant," the CSI supervisor said,

wincing at the unpleasant effect talking had on his aching ribs, "can you tell me what's going on here?"

"Who are you?" Maddox asked, sounding very distracted.

"I'm Gil Grissom, night-shift CSI supervisor for LVPD . . . and we're supposed to be working a crime scene up here on what I believe is a federal wildlife refuge. Are we in the wrong place?"

"Yes, sir, you are definitely that," Maddox said. "Wrong place at the wrong time; but it's not your fault."

"Then . . . whose fault is it?" Grissom asked reasonably.

"That would be First Sergeant Viktor Mialkovsky," the platoon leader answered, and then said something rapidly into his radio that Grissom couldn't quite comprehend.

"And why is this Sergeant Mialkovsky's fault?" Grissom pressed, thinking that he'd heard that name somewhere before.

"Well, mostly because we think he's trying to kill you and your team."

"Kill . . . us?" Grissom stared blankly at the young, green-faced officer. "Why would he want to do that?"

"I have no idea, sir," Maddox answered. "But it's definitely not a good thing, because First Sergeant Mialkovsky is, among many other things, a professional hunter-killer who is very good at eliminating people. Just about the best there is, in fact . . . except for Major Park," the platoon leader amended.

"And who is Major Park?" Grissom asked, not sure that he really wanted to know.

"He's the bad-ass ROK hunter-killer we just inserted between us and Mialkovsky a couple of minutes ago."

Grissom had no idea what those words meant.

"Is that a good thing?" he finally asked.

"Yes, sir, it very definitely is a good thing, because now Park and Mialkovsky are going to be real busy trying to kill each other; and that gives the rest of us a chance to get you and your team out of here before anyone else gets hurt."

"Anyone else?"

"Two members of your team are down, sir. Both with gunshot wounds, one pretty bad," the lieutenant explained.

"Do you know . . . who?"

"No, sir, I don't. All I know is we're using one of the Pave Hawks to medivac them all out right now, with the Apaches providing air cover. Have to be careful because Mialkovsky's probably still within rifle range, and we don't want him getting another clear shot at anybody. Bastard's too damned good with that rifle."

A sudden downdraft accompanied by the thunderous roar of twin rotor engines caused Maddox to grab Grissom and press him down against the nearby boulder for a few seconds until the crushing wind and brain-numbing engine noise finally died down.

"Your ride's here, sir," Maddox said as he released pressure against Grissom's back.

"My ride?"

"Our second Pave Hawk," the platoon leader explained, gesturing at the now–landed and waiting assault helicopter some fifty feet away, its rotor blades still spinning. "It's going to transport you to the Valley Hospital Medical Center, to get you checked out," the platoon leader explained.

"Is that where you're taking . . . the injured members of my team?"

"That's correct, sir. They're on their way there right now, ETA less than ten, and the emergency room's got two teams of surgeons waiting for their arrival."

Grissom blinked in sudden awareness.

"So there's nothing I can do for either of them right now?"

"No, sir," Maddox said with audible impatience. "You just need to get yourself out of here on that chopper, right now, so we can go ahead and do our job without you being in the way."

"I'm sorry, Lieutenant, but I can't leave yet," Grissom said in what he hoped was a reasonably firm and commanding voice.

The platoon commander looked as if he didn't quite believe what he thought he'd just heard.

"Mr. Grissom, *sir,* you must not have been listening. I just explained—"

"I understand, Lieutenant; believe me, I do," Grissom said hurriedly. "And I don't like being up here any more than you do; in fact, I don't like it at all. Frankly, the idea of being hunted by a professional sniper scares me to death, and there's nothing more I'd rather do right now than get on that helicopter and go check on my team. But I'm working a homicide scene that I'm sure has been rigged . . . and the man who rigged it may, in fact, be your Sergeant

Mialkovsky . . . and the only way we can prove that is to get at the evidence that's only a few yards away."

"Come back later, after we're done. The evidence will still be here," Maddox said reasonably.

"Perhaps, but most likely not," Grissom said, looking around and realizing that his fluorescent green paint had dissipated into a barely visible glow over an area the size of a basketball court. "My location marker's gone, and the ones my other CSIs made are probably fading away as we speak. And if the rain keeps falling like it is now, any blood evidence remaining at this scene will almost certainly be diluted and destroyed by the runoff and the prop-wash from your helicopters. And we can't use the luminol again to look for more evidence, because it won't be dark again for another eighteen hours . . . and by then, the chances of our finding anything useful in the way of blood samples will be virtually zero."

Maddox started to say something, and then hesitated.

"All I need is a few minutes to look under some of those rocks"—Grissom pressed, pointing to the general area in which, he was pretty sure, he'd discharged his spray can—"and then under those rocks out there." He pointed to a faint green spot some fifty yards away in the middle of the clearing.

"You'd be completely exposed in both locations," Maddox replied. "Understand that First Sergeant Mialkovsky is perfectly capable of putting a bullet through your head at eight hundred yards in this weather, and we have no idea where he is right now."

"But you *do* think he's over there somewhere, don't you?" Grissom asked, pointing his finger in a more or less westerly direction.

"That's his most likely location," Maddox agreed. "But Mialkovsky didn't make his reputation—or his seventy-eight documented kills in Afghanistan—by being predictable."

"Seventy-eight?" Grissom whispered.

"And those are the ones we know about," Maddox added meaningfully.

"So what I was thinking," Grissom went on, having to swallow to get the words out, "maybe if I could hide behind something that would move . . . ?"

As Lieutenant John Maddox and Sergeant First Class Ricky Gardez watched from cover with disapproving eyes, Gil Grissom scrambled on his hands and knees to a nearby pile of rocks, staying as low to the ground as he possibly could, pulled away several of the rocks, and then reached out, picked something up, and placed it in a plastic evidence bag . . . all the while hunched down against the swirling prop-wash of the Apache assault helicopter that had landed in a protective—and supposedly blocking—position some twenty yards away with its rotors churning and its 30mm chain gun pointing in a generally westerly direction.

Two hundred yards away in that same westerly direction, the second Apache was aggressively cruising back and forth—north to south and back again—at an altitude of one hundred feet, searching for any sign of movement.

"Gotta be the dumbest thing I've seen in a long

time," Maddox muttered as he watched the landed Apache suddenly rise up a few feet, charge forward about seventy-five yards like an enraged bull, and then drop back down again under the steady hand of its veteran pilot. Moments later, Grissom scurried forward, heading toward the distant faint green marker.

"Roger that, sir," Gardez agreed.

"I've heard these CSI people were dedicated, but I sure as hell wouldn't do something like that for a piece of evidence . . . no matter how important it might be. Would you?" Maddox asked.

"With Mialkovsky wandering around out there, looking to make a kill-shot?" Gardez snorted. "Hell, I wouldn't even—"

At that moment, an excited voice blasted over the radio.

"BAD BEAR TWO . . . TARGET SPOTTED . . . EN-GAGING!"

The concussive roar of a 30mm chain gun disgorging a three-second burst of its massive High Explosive Dual Purpose rounds at a rate of ten every second echoed across the Sheep Range and over the valley below, causing Catherine Willows and Warrick Brown to snap their heads up in surprise.

"What the hell was that?" Brown demanded.

The reverberations of another three-second burst thundered across the valley . . . immediately followed by a third.

"Automatic gunfire?" Catherine suggested, her eyes widened in shock.

The investigating team at the campsite had been

advised by Metro dispatch ten minutes earlier that military assault teams were responding to the Sheep Range clearing to deal with a rogue military sniper—and to extract Gil, Nick, Sara, Greg, LVPD Officer Carson, and Refuge Officer Lakewell from the immediate area; but that was the extent of the information offered . . . other than the admonition that they should stay alert for the approach of any individuals on foot, and not try to contact the CSIs up on the mountain because the rogue sniper would probably be listening in.

"Automatic cannon fire from one of those helicopters, more likely," Brown said. "Somebody up there is definitely in some serious trouble."

The two CSIs looked at each other, neither willing to voice the obvious concern: that the people—or person—in trouble might well be one of their comrades.

Patrol Sergeant Cooperson came running up to the two CSIs.

"I just got a report from dispatch that a military helicopter is transporting two injured investigators from the Sheep Range to Valley Hospital Medical Center," she said, pausing to catch her breath.

"Do they know who's being transported?" Brown demanded.

Cooperson shook her head. "No, the pilot just called in to report that he was inbound with two wounded on board, and requesting surgery teams be placed on immediate standby."

"Did the pilot say how badly they're hurt?" Catherine asked softly.

"Only that one is badly wounded, but both are stable," Cooperson said.

Catherine Willows looked around. "Are we done here?" she demanded.

Warrick and Cooperson both nodded their heads.

"Then let's pack up and get back to town," she said, visibly wincing as a fourth burst of very loud automatic gunfire thundered overhead. "We need to find out what's going on."

22

TWO HOURS LATER, when Gil Grissom finally entered the ballistics section of the LVPD Crime Lab—with a stainless steel cart bearing two small body bags and a smaller evidence bag, and Greg Sanders at his side—looking as if he'd been half beaten to death and nearly drowned, the scene before his eyes was chaotic.

Captain Jim Brass and DEA Assistant Special Agent in Charge William Fairfax were standing at the far end of the lab, dressed in muddy coveralls and boots, and engaged in what looked like a heated argument.

Warrick Brown and Archie Johnson were seated in front of a computer in the middle of the lab, visibly ignoring the argument and focused on the computer while DNA expert Wendy Simms watched over their shoulders.

Bobby Dawson and Catherine had their backs to the entire assembled group, talking back and forth with each other as they manipulated the objects mounted on their adjacent comparison microscopes.

For a long moment, no one noticed Grissom's arrival. It was Jim Brass who finally glanced up and saw the CSI supervisor.

"Gil! It's about time! Where the hell have you been?"

Grissom quickly found himself surrounded by Brass, Fairfax, and the members of his CSI and lab teams.

"Are you okay?" Catherine demanded, taking in Grissom's disheveled and drenched appearance with her detail-oriented eyes, and immediately spotting the bruises on his cheek and forehead.

"I'm fine," he said, looking around the lab with a sense of pending dread. "Uh, has anybody seen Sara or Nick?" he finally asked hesitantly.

"We're here," Sara called out from the doorway.

Grissom quickly turned around and sagged in relief. He started to say something, but then paused when he saw that both of their CSI uniforms were covered with blood. "I thought you . . . and Nick . . ."

"It wasn't us, it was Shanna and Joe," Nick said with a grim look on his face. "Shanna caught a bullet in her upper shoulder. The wound was through and through—a lot of tissue damage at the exit point, and we could tell her collarbone had been shattered—but we got the bleeding stopped right away in the helicopter . . . and the surgeon working on her sent word to us that she's going to be okay."

"And Joe?" Grissom asked, remembering the eagerness of the young, full-of-life patrol officer.

"Three surgeons were still working on him when we left," Sara replied. "His was a shoulder wound also; but the bullet entered through his right scapula, punctured his lung, and then shattered the shoulder ball-socket joint. The chief of surgery couldn't tell us much, other than to say his chances of surviving the initial reconstructive surgery appeared to be very good . . . but we got the distinct impression Joe won't be doing any major physical activity with that shoulder when he recovers."

"Definitely sounded like he's headed for an early retirement," Nick added solemnly. "Tough deal for a young kid like that."

"He ought to be grateful he's still alive," Fairfax commented sourly. "Not many people survive an encounter with an expert military sniper."

"Actually," Grissom said, "I get the sense our rogue sniper wasn't trying to kill either of them . . . or any of the rest of us, for that matter."

"Oh, really? Why would you say that?" Fairfax asked.

Grissom shrugged. "Everyone I talked with says he's an expert marksman under a wide range of combat conditions, and we were all out in the open and oblivious of his presence. If it had been his intent to kill us, I'm sure Jim and I would be wearing toe-tags right now, like the young man in that truck . . . instead of this young lady," he added, gesturing down at one of the small body bags on the cart.

"Young lady?" Brass asked.

"Correction, a young lady mule deer," Grissom amended. "But a very special lady deer who just happens to have a six-inch-square piece of hide missing from her right thigh."

"And that's supposed to mean something?" Fairfax asked.

"It definitely will, if the missing square of tissue matches this," Grissom said as he opened the evidence package and removed a wire-framed object with shreds of hide and tissue dangling from the middle of the frame.

"What's that?" Fairfax demanded.

"It could be a lot of things," Bobby Dawson said, smiling broadly as he moved in close to examine the object. "A makeshift flash suppressor, for one."

"Are you serious?"

"Actually, it could have that effect," Dawson replied. "Attach it so that the square of tissue rests precisely in front of a rifle barrel, and the targets downrange might not get a true fix on the shooter's position . . . especially if the targets were wearing night-vision goggles and that rifle barrel was fitted with a very precisely manufactured sound suppressor. Or, at least, I'm guessing that's what the shooter might want a crime scene investigator to think if the CSI happened to find this little gem and then started wondering what and why."

"You mean one of those odd pieces of evidence that might be misinterpreted at the scene, and thus end up being misleading . . . especially if the CSIs didn't know a great deal about guns and flash-suppressing?" Catherine asked.

Dawson nodded his head silently, giving Fairfax a contemplative smile.

"Certainly not a major component of *my* reading materials," Grissom conceded.

"But, of course," Dawson went on, "it could also be a very clever way of slowing down a seven-point-six-two hollow-point bullet, and causing that bullet to pick up a small chunk of female deer tissue in its expanding tip before going on and impacting our Mr. Toledano's neck. All in all, a perfectly valid explanation for a lot of open questions about that particular shooting—assuming, of course, that Wendy can match this piece of shredded hide with the tissue we pulled from the bullet," Dawson added, as he gently placed the gory bent-wire frame back into the evidence envelope, waited for Grissom's nodded approval, and then handed the package to Simms.

"I'm on it, right now," Wendy promised as she quickly exited the ballistics lab with her latest piece of genetics evidence.

"So, now all we need is the rifle that caused all this havoc in the first place, so we can start matching bullets," Dawson finished, looking at Grissom hopefully. "Unfortunately, I don't see a rifle pouch on your cart."

"Well, actually, you do," Grissom said as he reached down, zipped open the second small body bag, and carefully removed what was barely recognizable as a rifle.

"What the hell is that thing?" Fairfax demanded.

"That is—or was—a military M-24, bolt-action sniper rifle," Dawson said, frowning in dismay as he stepped forward to take the twisted, scarred, and gouged piece of metal out of Grissom's hands. "It used to be a precision-grade weapon. What happened to it?"

"It was on the receiving end of approximately one hundred and twenty high-explosive cannon rounds fired at relatively close range from a thirty-millimeter chain gun, if I'm using the correct military descriptors," Grissom said.

"You are," Dawson said, still examining the twisted metal with a pained look on his face. Then he seemed to remember something. "Hey, what happened to the sound suppressor?"

"An Army colonel by the name of Sanchez ordered that particular piece of equipment to be pried off the end of that . . . uh . . . rifle before he turned it over to me," Grissom replied. "He said something about the device being highly classified . . . and firearms examiners talking too much . . . and how he didn't give a damn if it would help or hurt our investigation. He seemed to think you could make your comparisons without it."

"Bastard," Dawson muttered, looking thoroughly disappointed. "I really wanted to take a close look at that thing."

"What about the shooter?" Brass asked. "You find anything remaining of him?"

"They allowed me to examine what they called the 'impact area' very briefly before they flew me out of there," Grissom said. "I saw that"—he gestured at the twisted remains of the rifle that Dawson was gently putting back into the small body bag—"and I saw a great deal of gravel that I assume had recently been large boulders, but no trace of a body, human or otherwise . . . or, at least, none that I could see."

"So our shooter's still on the loose?" Brass said, frowning.

"Yes, I suppose he is," Grissom said. "According to Sanchez, he was being actively pursued by a rather upset South Korean Army major who takes issue with military sniping instructors who misuse their talents. With any luck, the two of them are somewhere deep in the mountains far north of us by now."

"Yeah, we don't need a guy like that showing up at our crime scenes again," Brass commented. "It gives me the shakes just thinking about it."

"No, we don't," Grissom agreed, "but for a very different reason than you might expect."

"Oh?" Brass responded, his right eyebrow rising curiously.

"First Sergeant Viktor Mialkovsky," Grissom went on. "That's the name of our shooter, who happens to be a very dangerous man—according to Colonel Sanchez, who apparently knows him very well. Personally, I'd like to think that we'll never see or hear from Mialkovsky again; but that may not be the case, because, unfortunately, it turns out that he and I have met before."

"Are you serious?" Nick responded, looking dubious. "How can that be?"

"Yeah," Sara agreed, "how would you have ever run across a man like that? You weren't in the Army, were you?"

"No, I wasn't in the Army," Grissom said with a slight smile as he reached down to the lower shelf of the cart and pulled out a thick wire-bound handbook, "but I did attend an American Academy of

Forensic Sciences conference a few years ago, and found myself listening to a rather interesting breakfast talk about crime scene investigations on decomposed walruses. And, after the presentation, I remember having an equally bizarre but interesting and detailed conversation with a uniformed Army sergeant who'd been sitting at the same table. A sergeant who said he worked shooting-incident investigations and reconstructions for the Adjunct General's Office, and who had what I thought at the time was a rather unusual name."

"Mialkovsky?" Brass said softly.

Grissom nodded his head slowly. "I had to go back to the AAFS conference proceedings to be sure, but that was definitely his name." Grissom opened the handbook to a marked page. "Mialkovsky, Viktor, Staff Sergeant, U.S. Army, MS in Forensic Science."

For a long moment, the lab was deathly silent.

"So he's a military sniper *and* a forensic scientist?" Brass finally said in a hushed voice.

"According to the AAFS . . . and I do remember thinking at the time that he seemed to know an awful lot about forensics for an Army MP," Grissom added.

"A guy like that wouldn't have a whole lot of trouble rigging a crime scene, would he?" Greg muttered.

"No, he wouldn't . . . and that's something I'm afraid we're going to have to watch out for if he manages to survive his . . . uh . . . interaction with the good Major Park, and then heads back our way," Grissom said in agreement, turning to stare at

Fairfax, "which, coincidentally, reminds me that we have a second rigged scene to resolve."

For a brief moment, it appeared as if the DEA supervisor was going to lose control of his temper; but then he visibly recovered and stared at Grissom contemplatively.

"Mr. Grissom, I have no reason to believe that the scene of our shooting incident was rigged in any manner," he finally said in a calm voice. "Is there other evidence that I need to know about?"

"Yes, there is," Grissom said. "Before we returned to the campsite a few hours ago, my team and I processed the interior of the truck cab for gunshot residues."

"And you confirmed that our suspect did, in fact, fire his rifle once, through the roof of the truck—thereby covering the inside of the cab with gunshot residues—immediately after he'd been shot," Fairfax recited. "Yes, I recall you mentioning that. So?"

"What I didn't mention," Grissom went on calmly, "was the fact that the floor of the cab was also completely covered with a fine—and equally distributed—layer of GSRs . . . including the specific area under the passenger front seat where we found that Smith & Wesson hammerless revolver."

Fairfax started to say something, and then stopped.

"And since we found no area inside the cab—on the floor or the seats—with a no-GSR outline of a hammerless Smith & Wesson revolver," Grissom added with a shrug, "I think it's pretty obvious that the pistol was placed inside the cab at some point after the shooting. That is what we would call a rigged crime scene."

"That pistol could have fallen out of his jacket packet when he got hit—or when the truck came to a rapid halt," Fairfax pointed out.

"That's true," Grissom agreed, "but if that had been the case, I would have expected to find a great deal of the subject's blood inside the chambers and other recesses of the weapon, not just on the outer surface—like it had been dropped or tossed into some fresh blood splatters under the front passenger seat."

"So you're planning on accusing Jane Smith of falsifying evidence? Is that what you're telling me?" Fairfax demanded.

"No, actually, it's not," Grissom said. "I have no idea who placed that revolver in the cab of the truck after the shooting. But there are only a limited number of possibilities, and I'm sure that—at some point—a judge or jury will make the appropriate inferences. I think the more interesting question is: Who actually fired the fatal shot that killed the driver of that truck . . . and was that specific shot justified?"

"But to figure that out, you need to find the fatal bullet," Fairfax reminded. "And, as far as I'm aware, you haven't—"

"Actually, Agent Fairfax," Catherine interrupted, "I believe that Mr. Dawson and I can shed some new light on those questions." She looked over at Dawson. "Are we in agreement?" she asked the firearms examiner.

"We are," Dawson said with a nod, giving Fairfax another contemplative stare.

"What are you talking about?" Fairfax demanded, his eyes widening in apparent concern.

"We were able to place all of the shooters and the truck relative to each other during the few seconds that the questioned shooting actually took place," Catherine said. "And we were able to account for every relevant shot . . . except for the one that blew the subject's head apart and exited through the back window of the truck."

"That's the bullet you haven't been able to find, and probably never will find," Fairfax said impatiently.

"Actually, you're talking about the bullet we never *would* have been able to find, had it not been for all of the 3-D triangulations that Warrick made, based on those specific shooter-truck locations, which ultimately allowed Sergeant Cooperson to focus her search on a very specific—and a slice of desert with a metal detector . . . and find this," she said, walking over to her comparison microscope and removed a shiny green-tipped bullet from one of the two stages.

Fairfax stared at the projectile in Catherine's hand with visible disbelief.

"Sergeant Cooperson found an expended three-oh-eight hardened rifle bullet that Mr. Dawson was able to match to the three-oh-eight Winchester Seven Hundred scoped rifle you delivered to us earlier this morning," Catherine explained. "A rifle which I'm led to believe was in the hands of a DEA protection team at or near the location where the questioned shooting occurred. I just confirmed the match a few minutes ago; but I cannot tell you that this bullet passed through the head of our subject—and the window of his truck—because there was no blood on this bullet that we could use to make that specific match. If there ever was blood on this bullet, it was undoubtedly scrubbed off by its impact against the sand drift where it was found . . . or washed off by the rain . . . or both. Not that it really matters," the senior CSI finished with a shrug.

"We're not done with our report, Agent Fairfax," Bobby Dawson said firmly as he walked over to his comparison microscope and removed an object from one of the stages.

"What's that?" the DEA supervisor demanded, his face now a distinct shade of red.

"This is a bullet"—Dawson held the misshapen piece of metal out in the palm of his right hand—"with a very interesting history. It started out in Officer Grayson's forty-caliber Sig-Sauer pistol, punctured the right rear tire of the subject's truck, and then managed to strike Jane Smith a glancing blow across her forehead, setting a series of unfortunate events into motion . . . the most relevant being— and I'll admit I'm guessing here—the perfectly understandable decision of the DEA agent watching the entire shooting sequence take place through the scope of his Winchester Seven Hundred rifle to put the subject he believed to be Paz Lamos down with a single shot to the head immediately after he saw Jane Smith fall backwards and grab her head after being hit by Grayson's bullet."

Fairfax stood silently, looking confused.

"Wait a minute," he finally said. "I thought you people told me that Grayson couldn't have shot Smith because she was never in his line of sight?"

"That's true, she wasn't," Warrick confirmed.

"But then how—?"

"What we failed to take into account," Catherine went on, "was the possibility that the bullets Grayson fired at the rear tires of the truck might have ricocheted off some hard object after penetrating the tires."

"And we also didn't really appreciate the fact that Officer Grayson was firing at the truck from a somewhat downhill angle relative to the path of the truck, which kept the bullets from immediate burying themselves into the ground," Warrick added. "But once I was able to compile all of the data—including all of the laser-scanned rock formations—into a 3-D reconstruction of the scene, there were three rock formations that offered some interesting possibilities."

"Once I brushed all the sand away from the second formation, which had probably accumulated during the storm," Catherine continued, "I discovered what appeared to be a fresh streak of copper and lead on an angled face of a specific rock that seemed to line up with Smith's reported position . . . which, in turn, gave us a *second* vector leading to the third rock formation that apparently functioned as a very handy backstop, because that's where I found the bullet with a metal detector: buried under about three inches of sand. I matched the bullet to Grayson's pistol, and Bobby just confirmed the match."

"But how do you know—?" Fairfax started to ask when Catherine interrupted again.

"That Grayson's bullet actually hit Smith? We don't know that . . . yet."

"But we will know, for sure," Dawson said, glancing down at his watch, "in another hour or so, when Wendy's DNA comparison tells us if the little bit of tissue we found under the peeled-back portion of this bullet—the portion that started to mushroom out when it ricocheted off the rock before hitting Smith—matches the DNA sample we collected from Smith at the scene."

"I'm guessing it's going to be a match," Catherine concluded. "I could be wrong, but I doubt it."

"At the risk of speaking for Captain Brass," Grissom said, "it appears to me that we've reconstructed a questioned-shooting scene, as requested, and confirmed your initial assertion that the shooting was justified. Sadly, it's also apparent that a more or less innocent deer poacher managed to be in two very bad places—and at two very unfortunate times—within an hour of each other . . . decisions that ultimately led to his violent death at the hands of a covert team of federal and state agents who understandably misinterpreted his seemingly aggressive actions in the very few seconds they had to make a decision."

"That's assuming, of course, that our deer poacher and Ricardo Paz Lamos are not one and the same individual," Brass said.

"True," Grissom said, "but all of the evidence we found strongly suggests that's not the case. Setting aside the fact that our subject showed every sign of being desperately poor, it's difficult to imagine a criminal with a lethal history like Ricardo Paz Lamos engaging in a high-level cocaine deal with six well-armed individuals while only armed himself with a single-shot rifle and a homemade cross-bow. You described him as being deranged and un-predictable," he added, turning to Fairfax, "but I think that's stretching things here a bit."

"So if our subject isn't Paz Lamos, where is he?" Catherine asked reasonably.

Fairfax sighed heavily. "I'm guessing he either spotted our surveillance, or got the hell out of there when Toledano and his bodyguard arrived and took the high ground," he said.

"There's always the third possibility: that he ran into Mialkovsky while checking out Toledano," Brass said, "in which case, we may have another body up on that mountain."

"If that's what happened, the critters up there are welcome to feast on his rotting carcass," Fairfax growled as he turned to face Grissom. "I'm more in-terested in hearing the rest of your report."

"There's not much left to say, other than the ob-vious," Grissom replied. "Had Officer Grayson's rico-cheted second bullet not struck Smith at the time and place that it almost certainly did, one can only imagine how the incident would have resolved itself . . . because it's also apparent that none of the UCs fired their weapons with the intent to kill until they saw the muzzle blast from the subject's rifle in the cab."

"Justified?" Fairfax turned to Brass. "Is that really what your report will say?"

"I'm going to question the decision to allow an informant on the scene with a pair of pistols that had once belonged to your supposed suspect," Brass said, "and I will mention the fact that one of those pistols ended up in the cab of the victim's truck under questionable circumstances. But, yes, once I receive the final lab reports, I expect to issue a final report of my own that vindicates the actions of all the UCs at your scene."

Fairfax started to say something, but hesitated again, for the last time . . . and simply extended an open right hand to Brass. "Thank you," he said with apparent sincerity in his voice. "I really didn't expect things to work out quite as they did."

"Frankly," Brass said with a grim smile, "neither did I."

23

TWO HOURS LATER, the storm had returned, flooding the streets of Las Vegas with another deluge of rain that threatened to overwhelm the city's rarely pressed storm drains.

The timing of the storm coincided with the reappearance of a guest at the front desk of the luxurious Silver Garden Casino and Hotel. The nicely attired and extremely attractive desk clerk looked up with a warm smile of recognition. "Mr. Haverstrom, you're back early. We weren't expecting you until late—" The clerk hesitated and then blinked in shock when she saw his face. "Oh, my God, what happened?"

"A climbing accident." Mialkovsky shrugged easily. "I should have stayed in camp and waited out the storm, but I thought I could make it back down the mountain before the front hit. A bad decision on my part, as you can see," he said, holding up a bandaged right hand.

"But you're okay . . . not badly hurt?"

"Mostly bumps and bruises," the hunter-killer shrugged. "I was lucky. Another member of my party took a much worse fall."

"Worse?" the young desk clerk had a stricken look on her beautiful face.

"Both of us slipped. I managed to catch onto a tree branch that broke my fall; he didn't—a simple matter of luck and timing. He's a tough fellow, so I'm sure he'll be up and around in a few days. I suppose we both should know better than to try to act like we're twenty years younger," Mialkovsky added with an easy smile.

"That must be why your friends were trying to get ahold of you . . . wondering if you were okay," the clerks said.

"My friends called here?"

The clerk nodded. "I told them we weren't expecting you to be back from your climbing trip until tomorrow at the earliest. I hope that was okay. We're really not supposed to be giving out information on our guests; but they sounded real worried and I—"

"Don't worry, it's not a problem at all," Mialkovsky said reassuringly. "I'm just surprised they managed to find me here. I upgraded to the Silver Garden at the last minute—one of those impulsive decisions I'm probably getting famous for among my friends."

"Actually, they didn't know for sure that you were staying here," the clerk confessed. "They said they were looking for a friend who was staying in town, and the description they gave just fit you perfectly—

especially the part about your . . . uh . . . hand," the young woman added, looking embarrassed.

"Oh, this?" Mialkovsky held up his gloved left hand with the missing little finger. "It happened so long ago, I keep forgetting that it's missing."

"Well, it is pretty distinctive . . . and, kinda, you know, hot . . . I mean, the fact that you can climb mountains with it, and all that," the young clerk stammered, blushing.

"Hot, huh?" Mialkovsky chuckled appreciatively. "I can't wait to tell my friends . . . they're going to love to hear that. When did you say they called?"

"Oh, just a few minutes ago," the clerk said, looking relieved but still a little embarrassed. "That's why I was so surprised to see you—"

Mialkovsky quickly checked his watch.

"Well, in that case, I'd better get going before we miss each other again. Are we clear on my bill?"

"Oh, I believe you have a refund coming for to-morrow—"

"That's okay, just add it to my tip to the staff," Mialkovsky said casually as he picked up his duffel bag with his undamaged left hand. "I had a very nice time here, in spite of my misfortune. I hope to be back soon."

"We'd love to have you back, sir, anytime," the young clerk said, still blushing as she watched the ruggedly handsome Mr. Haverstrom walk quickly out the door, telling herself that he really was too old for her, but . . .

As the taxi bearing Viktor Mialkovsky made the turn onto Flamingo Road, the hunter-killer looked back through the rear window and observed what looked to be a combined military MP and LVPD raid team exiting their vehicles and rapidly surrounding the front, side, and rear entrances to the Silver Garden Casino and Hotel. He muttered something unpleasant under his breath.

"Excuse me, sir?" the taxi driver said, looking back over his shoulder.

"I said 'Never again,'" Mialkovsky replied calmly.

"You didn't like staying at the Silver Garden?" The taxi driver blinked in amazement.

"Oh, the hotel was fine: excellent accommodations and first-rate staff. Things just got a little warm at the end," Mialkovsky said, his mind elsewhere. "I usually prefer a much cooler environment."

"Oh, yes, sir, I do too," the taxi driver agreed, and then shut up when Mialkovsky's cell phone began to ring.

"Hello?"

"There was an incident out in the desert last night," a deep voice rumbled ominously.

"Yes, so I've heard," Mialkovsky acknowledged.

"We weren't pleased."

"No, I suppose not." Mialkovsky's voice remained calm, but his eyes were now scanning his environment closely.

"What I mean to say is, we were not pleased with the decision of your client to hire your . . . services," the deep voice amended. "We consider *your* actions to have been of a professional nature."

Mialkovsky hesitated a brief moment. "That might be a matter of opinion," he finally said. "I wouldn't say that I earned my fee in this particular instance."

"We understand your final product wasn't up to your normal standards. Perhaps you'd like another opportunity . . . to make amends, and to properly earn your fee?" the deep voice suggested.

Mialkovsky hesitated again. "Do you have a time frame in mind?"

"Sooner would be better than later. We wouldn't want your former client to make any more unfortunate mistakes . . . or say too much about his previous ones."

Mialkovsky hesitated again for another three seconds as he made his decision. "Yes, I suppose I could change my travel plans and stay another day or two."

"Excellent," the deep voice responded. "We'll be waiting to hear from you."

Click.

"Uh, back to your hotel?" the taxi driver asked hesitantly after a long moment.

"No, I think I'll try something at the other end of town. Take me to the Orpheus Hotel," Mialkovsky replied casually. "I've always found a nice change of scenery to be refreshing."

About the Author

A former deputy sheriff, CSI police forensic scientist, and crime lab director, Ken Goddard is currently the director of the National Fish and Wildlife Forensics Laboratory. Over the past thirty-nine years, Ken has taught CSI techniques to local, state, federal, and international law enforcement investigators, and is currently adapting police/wildlife CSI techniques to investigate damaged coral reefs. His previous novels include *Balefire*, *The Alchemist*, *Prey*, *Wildfire*, *Cheater*, *Double Blind*, *First Evidence*, and *Outer Perimeter*. Ken and his wife live in Ashland, Oregon.

THE DNA OF GREAT DVD

AVAILABLE:
10.09.07

AVAILABLE:
10.30.07

AVAILABLE:
11.20.07

OWN THEM ALL!